Pearl Sydenstricker Buck was born in West Virginia and taken to China as an infant before the turn of the century. The daughter of Presbyterian missionaries, she lived with her family in a town in the interior instead of the traditional missionary compound. Buck grew up speaking Chinese as well as English and received most of her education from her mother. She received an M.A. from Cornell and taught English literature in several Chinese universities before she was forced to leave the country in 1932 because of the revolution.

She wrote eighty-five books and is the most widely translated American author to this day. She has been awarded the Pulitzer Prize, the William Dean Howells Award, and the Nobel Prize for Literature. She died in 1973.

Once more, Mrs. Buck is magnificent with her background and her handling of incident and the main story. Nowhere have I come across a more vivid description of Burma, and the Burmese fighting, and especially the Burmese jungle.

—*Saturday Review of Literature*

Pearl Buck needs no introduction as the voice that speaks for China . . . In her new novel she once again calls to a sleeping world to awake and take thought and action for an ally that holds the fate of the Eastern Hemisphere in its hands. There is indignation and bitterness in her call; there is accusation and challenge.

—*Weekly Book Review*

Other Novels by Pearl S. Buck

All Men Are Brothers *(translator)*
Dragon Seed
East Wind: West Wind
The Good Earth
A House Divided
Imperial Woman
Kinfolk
Living Reed
Mandala
The Mother
The Pavilion of Women
Peony
Sons
Three Daughters of Madame Liang

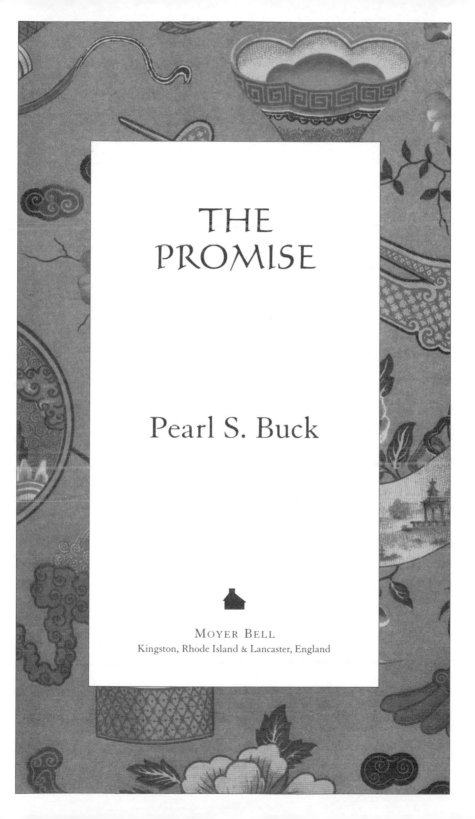

THE
PROMISE

Pearl S. Buck

MOYER BELL
Kingston, Rhode Island & Lancaster, England

Published by Moyer Bell
Copyright © 1948 by Pearl S. Buck.
Copyright © renewed 1968 by Janice C. Walsh,
Richard S. Walsh, John S. Walsh, Henrietta C.
Walsh, Mrs. Chico Singer, Edgar S. Walsh, Mrs. Jean
C. Lippincott, and Carol Buck.

Second Printing, 2004

LIBRARY OF CONGRESS
CATALOGING-IN-PUBLICATION DATA

Buck, Pearl S. (Pearl Sydenstricker),
1892-1973,
The promise / Pearl S. Buck. 1st—
ed.

p.   cm.
Sequel to: Dragon seed
1. China—History—1937-1945—
Fiction. I. Title
PS3503.U198P7   1997
813'.52— dc21   97-6889
ISBN 1-55921-209-8   CIP

Printed in the United States of America
Distributed in North America by Acorn Alliance,
549 Old North Road, Kingston, Rhode Island 02881,
401-783-5480, www.moyerbellbooks.com and
in the United Kingdom, Eire, and Europe by
Gazelle Book Services Ltd.,
White Cross Mills, High Town,
Lancaster LA1 1RN England,
1-44-1524-68765, www.gazellebooks.co.uk

THE
PROMISE

I

I n their despair men must hope, when a promise is given, though
it be only a promise.

Thus, though his second son always shook his head when
Ling Tan spoke of the promise, still the old man believed in it. The
truth was that Ling Tan, as many did, believed the men of Ying and
Mei to be the strongest and fiercest of all men on earth, and he and
all others in this enemy-ridden land daily hoped that by some provo-
cation the enemy would overstep themselves and enrage those foreigners across the sea and force them to come into the war, and thus
bring an end to it. For, evil and strong as the enemy was, none believed even this enemy could conquer the foreigners, the hairy men
of Ying and Mei.

Nor would Ling Tan listen to his sons when they told him that
these foreigners were not so strong as they had once been. Thus in
the city one day where Lao Er had gone to sell some salted duck
eggs, he saw an enemy guardsman spit into the face of a foreigner,
and the foreigner did no more than wipe it off with a white cloth he
took out of his pocket.

"He keeps that white cloth in his pocket, doubtless," Lao Er said
to his father when he came back, "and he keeps it just to wipe off
enemy spittle from his face. All we who saw it were amazed, and a
man who stood near me to sell his dumplings to those who passed
said that he would never have believed it. He said that it used to be
when a foreign man or even a foreign woman was given an insult,
or so much as what they thought an insult, men with guns came
down from foreign warships that lay always ready in the river."

"Where are those warships now?" Lao Ta asked. "There are only enemy warships in the river these days. And one day when I went into the city gate from the river side, I saw foreigners stopped even as we are stopped and their clothes taken off and their bodies searched by the enemy guardsmen, and they were as meek and helpless as we are, having no guns. Do not hope too much now, old father."

Thus his two sons begged Ling Tan lest he be too grieved for his own good when the promise the foreigners had made was not kept. But he still hoped, for where was there hope in any other place?

All through that evil autumn, though the skies were so tranquil and clear above the harvest fields, the times grew steadily worse. The village of Ling lived as though it were in the middle of a silent world. No news came in from the outside except such as could leak in by the whispers of men hastening through on plans of their own. From these Ling Tan and his sons heard that the war still went on in the free land. They heard, too, that though the capital of the country was moved far inland, even there the enemy went and sent down the great bombs which had torn up the earth near the village, a single bomb strong enough to make the large pond. That hole was full of water now, and on the day that Ling Tan heard how the inland capital was bombed he went and looked at the hole and thought to himself how it would be if great pits like that were dug into a city and what of the people? Even if they hid in the rocky hills, as it was said they did, could it go on forever? He was compelled the more to hope that from the world outside there might come help against this bitter enemy.

And again in the eighth month of that year Ling Tan and his sons heard that outside in the free land there was now war made on the enemy in five provinces at once, and this was the first time they heard of Lao San. The word came through a traveling priest, who said that all young and strong men were gathering together for that new war. Then he took out a paper from his gray robe, and in the paper was a piece of black hair that lay in a curl and he said, "This was given to me by the tallest young man I have ever seen, and he told me to go out of my way to pass this house and that you would give me food when you saw this piece of hair which he cut from his

2

own head as he stood before me. He took his short sword and cut it off and gave it to me."

Now when Ling Sao heard the priest say this she cried out that this was surely her third son's hair who had gone away many days before this and with him some of the hill men whom he led.

"Whose hair curls like this except my third son's?" she cried. "I never saw any hair like it, and I always said it was because when he was in my womb I craved eels. Do you remember how I ate eels when I carried your third son, old man?"

"I do remember," Ling Tan said, "and when he was born we were all grieved at the way his hair was. It curled on his head, like eels, as you say, old woman. But it was too late then. And it has always grown out of him like that. Where did you say you saw him, good priest?"

"Near the city of Long Sands," the priest said.

"Was he in rags?" Ling Sao asked anxiously.

"No, he was in whole cloth," the priest said, "and he looked full fed and happy enough. But he was on the way to battle, as all young men were in those parts, for it is expected that the enemy is gathering itself for a new attack upon that city."

Ling Sao took the hair from the priest's hand and wrapped it in a bit of red paper that she had kept in a drawer of the table in her own room, and Ling Tan told the wife of his eldest son to prepare food for the priest, as much as he could eat, and then more to take with him. This the woman did, for she had become in this house a willing, faithful soul whom all called upon and she never said she was weary. Even the work that Jade once did this woman now took for her own duty and if Jade mentioned it, she laughed and said, "If you suckle those two boys of yours what else can be asked of you?" And it was true that Jade's twin sons were always hungry, and it seemed however much Jade ate and however she drank rice gruel mixed with red sugar and however she supped broths and ate eggs boiled in tea she could never turn the food fast enough into milk for those two thirsty boys at her breasts.

That day after the priest had gone, his belly swelled under his girdle with what he had eaten and his basket full of food for tomorrow, they all sat and wondered about the third son and whether he

3

would be killed in the battle or not, and what would become of him.

It was not long after this that Jade had a letter and when she opened it she found it was written by Mayli, and it came from that province which is called Yünnan, or South of the Clouds, and it was from the city of Kunming. There Mayli had told Jade she would go, and there she was. It was a short letter, seemingly full of playful talk and yet it ended with this question, "How is it your husband's younger brother has not brought me back my little silk flag?"

Now none but Jade and Lao Er knew about that small silk flag or how Mayli had given it to Jade to give to Ling San as a sign that she was going to the free land if he cared to follow her. So now when Jade was reading the letter to them aloud as they sat in the sunshine in the court one day in the autumn of that year, she saw that question ahead and did not read it aloud to them, lest they press her with questions she could not answer. But afterward when she was in their own bedroom she told Lao Er about it and he smiled.

"He will be there one of these days," he said.

And so it was that something more than a month later there was another letter to Jade and this time Mayli said, "Tell your parents that their third son has come here to this city, and he has fought in the battle of Long Sands, and he is full of the great victory we won there against the enemy."

More than this Mayli did not say, but so much they all heard and were greatly cheered to know that somewhere there was a victory and that Lao San was alive. Only Ling Sao fretted because there was not more in the letter to tell her whether her third son and this Mayli were to be married or not. But no, there was not a word of marriage, not in this letter or another that came afterward, and Ling Sao grew angry and said:

"I wish I had that third son of mine here and I would jerk his ears! When did a son of mine ever go smelling around a woman when she was not his wife? If he is hungry for her, why does he not marry her? And she is worse than he is, to let him come near her, the bold daughter of a rotten mother—"

"Give over cursing, woman," Ling Tan said. "Why is it that women will curse each other so easily?"

"Perhaps she will not marry my brother," Lao Ta said. "You must

4

remember, mother, that she is full of learning, and my brother does not know even his name on paper when he sees it."

But Ling Sao flung up her head at her son. "If she has her belly full of ink, she is not the woman for him anyway," she said, "and all the more he ought not to go near her."

By this time they were all laughing at her and she seized one of the twins from Jade's arms, and bore him away to comfort herself in the kitchen. For this woman could always be comforted by one of her grandsons. Her older children she could find fault with but the little ones were perfect in her eyes.

These were the small things of Ling Tan's house, and somehow the house went on, even though the countryside was under the heavy rule of the enemy. Somehow they got enough food out of the earth for themselves, and Lao Ta and Lao Er grew clever in ways of deceiving the enemy. Since he had married the woman he found one day in his trap, Lao Ta had ceased to set traps any more, for she loved him beyond all reason, and she would not have him risk his life. So she wept until she had made him come home and live in his father's house again, and till the fields, and be once more a decent farmer. Yet though this family seemed nothing but a common family such as in any country may be found upon the soil, they never for one moment gave up their hatred of the enemy nor their will that, when Heaven set the day, all the people, and they among them, would sweep the enemy into the sea.

To himself Ling Tan always said that the day would be that one when the men of Mei could be made so enraged that they, too, would join this war.

"On that day," he said to his sons one night, "when we hear that the men of Mei have come into this war on our side, we shall all be given strength to rise up and fall upon the enemy and drive them out. Each man in his place will rise and fall upon the enemy next him, even though he has only his bare hands to put at the enemy's throat, and then we shall all be free."

It was on a cool night at the end of that month when he said this —so cool that Ling Sao had bade her two sons move the table from the court and set it inside the main room, so that they could eat

5

their night meal in warmth. There had not yet been frost, but she lifted her head and sniffed the night air before she shut the door.

"I smell winter tonight," she said.

"The fifth winter of this war," Ling Tan said gravely. "But next winter we shall be free again."

None spoke when he said this, not wanting to take away hope from him. He had come to believe too much in that day of his hope, plucking his belief out of the air, for there was still not one word of news from the outside world to tell him that the promise would be kept by the men of Mei and Ying. Even the random news they had been used to hearing from their old cousin who had lived in the city was now gone. For that old scholar had one night taken too much opium and had not waked again. The man who owned the poor room where he slept his life away found him dead the next morning, and was about to throw his frail body outside the city wall, for in these times the dead were not valuable as they once were. There were too many dead bodies in the streets each dawn, some starved and some diseased and some stabbed by who knows what dagger? Then the man saw that the dead one wore a good cotton vest under his ragged scholar's robe, and so he thought he would take the vest off for himself, and then he found tied to it with a bit of thread a command from the dead man. "Should I be found dead," the old scholar had written, "take my body to my wife who lives in the village of Ling outside the south wall of the city."

This the man had done, wishing a reward for it, and Ling Tan gave it to him, be sure. But what a day that had been, when at last the cousin's wife got back her old man! It was a day of mixed rage and sorrow, for she was so vexed that she could not mourn properly because however she scolded her old man could not hear her as he lay in the coffin Ling Tan gave him. It was Ling Sao's own coffin, for both Ling Tan and Ling Sao had their coffins ready in an outhouse, and this had been done in the summer when Ling Tan was sixty years old. It was a comfort to them both to know that should death come down upon them, unseen, their coffins were ready and waiting for sleep.

But now Ling Sao let the cousin's wife have hers. "I can get another the next time my sons go into the city," she said, "and let the old scholar's bones rest at last."

So they did as she said, and the cousin's wife wept and grew angry by turns. First she wept and moaned and then when she fell to thinking of those many months this old corpse had hidden himself in the city and how he had put all he earned into opium she grew angry and she stopped weeping and washed her face and combed her hair and cried out that she was glad he was dead, for he had been no use to her alive, and then she would remember that now indeed she was a widow and so she wept again, and all in all she made such commotion in the village that all were glad to have the old man under ground.

Once during the day before he was buried, Ling Tan looked down into the coffin and smiled. The old scholar, though wasted to his skeleton with opium, looked so peaceful that Ling Tan knew he was pleased as he lay there. He told Ling Sao that night, "I swear I believe the old rascal knows that he has the best of it because she cannot make him hear any more."

Still, after the dead scholar was under ground, there was no other way of knowing what was going on beyond the seas, and Ling Tan had now only the promise to hold to, for hope.

How then could he be ready for that most evil day which came down upon them from heaven? On that day the enemy took by surprise the men of Mei. They fell upon the foreign ships as they lay side by side in a foreign harbor, and they set fire to the airplanes, resting wing to wing upon the ground. And those who had the keeping of these ships of sea and cloud were sleeping or finding their pleasure on a day when all were idle. Be sure that the enemy made known everywhere their victory. They cried it upon the streets and it was written upon the walls in great letters, and voices took it over the land faster than the winds could carry it. So the news reached the village of Ling. It was a clear cool day, such a day as in better times Ling Tan would have cried out to Ling Sao to make him noodles of white wheat flour. He had smelled the frost at the door that morning and he looked out and saw it white on the threshing ground.

7

"If it were the real times," he said to her, "I would eat wheaten noodles today."

"There is only the same millet," she said, "but it is hot."

So he ate his hot millet and the day went as it always did, his sons busy with their tasks, and he sitting in the sun to smoke his water pipe. Then suddenly one came running toward the house. It was a young fellow, the son of a neighbor in the next village and he came to Ling Tan first. He was weeping as he ran, and Ling Tan shouted at him.

"What now? Can there be anything more than what has happened to us already?"

"There is worse and it has happened," the lad said, and then gasping and sobbing he told him. In the early morning of that day the enemy had fallen upon the ships and the airplanes of the people of Mei, thousands of miles across the sea, and had destroyed them utterly. The men of Mei were full of rage—but helpless.

Ling Tan sat, his water pipe in his hand and heard this black news. "I will not believe it," he said.

But his mouth went dry. For the young man went on with such a close story that Ling Tan saw it might have happened thus to a people unwatching. If the men of Mei were unmindful, it might have been so. And well he knew the cunning of this enemy. He called the young man in and before his sons he made him tell the story over again. Then he sent his sons for the other men in the village and they all came into Ling Tan's court, and once again the young man told his story. Each time it seemed more possible.

When it had been told for the third time, Ling Tan knocked the cold ash from his pipe which he had forgotten to smoke. Then he turned to Ling Sao.

"Get my bed ready," he said. "I must lie down, and I do not know whether I shall ever get up again."

They were frightened at his words and all urged him not to give up his hope. They told him that there were yet the men of Ying who had not been destroyed, but well he heard the faltering in their voices, and he shook his head.

"Get my bed ready, mother of my sons, get my bed ready," he said.

8

He lay in his bed with eyes closed for eleven days and in all that time he would not eat a full meal nor did he wash himself all over. On the twelfth day Ling Sao came in with ashes on her hands and face and a length of coarse white mourning cloth in her hand and she let out her voice in loud weeping.

"If you die I will swallow the gold earrings you gave me," she said, "I cannot live on without you, old man."

Then his sons came in and their wives and children, and they wept and begged him for the sake of all to rouse himself and to wash and to eat.

But it was Jade who said the word that made him move. "Will you let the enemy kill you at last, when in all these years you have been the one to give us courage?" she said.

He thought for a moment, she looking at him shrewdly. Then he dragged himself up. "You would find the right word to make me live when I long to die," he said in feeble anger.

He rose, nevertheless, and his sons leaped forward to help him, and the women went away and with his sons' help he was washed and dressed, and he ate a bowl of broth with two eggs in it, that Ling Sao had ready, and so he began to live again.

But he was never what he had been. His withers were weak, and when he walked he clung to the wall or the table or to the shoulder of a son, or he leaned on Ling Sao. Nor did he ever mention the war again, nor the enemy, nor the hope he had lost. From then on Ling Tan was an old, old man, and they all saw that he was, and they took turns caring for him, and never leaving him alone.

After that day Ling Tan could never remember well again anything that he was told and most of all he fretted because he could not remember where his third son was. He forgot again and again that Jade had read him a letter which had come last from Mayli, and he asked for it each day saying that he had not heard it. So she read the letters to him patiently. One day when she had read for the sixth time a letter which had come six days before, he put out his hand.

"Give the letter to me," he said.

Jade gave him the letter and he took it in his right hand and as he held it his hand began to tremble with that small tremor which he

9

could not still, however hard he tried. It had come on him with his weakness and it always made him angry.

"Look at that hand," he now said with scorn, as though the hand did not belong to him. "See, it shakes like an old leaf ready to drop from the tree!"

Jade moved the weight of the child she held. One or the other of her twin sons she had in her arms all day, and whichever she did not hold, Ling Sao held. Between them they were never without a burden, whatever they did. "It is only one hand," she now said to soothe the old man.

"But it is the hand I used to sow seed in the earth," Ling Tan grumbled.

"Therefore the more weary," Jade said gently.

Ling Tan gave a great sigh and took the letter in both hands and turned it slowly around and around. He would not for pride's sake ask which was top and which bottom, and Jade would not tell him when at last he held it wrongly, after all. Why should she shame an old one? So he held the letter and stared at it carefully, imagining into the marks he saw the things which he had just heard from her lips.

"It is strange she writes about him and they are not wed," he said at last. "Why are they not wed?"

"How can I tell why another woman will not wed one of your sons?" Jade said laughing.

Ling Tan did not smile.

"I will never see my third son again," he said sadly. "Foreign winds and foreign waters—they are ill things."

"Do not allow such thoughts," Jade replied. The child in her arms was asleep and she was thinking that she might lay him on the bed and rest her arms a while. Thus thinking she rose and tiptoed through the court where she had been sitting with the old man and so he was alone.

For a while he continued to stare at the letter which he could not read, but at last he folded it up small and put it inside his girdle. There he would keep it until it wore into dust, as he had kept the other letters which the woman had sent, the woman whom his third son loved. Yes, he could not understand this woman who though she would not marry so fine a man as his third son yet faithfully wrote to them now and again, sending the letters by any messenger whom she could find. But nothing was usual in these years of war and men and women were the strangest of all. He sighed again and laid his head on his arms on the table. The sun came down warm into the court and all around him was still. He heard the sound of the loom again, the loom which had been silent since his third daughter Pansiao had been sent away to the inland mountains to school. They had not heard of Pansiao now for many months. He had almost forgotten how that small daughter of his looked. But he thought of her now when he heard the loom.

He knew it was not Pansiao who now sat at the loom but the widow whom his eldest son had married. She was a good weaver, good everywhere in the house, though Ling Sao was often impatient with her because she was always anxious lest she did not please and, being too anxious, she did not please, and she would creep away to weep. Then Ling Sao cried after her angrily: "Give over weeping, poor stupid good soul! It is true you always try to please me, but I swear it would be easier if you were not always at my side, like a cat rubbing my legs and in my way. Do not try so hard, daughter-in-law, and I will like you better!"

But this the woman could not understand. She would only roll her tearful eyes at her mother-in-law. "It seems to me I cannot try too hard to please you," she whimpered.

Time and again this quarrel had come between the two women until one day Ling Tan had taken it upon himself to say to Ling Sao, "Since my eldest son has found this woman for himself and likes her, leave her alone. Am I to have a miserable old age because of you and this woman? Since there is no peace in the world, can I not have it in my own house?" Ling Sao did her grumbling out of his hearing after he said this and so he had peace.

Now the light clack of the loom beat through the warm sunshine of a mild winter's day and carried him away from all thought and he slept.

II

A THOUSAND and more miles away from where this old man slept in his courtyard in the sun, his third son, Lao San, stood in another courtyard.

This Lao San had in these days another name. Lao San, or Lao Three, is well enough for the name of a farmer's son, but after the victory of Long Sands he had been made into a commander of other men, and his General, with his new rank, had given him a new name and this name was Sheng, and Sheng he was called from that day on.

He had been sitting until a moment ago, talking across a small porcelain garden table to the woman he loved who would not marry him. It could be said rather that she persuaded him to talk, drawing out of him by her shrewd questions all that he had been doing since they last met, more than two months ago. Then she fell silent, and her handsome head drooped as though she were thinking of what he had said. What she thought about he did not know, indeed. He loved her very well but he did not pretend that he knew her thoughts. She was not a usual woman when it came to the stuff of her brain. He could talk to her as though she were a soldier and she to him. But when she was silent she seemed always beyond him. Now she lifted her head suddenly, as though she felt his eyes, and smiled a small smile.

"You look beautiful in that uniform," she said. Her smile twisted. "But why do I tell you? You know it."

He did not answer this, for he never answered her when her red mouth twisted.

"How many characters can you write now?" she asked again.

"Enough for me," he said.

"Then why did you not write me a letter?" she asked.

"Why should I write when I knew I was coming here in a month or two at most?"

"If you see no reason for writing to me, then there is no reason," she said.

She took up her tea bowl in her hand and held it and he looked at that long narrow hand of hers, its nails painted scarlet. He knew the scent in her palm. But he did not move toward her. Instead he put his hand into the breast of his new soldier's uniform and took out a handful of colored silk. She sat sipping her tea, her lips still smiling, and her great black eyes smiling.

"Here is the flag," he said.

"You still have that flag?" she said.

"You gave it to me," he retorted. "It was your command to me to come to you."

It was true that when Mayli left Jade that day now six months behind them she had given this small bright flag to Jade and she had said, "Tell him I go to the free lands—tell him I go to Kunming." To Kunming he had come after the victory. But when he had come she was not willing to marry him. She was still not willing, though he had been here for days and each day he had come to see her.

"Why do you keep that flag in your bosom?" she asked him.

"That you may remember you bade me come here," he said.

He leaned over the porcelain table and looked down upon her upturned face. Behind his head, over the wall of the courtyard, she could see the high tops of the mountains which surrounded the city, bare mountains, purple against the clear winter sky. The day was not cold. It was seldom cold here, and in another climate it could have been spring. The light of the sun fell upon her face and his, and each saw the other's beauty, how fine their skin was, the golden fine skin of their people, and how black were their eyes and how white.

"I ask you again if you will marry me," he said. "Yesterday I asked and today I ask."

Her eyelids fell. "You are very bold these days," she said. "When you first came you would not have thought of asking me yourself. Do you remember how you found some one who knew a friend of mine and then through the two of them you proposed marriage to me?"

"I have little time now," he said. "A soldier must go by the straightest road to what he wants. I ask you this—will you marry me before I march to my next battle?"

She lifted her lids again and he saw what he feared in her more

13

than anything—her laughter. "Is it the last time you ask me?" She put the question to him as playfully as a kitten tosses a ball.

"No," he said. "I shall ask you until you yield."

"At least wait until you come back before you ask again," she said.

Each of them thought the same thought—what if he never came back? But neither would speak it aloud.

"Do you know why you will not wed me?" he asked her at last.

"If I did I would tell you," she said.

There was one more long moment between them, eyes looking into eyes. Then he took up the bright silk flag that lay between them and crumpled it and put it back into his bosom.

She rose. "Do you go?"

"Yes," he said.

"Do you go because you must or because you wish?" she asked him. Now that he was going away she felt her heart pull at him to stay.

"What does it matter?" he said. "I have said what I came to say. There is no reason for staying longer today."

She did not answer him. She stood near him, tall for a woman, but still only a little beyond his shoulder.

"I swear I think you are still growing," she said willfully. "Can you blame me that I do not want a growing boy for my husband?"

"I do blame you for not wanting me," he said gravely. "I blame you because you know we are destined for marriage. Do not our horoscopes promise us to each other? Are you not gold and am I not fire?"

"But I will not be consumed!" she cried.

"I am the man," he said, "and you are the woman."

The air around them was so clear, so still, the sunshine so pure, that their two shadows lay on the white stones beneath their feet as though they were one. She saw the closeness and stepped back from him and the shadows parted.

"Go away," she said. "When you are finished growing you may come back."

He gave her a long look, so long and fierce that she stamped her foot. "Don't think I am afraid of your eyes!" she cried.

14

"Don't think I am afraid of you," he said sturdily, and turned and without another word he went away.

And she, left alone in the courtyard, walked here and there, and back and forth, and stopped in front of a cluster of bamboo trees and plucked off a smooth hard leaf, and tore it between her teeth into sharp shreds. When would she be sure of this man for whom her flesh longed? She would not marry a lout, and was he more than a lout? Who knew? A month ago he had been chosen by those above to lead other men. But it had taken him months to prove that he could lead something more than the handful of ragged men who had escaped with him out of the hills near his father's house. For those months he had drilled in the common ranks of soldiers and at night he had learned like a schoolboy the strokes and dots and hooks that go to make writing and reading. He could read a book today but only if it were simple. And she did not yet know whether or not his mind were simple. Marry him she could, as women did marry in these days, and then cast him off. But she was not of such hot blood that she must marry for nothing but that. She wanted to marry a man whom she could love until she died and to keep her love he must have more than beauty—he must have the power to be great. Had he that power? She did not know.

An old woman in a black coat and trousers came to a door that opened upon the court.

"Your food is ready," she said. She looked about the court. "Is he gone? I went out and bought a pound of pork and some chestnuts because I thought he was here."

"I will eat them," Mayli said.

"No, you will not," the old woman said. "You are the child of your mother, who was a follower of Mohammed, and not while these hands of mine prepare your food will flesh of pig enter into you. I, who nursed you as a child in your mother's house!"

"Why did I ever find you?" Mayli pretended to complain. For she had found this old woman in the city of her birth where now the puppet of the enemy ruled. In that way which poor people know everything about those above, this old woman heard that Mayli had returned from over the seas and so one day she came and told Mayli who she was and told such things about Mayli's mother that she

15

proved herself as the one who had been Mayli's wet nurse. She, too, was a follower of Mohammed, else would the child Mayli not have been allowed to suckle her, and yet it was often an inconvenience now that she still made much of rites and foods which had no meaning for Mayli, reared far off from such ways in the land of the foreigners.

"Your dead mother put it into my mind to come to you," old Liu Ma now said. "I felt her ghost stirring the bed curtains for two nights and I knew it was she because I smelled the cassia flowers she used always to wear in her hair."

"My father still loves cassia flowers," Mayli said. One reason why she had wanted the old woman near her was that she might hear these small stories about the mother who had died when she was born.

"Do you think you can tell me anything I do not already know?" the woman said. "What happened to your mother happened to me. I have forgotten nothing. Now come and eat."

She seized Mayli's hand in her dry old hand and pulled her toward the door into the main room of the house where Mayli lived alone with this one old woman. "Sit down," she commanded and when Mayli had sat down she brought a brass bowl of hot water and a small white towel for hand washing. And while she did this she grumbled steadfastly.

"I will throw the pork to the street dogs," she said. "It is dog's food, anyway. But that great turnip of a soldier who you say is your foster brother—though it is only in days like these when all reason has gone from the minds of the people that a young girl has a foster brother! A brother or nothing—what is a foster brother but a man, and what have you to do with a man who is not your brother? It spoils the name of this house to see a tall soldier stoop his head to enter the gate. I lie for you, but can lies deny that he is here when any one on the street can see him come in? That hag in the hot water shop next door, she says, 'I see your master is home again.' And how can I say he is not the master here, when she sees him come into our gate?"

To such talk which the old woman poured out all day like water from a dripping fountain, Mayli said nothing. She smiled, smoothed

16

her black hair with her long pale hand, sat down at the table in the main room of the house and ate heartily of the lamb's meat and rice and cabbage on the table, while the old woman hovered about her, keeping her tea hot and watching her while she ate and always talking.

Now suddenly Mayli broke across that talk with a sharp look of mischief. She had eaten well but she did not put down her chopsticks.

"Where is that pork, Liu Ma?" she asked.

"It is in the kitchen waiting for me to throw it to the dogs," the old woman said.

"Give it to me," Mayli said, "I am still hungry."

Liu Ma opened her old eyes and thrust out her under lip. "I will not give it to you, and you know it, you wicked one," she said loudly. "I will let you starve before with my own hands I give you so vile a meat."

"But if Sheng had stayed to eat with me as he often does, I would have eaten the pork," Mayli said.

"I always know my place," Liu Ma declared. "Of course then I would only wait to scold you in private."

"Oh, you old fool," Mayli said, still laughing. And she rose and swept past the old woman and into the kitchen and there on the edge of the earthen stove was the bowl of pork, very hot and fragrant, with chestnuts cooked in it. "It does not look like a dish ready to throw to a dog," Mayli said, her black eyes still bright with mischief. "It looks like a dish an old woman puts aside for her own dinner."

"Oh, how I wish your mother had lived!" Liu Ma groaned. "Had she lived she would have beaten you with a bamboo and made you into a decent maid! But your father was always a man as soft as smoke. Yes, he never made a shape for himself in anything. It was she who would have beaten you."

By now Mayli had the dish on the table and she dipped into it with her chopsticks and brought out the best bits of sweet pork, crusted with delicately brown fat and tender parboiled skin.

"How well you do cook pork when it is a dish you never even taste," she said to the old woman.

17

She looked at Liu Ma and suddenly Liu Ma's brown face crinkled. "You young accursed!" she said laughing. "If you were not so much taller than I am, I would smack the palm of my hand across your bottom. I am glad that dragon's son whom you call your foster brother is bigger than you. When he loses his temper with you after you are married I will not beg him to stay his hand. I will call out to him, 'Beat her another blow, beat her another one for me!' "

"You old bone," Mayli said gaily. "How do you know I will marry him when I do not know myself whether or not I will?"

. . . At this moment Sheng stood at attention before his General. This General was a man of the southwest, a man still young and hearty, who was in command of the armies of this region. He had a notable story of his own, being sometimes a rebel but now a loyal soldier against the common enemy. For in times of peace men will fight for this or that small cause, but when an enemy from outside the nation comes down upon all alike, then no man may fight for his own cause, and so this General had brought all his soldiers behind him and he had gone to the One Above and given himself and his men to the common war.

When he saw Sheng stand at attention before him he made a motion to him. "Sit down," he said. "I have something to say to you, not as your superior but as a man to another man. I have had an order from the One Above that our two best divisions are to march into Burma. It is against my will and I cannot obey the One Above and put my command on you without letting you know that I do not approve the thing I am compelled to command you. Sit down—sit down!"

At this Sheng sat down, but he took off his cap and held it and he sat down on the edge of his chair so as not to show himself at ease before his superior. He kept silent, too, and waited, so that he might prove his respect. There were two guards in the room, standing like idols against the wall. To these the General lifted his eyelids and they went out. So the two of them were alone. The General leaned back in the wooden chair in which he sat and played with a small clay buffalo that was on his desk.

"Your father is a farmer, you told me once," he said to Sheng.

18

"I am the son of the son of farmers for a thousand years," Sheng replied.

"Are you your father's only son?" the General asked.

"I am the youngest of three," Sheng replied. "And all are living."

The General sighed. "Then I may send you out to an unlucky war without cutting off your father's life."

"My father's life is not in me," Sheng replied. "He has my two brothers and they have sons."

"And you, are you wed?" the General asked.

"No, and not likely to be," Sheng said bitterly.

The General smiled at this. "You are young to say that," he said.

But Sheng did not answer this for a moment. Then he said, "It is as well for one who is about to be sent into battle not to have a wife. At least I go alone and free."

"You are right," the General said. He put down the clay toy in his hand and picked up a brush. "Where is your father's house and what is his name? I shall write him myself if you do not come back from this battle."

"Ling Tan of the village of Ling, to the south of the city of Nanking, in the province of Kiangsu," Sheng said.

The General dropped his brush. "But that is land held by the enemy," he said.

"Do I not know that?" Sheng replied. "They came in and burned and they ravaged and they murdered wherever they could. I fought there together with the hillmen and we killed the enemy by the handsful, and then I came out because a handful now and again was not enough for the thirst in me for their blood. I shall be thirsty until I can kill them by the hundreds and the thousands. So I came out and I have spent the months learning until the battle of Long Sands."

"That tells me why you have learned so well," the General replied.

When he had brushed quickly the name of Ling Tan and where he lived he put down the brush and put his hands on the sides of his chair and fixed his eyes upon Sheng's face.

"It is against my will that I send these two divisions to Burma," he said. "I have reasoned with the One Above. I have told him that we must not fight on soil that is not our own, and this for two

19

reasons. In the first place the people of Burma are not for us. They will not welcome us when they know we come to help those who rule them. They do not love the men of Ying who have been their rulers and when we come to aid the men of Ying they will hate us, too. In the second place, the men of Ying despise those not of their own pale color, and even though we come to help them they will not treat us as true allies. They will look on us as servants and they the lords, and shall we endure this when we go to succor them?"

"What does the One Above say when you tell him these true things?" Sheng asked.

The General leaned forward. "He says the men of Ying must know how small are their chances to hold their rule in Burma and they will be grateful to us. He says that since they need our help they will show us courtesy and we will fight by their side and win a great victory over the enemy at last."

"Is the One Above so sure that we can win?" Sheng asked.

"Is he not sending our best divisions? You are all seasoned and young and strong."

The General sighed and it was like a groan. "So he says, even though Hongkong has fallen to the enemy, and all know that the men of Ying gave that great city to the enemy as though it were a present for a feast day. I say, the men of Ying are doomed and if we go with them we are doomed. I have had all my life a knowledge of which way doom lay ahead, and I have that knowledge now. We ought to stay on our own earth and fight only from our own land. These men of Ying—have we reason to think they will change suddenly in their hearts to us? Have they not always despised us?"

The General fell silent and sat like a man of stone for a moment. But Sheng saw the veins begin to swell under his ears and on his temples and his clenched fists, which lay out on the table before him like two hammers, grew white on the knuckles and the veins in his wrists swelled. He did not lift his eyes to Sheng's face and Sheng could not see what was in them. But after a moment this man began to speak in a low voice, thick as though he were choking.

"The men of Ying have treated us like dogs on our own earth! They have lorded it over us since they won those wars against us—

20

opium wars, they called them, but they were wars of conquest. Their battleships have sailed our rivers and their soldiers have paraded our streets. They took land from us for their own. They refused to obey our laws and here in our country they have set up their own laws for themselves, and their own courts and their own judges, and when one of them robbed us and even when one of them killed one of us, there has been no justice. Their priests have paid no taxes. Tax free they have gone where they liked and preached their religion which is not ours. They have turned the hearts of our young away from our elders. They have sat at our customs gates and taken the toll of our merchandise."

Suddenly he leaped to his feet and his wrath burst out of his eyes like lightning. He paced back and forth in the long narrow room in which they were. "And I am commanded to send my best young men to fight for these men who have despised us and trodden us down for all these years!" he shouted.

Now Sheng himself had lived always in his father's house outside the city and the few times he had ever seen these foreign men whom the General so hated could be counted on the fingers of his right hand. Once or twice he had seen them on the streets, and once or twice hunting wild beasts in the autumn when the grass was long on the hills. He had stared at them and heard their loud voices and harsh language of which he understood not one word. But he himself did not know of all these hateful things they had done to his people. So now he listened and said nothing, because he had not knowledge of it himself. Moreover, he was a soldier. In these months he had learned to obey the one above him as he made his own men beneath him obey his smallest command, and he did not answer. He waited to see what the General would tell him to do.

So the General walked back and forth a few times, grinding his teeth together under his mustaches, and then he sat down again and slapped the table with both his hands outspread.

"What must be done must be done!" he said still loudly. "For many days I have resisted the One Above and I have held back my men. Now his commands have come down on me as commands from heaven and either I must obey or take my life. What use is it to take my life since then another would obey his same commands?"

21

He had told Sheng to sit down, but now Sheng rose, and he stood to receive his orders for battle.

"You will prepare your men to go to Burma with the others," the General said harshly. "I myself will lead you. When we are at the edge of Burma we are all to encamp upon our own soil until we receive orders to march on."

Sheng put his heels together and saluted and then he waited.

"Where we shall go from there is not yet clear," the General went on. "It is said some of our men will be sent into Indo-China and it may be we will invade that land. The enemy promised that they would not enter the land of the Thai. But they did enter it. The Thais yielded to them in five hours. Everywhere the enemy is winning. They do not need arms to win—everywhere all are ready for them. It is only we who resist, though we die."

The General sighed and leaned forward and clutched his hair in his two hands. "We go to fight in a battle already lost," he sighed. "I know it but what shall we do to make the One Above know it?"

"Let your heart rest," Sheng said sturdily. "If the battle has not been fought yet, how can we have lost it?"

The General sighed again. He lifted his head and looked at Sheng's brave and honest face. He remembered this man when he had first come from the hills six months before. In six months it was hard to believe that so great a change had been made. Sheng had come as wild as a tiger, his hair long and shaggy over his eyes, and his garments ragged blue cotton such as peasants wear. Had he been a smaller man none might have noticed him and he might have been put into the common ranks and left there to work his way up. But Sheng was not a small man. He was a head taller than most men, and the strange thing was that he was still growing, though he was more than twenty-two years old. His hands were twice as large as a usual man's, and his feet were too big for any sandals except such as were made to his measure, and all of his body was large to match. Even his eyes were large and the look he gave out of them was large and clear. Wherever he went men's heads turned to stare after him and to cry out at his size. Thus because he was so large he was the more easily a leader among his fellows.

22

Yet had he been stupid or timid, of what use would his size have been to him? He would have been only a bigger lump of clay. But he was sensible and high-tempered and he learned eagerly, and he obeyed faithfully until he had learned. When he in turn taught another, he saw to it that he himself was obeyed, and while all his men liked him, still they were afraid of him, too, and so men should be of the one who leads them.

Besides all this there was yet another reason why he had risen so quickly to be a commander. He had proved himself well in this war. In the eighth month of the year the war was pushed into many new places, and Sheng had fought through that campaign, always well. He had come out with his life, too, and with only small wounds, and so when those higher than he were killed, he was moved quickly upward. Then in the ninth month in that great battle of Long Sands, it was he who led his men and another officer's who had fallen, and had driven the last of the enemy out of the city. Behind that young giant the men gathered and followed with fresh courage, and he was so tall that he could be seen above them all and always at the front. When at last the battle was won it was the men left alive that day who sent their messengers to the General and begged him to give them Sheng for their leader. This wish was granted and these men were put, Sheng at their head, with others into that division which was famous for its bravery. And the General was so proud of them that he saw to it that these men had the best of everything, the best food, the best guns.

As for Sheng, he learned to cut his hair short as his General did, and he kept himself clean, and he wore a uniform, not better than his men had, for all dressed alike, but better that the ragged blue garments he had worn in the hills.

And still besides all this there was Mayli. Mayli had taken trouble to know the General, and to speak good words for Sheng here and there, gay words, half fun, so that none might think she cared whether this tall fellow lived or died. But she praised him sometimes where the General heard, and she told of the brave things he had done in the hills.

"I come from the city near where he lives," she told the General, "and he is famous there for his strength and his bravery. Why, it is

23

told there that wherever he met a small company of the enemy he would capture them alone with his two hands and an old gun. And his skill at surprising the enemy made him the talk of all the countryside and the children and the common people made songs about him in the streets."

This was true, and she sang one of these songs which she had heard on the streets of Nanking.

> *"A dragon sits upon the hills,*
> *He sleeps by day, he hunts by night.*
> *His belly fills*
> *With what he kills*
> *He wins in every fight."*

The General laughed at the rough song, but still the next time his eyes fell on Sheng he remembered it and it made him think even better than he had of the huge young soldier under his command.

And be sure that Mayli had something too to do with Sheng's looks. She could by her laughter send him away determined to change himself, though at the time he might refuse to do what she wished. He swore to her always that he would stay what he was and that if she would not love him as he was, then let it be so. But as long as she did refuse to love him, when he left her he made the change she wanted, and she was clever enough when he came back to her with some change she had wanted, not to speak of it or seem to notice it, so that he would think she had forgotten it. But she was kinder to him by a little each time that he did what she had wanted him to do.

And yet she knew that she could never rule him. He loved her and told her he did, but she knew that he would never love her better than all else. Yet she knew that she must love him better than all besides or else she did not love him enough.

Here was the middle of the road where these two stood on that day when the General told Sheng to prepare to lead his men to Burma to fight by the side of the men of Ying.

"I have only one thing to ask," Sheng now said to his General. "How shall we get to Burma?"

24

"How can we, except on our own feet?" the General retorted. "There is no railroad. We go by the Big Road."

Sheng considered this awhile. "And our food?" he asked.

"We will get it where we can as we go," the General replied.

Sheng considered again. "And when do we go?" He inquired.

"In four days," the General answered.

Now as soon as Sheng had received these orders, he saluted his General again and turned and went out. It would take two days to prepare his men for the long journey, but not more, for they were hard and ready. But they ought to have some hours in which to tell their women good-by and to eat a good meal or two of the sort they would not get while they fought, and a few more hours to make an extra pair of sandals apiece, and all such things that men must do when they prepare for a journey which is new to them and from which they may not return.

And then, when he came out of the room where the General was, when he had passed the guards who saluted him, it suddenly came to Sheng that he, too, was one of those who might never return. For he knew very well that this would be the bitterest battle that he had ever fought. To lead his men a thousand miles by foot over mountain and river, dragging their field guns with them as they went, carrying their guns on their backs, eating as they could find food, and then at last to fight on foreign soil, their comrades men of strange blood and unknown temper, this was gravest hazard.

He stood for a moment outside the gate and the people passed him. The street was bright with the hard clear sunshine of winter, but it grew gray before him. It would be a long time before he could see again that woman whom he loved. What if he never saw her again? He turned to the left instead of the right and strode through the crowd, head and shoulders above them, toward the south of the city where Mayli lived.

III

MAYLI'S house, at the end of the narrow street, was very still when Sheng entered it. It was mid-afternoon. In a corner of the court under the scattered shade of a clump of bamboos, Liu Ma sat asleep. She had fallen asleep as she sewed, and over her left hand was drawn one of Mayli's long foreign silk stockings. On the right hand she wore a brass thimble like a ring about the middle finger, but the needle had dropped from this hand and hung dangling by its thread. A small dog, which Mayli had found lost one day on the street and had brought home with her, lay asleep on the flag stones beside the old woman. It opened its eyes at Sheng and, seeing who he was, went back to sleep again.

Sheng smiled at the two and tiptoed across the court and into the main room of the little house. Perhaps Mayli was asleep, too, for the house was as quiet as the court. He entered. She was not in the main room and he was about to sit down and wait for her when his eye fell on the door into the room where she slept and which he had never entered.

The door was open, and through it he saw her standing before the window. She had washed her hair and was tossing it, long and wet, into the sunlight which streamed in, and she did not see him. He stood watching her, and his heart beat hard. How beautiful a woman she was, how beautiful her black hair! He was glad she had not cut her hair as the students and girl soldiers did. She wore it coiled on her neck, but not oiled, so that the fine black hairs sprang out about her face.

His heart suffocated him. "Mayli!" he called roughly.

She parted her hair with her hands and looked and saw him, and instantly she leaped forward and slammed the door between them. He heard her push the wooden bar into place. "Oh, you big stupid!" he heard her breathe through the cracks of the door. And in a moment she was calling for Liu Ma.

Sheng sat down quickly at the right of the table, laughing to himself. Liu Ma was stumbling across the threshold, rubbing her eyes.

26

"How did you get in, Big Soldier?" she asked crossly. "I swear I did not see you come in."

"What would you say if I told you I have a magic dagger?" he asked to tease her. "I carry it in my girdle, and when I say 'Small!' I am so small I can blow myself over the wall in a particle of dust and when I say 'Big!' I blow myself over the wall like the west wind." This he said knowing the old woman must often have heard the wandering story-tellers tell their tales of such daggers.

But she thrust out her lower lip at him and would not smile. "We ought to have a better watch dog," she said. "This dog is only a sleeve dog, and it is no better than a cat for barking at a thief when he comes in."

"Do not blame the dog, good mother," Sheng called after her.

By this time the old soul was out of the room and in the kitchen to heat some water for tea, and the little dog came in wagging its tail, and Sheng leaned over and pulled its long ears. It was nothing but a toy, this small creature, left behind by some mistress fleeing the city when the enemy bombs had fallen in the year just past. He was not used to such little city dogs. The dogs he knew were the village beasts whose ancestors were wolves, and they were still wolves in their fierceness toward strangers. Such a dog had been in his own father's house, and when a stranger came, he had often as a boy to hold back the dog by the hair of its neck, lest the beast spring at the stranger's throat. But there were not many of these dogs left now. The enemy taxgatherers and soldiers, coming to villages to rob and to rape, always killed first the dogs who sprang at them so bravely.

"Of what use are you?" Sheng now inquired of the small dog. Its large brown eyes hung out of its small face like dark glass balls, and its body quivered. When it heard Sheng's voice, it put out a paw and touched his foot delicately, then wrinkling its black nose, smelled him and shrank back. Sheng burst into loud laughter, and at that moment Mayli opened the door. She had put on an apple green robe and her hair was bound in its coil on her neck. On her finger was a ring of green jade.

"Why are you laughing at the little dog?" she asked.

27

"I am too strong for him," Sheng said. "He smelled me and drew back afraid."

"He is a wise little dog,'" Mayli said.

She came in and picked up the tiny creature and sat down with him on her knees and Sheng watched her.

"Why do you hold a dog as though it were a child?" he asked. "It is not fitting."

"Why not?" she asked. "He is clean—I washed him only yesterday."

"That also," Sheng replied. "To wash a dog as though it were a child! It makes the hair on me rise to think of it. To treat a beast as though it were human—is this decent?"

"It is a nice little dog," Mayli said fondling it. "At night it sleeps on my bed."

"Now that is the worst of all," Sheng said impatiently.

Mayli did not cease to smooth the silk smooth hair of the little dog which lay curled tightly on her knees. "You should see the foreign ladies," she said smiling, "how they love their dogs! They lead them on chains, and they put little coats on them when it's cold—"

Sheng gave a loud snort. "I know that you learned all the ways of the foreigners," he said. "But of them all this love of a dog is the one that sickens me most."

Suddenly as he spoke he leaped up from his chair and in one instant before she had time to see what he did he seized the dog from her lap and flung it across the room and out of the door into the little pool in the middle of the court.

"Oh you—you beast, yourself!" Mayli cried and she ran into the court and took the dripping, crying creature out of the water. But now she could not hold it against her silk gown, and so she cried out again for Liu Ma, and Liu Ma came running.

"Fetch a towel!" she commanded the old woman. "Look what Sheng has done—he threw my little dog into the cold water."

But for once the old woman did not take her mistress's part. "Let him be dried in the sun," she said coldly. "I am busy and I cannot take my time to dry a dog."

"The old woman is wise," Sheng said.

But Mayli herself ran for a towel, while the dog shivered and

28

looked sadly at Sheng as he stood there, and then Mayli rubbed the dog dry and laid it down on the towel she first folded upon a stone which the sun had warmed.

And all through this Sheng stood watching her as she moved so swiftly and willfully and full of grace. She was as foreign, he thought, as though she had no blood of her people in her body. For the first time it seemed to him that perhaps he was not wise to love her and that if he married her his life would be war at home as well as on the battlefield.

"I came to tell you, before all this foolish noise, that I am to be sent with the armies to Burma," he said.

She forgot the beast at the sound of these words, and she stopped where she was in the court, and the sunlight fell on her green robe and on her hair. He stood in the doorway, watching her.

"When do you go?" she asked.

"In a few days," he said, "two or three—perhaps at most four."

She sat down on a porcelain garden seat and looked up at him. The sun shone down on her fine smooth skin, and he saw each hair of her long straight eyelashes, black against her pale skin, and he saw each hair of the narrow long brows above the eyes. Into her eyes he looked, and the white was white and the black divided from it clearly. But now that he looked into the blackness of her eyes, he saw that there were flecks in them, like light.

"You have gold in your eyes," he said. "Where did it come from?"

"Do not talk about my eyes," she said. "Tell me why it has been decided that you go so quickly?"

"It only seems quick to us," he said. He came out and drew up the stool upon which Liu Ma had been sitting asleep and he sat down, too. The little dog crawled, still shivering, nearer its mistress and away from him, but neither of them thought of the dog now.

"It has been talked of for weeks," he said. "My own General is against it. But the One Above is for it. And when that one says 'yes,' what 'no' is strong enough to balance it? We go."

These words, "We go," he said so firmly and his face was so stern as he did so, that Mayli said not one word. She looked at him, seeing in a moment what her life would be without this man with

29

whom she quarreled every time he came. But when did she ever wish a quiet life?

"So now we go to ally ourselves with white men," Sheng said.

"Why is your General against this?" she asked.

Sheng reached to the branch of bamboo above his head and plucked a leaf which he tore to shreds as he spoke, and she sat watching not his face but his hands as they moved, with strong slow strength. The thing they tore was slight and fragile, but he tore it to pieces with precision. His hands were delicately shaped, as the hands of all were in her country, even the hands of the sons of farmers.

He did not look at her. Instead he too watched the bits of green that fell away from his hands. "My General says that already it is written that the white men will fail," he said.

"Oh, why?" she asked. Her mind flew across the sea to the land where she had spent most of her life. When she was born her mother had died, and before she was a year old her father had taken her to America. The first words she had spoken were in the language of that land, and they were taught her by a dark-faced woman who was her nurse. The Chinese nurse whom her father had brought with him to care for her had grown sick for home by the time the ocean was crossed, and he had sent her back from the coast. And now Mayli thought of those great cities and the factories and the rich busy peoples, and all the wealth and the pride everywhere.

"How can the white man fail?" she asked.

"It is so written," Sheng replied.

She curled her red lip at one corner of her mouth. "I am not superstitious," she said. "There must be a better reason for me than the prophecy of some old geomancer who sits on a street corner and wears a dirty robe. Has your General ever spoken to a white man— has he ever been in those countries?"

"I do not know," Sheng said. "I do not ask him anything."

"Then how does he know?" she asked.

"He has seen them here on our own earth," Sheng told her. He blew the bits of green from his hands and then he sat, his fingers folded together, and now as he spoke he looked at her, but she knew

30

he was not thinking of her. He was thinking of his own words and their meaning.

"My General has seen the pride of the white men in Shanghai and in Hongkong and he has seen them on the pieces of land they took from our ancestors and made into their own cities. He says they have always considered us as dogs at their gates, and he says that wherever they have lived among the peoples near us, whom they have ruled, they have so held them as dogs, and that now those people will join even with the enemy they hate, because more than they hate the enemy they hate the pride of the white man, who has despised them and their ancestors."

This Mayli heard without understanding it. How could she understand it when all her life until now she had lived in a country where all had been kind to her? Her father had held an honored place in the capital city and she was his daughter, and if the citizens of the city despised the dark ones who were their servants, was that to say they despised her?

"The people of Mei do not despise us," she said. "They despise only the black-skinned people."

"Well, we are not going to Burma to fight beside the people of Mei," Sheng replied. "It is the people of Ying who rule there and it is the people of Ying whom those people hate."

"There is no great difference between these two peoples ot Mei and Ying," she said.

"If that is true," Sheng said, "then it is the worst news you could have told me."

She fell silent, biting her red lip and thinking what to say next. "Perhaps it does not matter whether we are liked or not," she said. "Perhaps the only thing we need to know is the strength of the peoples against our enemy. If the people of Ying are against the Japanese, then we must be with them."

"If we can win with them," he said gravely.

"Who can conquer the peoples of Ying and Mei together?" she cried. She remembered again the great factories, the iron wheels of factories, the terrible precision of the wheels, shaping out iron and steel as though they were wood and paper.

"The dwarfs have conquered thus far," Sheng said in a low voice.

31

"Do not forget—the dwarfs took them by surprise. Well, you say, any man may be taken by surprise once. But on the same day and hours later, they were taken by surprise again in the islands to the south. Wing to wing, their flying ships sat on the ground again and once more the dwarfs destroyed them. It is not enough to be strong only! One must also be wise."

He rose in sudden impatience and stretched out his great arms. "Look at me!" he commanded her. "Look at this great piece of meat and bone that I am! Is it enough that I am so huge? Is it enough that I can bend a piece of iron in my two hands? If I am a fool, is all this size and strength of any use to me? No, I must have wisdom here!" He tapped the side of his great skull as he spoke.

She did not answer. Instead she sat looking up at him as he stood against the sky above her, and she was filled with the sense of his power. How many times she had asked herself if this man had power in him! Had he not? She trembled and she felt the blood run up her body to her face. He dropped his arms and stood there, looking down on her, and she rose quickly and slipped sidewise as though to escape him. For not once did she dare risk his power over her. He must not touch her.

She walked back and forth in the little court once and twice and the small dog dragged itself to its feet and walked after her, still shivering. Then she stopped and sat down on the edge of the pool and she put her arms about her knees. She did not look up at him but he could see the reflection of her face in the still water of the pool. He sat watching this clear reflection. Since it was winter there were no lotus leaves, and the pool was a clear mirror under the sky.

Liu Ma came out, her under lip thrust far beyond her upper one, and she set down the tray she carried on the garden table near the porcelain seat. She poured the tea from a blue and white teapot into the bowls and then to show that she did not approve of these two sitting together in talk, she did not hand them their bowls, but went away again into the kitchen. In a moment the quick smoke of grass-fed fire poured out of the low chimney and hung above the court like a cloud. Mayli laughed.

"Liu Ma hopes that the smoke will choke you," she said to Sheng.

32

"I am too good to that old crone," Sheng said with heat. "I give her very often a silver coin to make my way here easy."

"She is old," Mayli said, "and she loved my mother, and she does not think I am good enough to be my mother's daughter. She thinks I am too foreign."

"And it may be that you are," Sheng retorted.

He saw the painted reflection of her pretty head shake itself in the water, and then he saw her reflected face grow grave.

"Whether one is foreign or not," she said, "today what does it matter? It is not sensible any more to hate something—or some one— because he is foreign. It is better to ask ourselves whether we should not ally ourselves with the strongest people in the world, and these are still the peoples of Ying and Mei."

"Are they so strong?" he asked. "Then why have the dwarfs beaten them so easily, and us they have not beaten although we have fought all these years?"

"Do not take a trick for a victory," she said. "I know so well those people of Mei! It is quite easy to believe that the enemy tricked them. They are so rich, so used to their own skills and power, that they would not believe they could be tricked. But now in their fury they will be twice as fierce and ten times as wary. In one day they learned what it might have taken them a year of usual war to learn."

"It is a pity for us that it had to be learned at such cost to us also," Sheng said grimly. "With a few of those airships that were destroyed in an hour or two, we could have driven the enemy out of our land. It is not only they who were the losers."

Mayli dipped her hand into the pool and stirred the water gently in small circles. "All that you say is true," she said, "and yet when I remember them—I know they cannot lose—no, whatever has happened, and whatever will happen, they will be the victors in the end and for this we must stay with them."

"What do you remember?" he asked. The tea grew cold in the bowls but neither of them thought of it. The small dog had lain down on the folded towel and now it rose again and whimpered beside its mistress but she did not hear it. She let her hand lie in the water, as she remembered, and she sat gazing across the court, seeing only what she remembered.

33

"It is the most beautiful country," she said. "I do not love it as my own, and yet I can say that. The great roads go winding over the hills and the mountains and the deserts and the plains. The villages are so clean, and the people are so clean and fed well. Upon the land the farmhouses are clean, too, and there are no beggars with sores and no hungry wolves of dogs. The forests are deep and the streams are clear—"

"These will not win a war," he said sternly.

"No, but there are the factories," she said quickly, "the factories make ships and automobiles—everybody has automobiles, and they know all the strength and the secrets of machines. Why, they can make enough airplanes to cover the earth!"

"It is strange they have not been able to send us a few," he said bitterly.

"No, but they have not begun yet," she cried. "You do not understand—" she cried. "A people who are so happy and so well fed— they cannot wake up in a moment. They must suffer and feel the war on their own bodies first—"

"We have been feeling it now for five years," he said. "Are we not flesh and blood to them?"

"You must understand," she said, "that we are very far away from them. They do not know us."

"If they are so far away from us, will they help us?" he asked.

"I tell you they will help us," she insisted. "You do not know them and I do. It will be to their interest to help us. Will it not be to their interest to use our soil for their airfields to attack the enemy? But you must give them time to waken—you must give them time to understand—"

"They have had time," Sheng said somberly. "And can we wait now when in a few days we march westward to fight on foreign earth? It may be too late when they have taken their time to waken. No, a few airplanes now might save us all, and thousands may be useless when it is too late."

When she did not answer this, he said, "I speak as a soldier."

"And yet," she said, after a moment, "soldiers do not always speak with all wisdom. For you think in battles and a war is not only made of battles."

34

"What else?" he retorted.

Now at this moment the little dog threw up its tiny head and shut its eyes and howled. They stopped their talk and both looked at the beast.

"What does this dog hear that we do not?" Sheng asked. He looked up to the sky and around the court.

"Listen!" Mayli whispered.

They listened and heard the rising wail of a siren.

Sheng leaped to his feet. "It is the enemy!" he shouted.

In all the time that Mayli had been in Kunming no enemy planes had come over the city. She had heard talk of their coming and she could see the ruins of the times that they had come before, but still it was but hearsay to her. When she went into a shop and saw a broken roof, or a wall that was still a heap of rubble, the shopkeeper would tell her with zest and horror how he and his family had escaped, and this one or that of his neighbors had been killed or maimed, but still it was all hearsay.

The noise grew louder and more loud and the little dog was in an ecstasy of pain. It groveled on the ground, moaning.

Liu Ma came running out, wiping her hands on her apron. "Now, now—where shall we go?" she cried. "Big Soldier, think for us—be of some use to us—we are only two women!"

Sheng ran to the gate and threw it open. In the street the people were already running, some here, some there. The keepers of shops were putting up the boards in front of their houses as though it were night. He heard the slamming of doors and the barring of gates.

"If we were outside the city! To be caught in the city is like being in a pen!" he shouted over his shoulder. And he remembered how when the first bombs had fallen in that city near his father's village he had grown sick at the sight of men and women and children crushed and scattered into scraps of meat and bone, blood and brains mingled together in refuse. But Mayli did not move from where she stood. She could not fear what she had not even seen.

Then he considered quickly. It was perhaps a mile to the south gate. If the gates were not closed, it might be they could gain the countryside before the enemy came. Outside the gate they could

35

take refuge in the bamboo groves. At least the beams of the roofs and the masonry of thick walls could not fall upon them and crush them. They would have only the danger of the chance of a bomb falling upon them.

"Come!" he shouted. The two women ran to follow him. But Mayli remembered the little dog and she ran back to pick him up, and now even at this moment the two must quarrel. For when Sheng saw she had the dog in her arms, he cried out at her a name for her folly, and he wrenched the dog out of her arms and threw it on the ground. Then he pushed her out of the gate and held her to his side so fast that all her struggles could not free her.

"Oh, you daughter of an accursed mother!" he shouted. "When your two feet must run faster than a deer's four feet, you stop for a dog—a worthless dog that does not earn its food—"

But she was wrenching and twisting to be free of him, and the more she wrenched and twisted the more he held her and all the time he was hurrying her down the streets to the south gate, and a few people even in their haste wondered at this tall man who forced the struggling girl. Behind them Liu Ma called and panted, but Sheng would not stay to hear her.

"Her feet are not bound," he muttered, "and let her use them."

Once an old man shouted after him, "Do you force a woman at such a time as this, you soldier? Give over—give over—lest you be killed and enter hell—"

For he thought that Sheng had seized a young woman against her will as soldiers sometimes did, and that Liu Ma was the girl's mother, screaming and calling behind. But Sheng only shouted at the old man, "You turtle!" and hastened on. And at last Mayli gave up her struggling and went with him in silence, and only then did he let her go, except that still he held her hand in a great grasp and he did not let that go.

By now they could hear the drone of planes coming nearer and still they were only in sight of the city gate. But they could run freely enough for the streets were empty. The people had hidden themselves in their houses to wait for whatever came down out of heaven. But the great gate was ahead, and in a moment they had entered the cold shadows of the city wall thirty feet thick which arched over the road, and at the end of this long arch was the gate.

In that moment when he entered the shadows Sheng saw that the city gate was closed. Many a time he had passed through under this city wall to go out into the country, for he was one who had not lived for many days inside encircling walls. It had always been a pleasure to him, when he entered these shadows where the cobbled road was wet from year's end to year's end because the sun never shone here, to see the shining countryside through the open gate beyond. Now there was only darkness, and into this darkness they entered. It was full of other people who had come here for shelter, people who had no homes, travelers caught in the city and beggars.

In the chill dimness under the wall Sheng and Mayli now saw these people, crowded together, the ragged beggars pressed against the others. At such a time none drew away from any other except that one beggar, who had his cheeks rotted away with leprosy, of his own accord drew as far away as he could. But still this was not very far, and it happened that he had been the last to come in, and so he was nearest to the entrance when Sheng and Mayli came in. And Mayli before she took thought cried out at the sight of this wretched man.

"Oh Sheng, look at the man—he has leprosy!" And she turned to run out again.

But by now the airships were over the northwest corner of the city and already the heavy thunder of the bombs had begun. Sheng put out his arms and held Mayli, and yet he, too, was torn between his horror at the leper and his fear of the bombs.

"Wait," he cried, and he put himself at least between her and the man, though himself careful not to touch him.

Now there were voices that cried out against the leper that he ought not to come in where other people were, and one voice after another complained at him.

"Is your life worth saving, you rotted bone?"

"Are we all to escape from the devils outside only to come upon another here?"

Such things were called out and especially the mothers of children were harsh in their anger against the leper, and Liu Ma's voice was loudest of all.

"Stay far from us, turtle's egg!" she cried to the leper. "Fair flesh sickens as well as foul!" And she cursed the leper and his mother, and his ancestors.

Through all this the leper said not one word. His lashless eyes blinked now at this one and now at that one. In the midst of the unrest in the gateway, and some were for going out because of the leper and yet the bombs were now thundering down all around them, there came out from the far end of the tunnel a Buddhist priest. He wore his gray priest's robe, and in his hand he held his begging bowl and he was a young man, and only a new priest, for the nine sacred scars on his head were still red and fresh.

As for the leper, though indeed he felt himself vile and unclean, yet he clung to his life, for it was all he had, and he made no move to go outside where the bombs were. By now the noise was so loud that none could hear a voice, and so without speech the priest put the leper against the wall and himself stood between him and the others, and so all stood, their heads bent, while the fearful rain from heaven came down.

The air in the gateway under the wall grew thick with dust and once or twice the old wall shook around them. A thousand years before this day the wall had been built, and who of those whose hands had built it could have dreamed of such an enemy? Yet because they had laid the foundations so deeply and so well, the old wall stood, and by heaven's kindness, no bomb fell directly upon it as it went curving in and out between the hills about the city. So now it did not fall upon the heads of those who took shelter under it, and they stood speechless and gasping under this rain.

Then it was over. The enemy flew away, and Sheng stepped out of the shelter to see them go. He had seen them come in a line drawn against the sky as clearly as though a painter's brush had drawn wild geese flying. And that he might see them go he climbed quickly up on the wall. They flew home again as evenly as they had come and as full of grace. And Sheng felt such bitterness in his heart that he could not swallow it down. There had been nothing that any could do that could so much as break the perfect line of those ships in the sky. They had come and done their evil work and gone away, maintaining even their shape.

38

And as he watched he remembered what Mayli had told him, how the machines and the factories in the land of Mei could grind out such ships by the score every day, and yet they would not send a few hundred across the sea to beat off the new enemy. A day's harvest of airships would have been enough! And as Sheng stood watching from the city wall he thought to himself how earthbound he was and all his men were, and he longed to be able to fly too, so that he could follow after that enemy. But no, he was earthbound. Upon his feet, plodding ahead of his men, he would have to march a thousand miles to do his share of the battle, while here, where she whom he loved must live, the enemy came on wings and did what it willed.

He leaned over the edge of the grassy inner side of the wall and shouted to Mayli that she was to come up. Now all the people were going back into the city whose homes were there, and those who were travelers went on their way, for the gate was opened. Only the leper sat down beside the gate, for he had no home. As for the priest, he went outside the gate toward his temple in the hills, for he had only come into the city that day to beg. But before he went he took out some coins from the bosom of his gray robe and dropped them into the palm of the leper. When they fell there they made a sound as though that palm were of metal, so hard and dry and white it was with leprosy.

But now Mayli was climbing up the wall and soon she was beside Sheng and he saw distress in her eyes.

"I must go home and wash myself," she said. "I shall not feel clean until I am washed."

He was astonished that she made such ado about this leper and told her so. "You did not touch the man, and he cannot hurt you if he is not touched," he said. "I took care, too, that my body did not touch his, and it is only that priest who touched him, and he is holy and no hurt will come to him."

"But a leper ought not to be allowed to come out," she cried. "If it were in the Mei country, or the Ying, do you think a leper would be allowed to wander among the people?"

"Why, what would they do with him?" Sheng asked amazed.

"Surely they would not put to death a man who cannot help what he is?"

"No, of course they would not," she said. "But they would put him into a place where there were others like him and where none would touch those who are not lepers."

"Yet that is unjust, too," Sheng said gravely. "Is a man to be kept in a prison because he has an illness he cannot help?"

"Oh, you who understand nothing!" she cried impatiently. "It is for the sake of the ones who are not lepers!"

He looked at her and saw her dusty face and hair and her cheeks, which were always rosy red, now pale.

"Let us not quarrel when we have only escaped death together," he said. "You and I, we quarrel whatever comes to us. It will be better perhaps that I go away and leave you. For I begin to see that you will always quarrel with me because I am not what you want."

He saw her red underlip begin to tremble and she turned her head away, and then she saw the city. They had forgotten the city for a moment, but there it lay, smitten under the enemy. Four great fires blazed, and the coils of smoke rose against the fair evening sky. Suddenly she began to sob.

"What now?" he cried, frightened, for he had never seen her weep before.

"I am so angry!" she cried. "I am so angry that we are helpless. What can we do? We wait for them to come and kill us and we can do nothing but hide ourselves!"

He reached for her hand and they stood watching the fires. A roar of far-off voices rose as the gathering crowds began to throw water on the fires, but they did not move to go to help. There were people enough—all that the city had was people!

Liu Ma's voice came scolding up to them from the street. "Are you staying there in the cold? It will soon be night. I go home to cook the rice."

They came down at the call, and followed her, and they felt themselves tired and their hearts were cold with what they had seen and each was weary.

"I must go back to my men," Sheng said.

"Will you come to me again before you go to Burma?" she asked.

40

He did not answer. For they were stopped in their way. Here where the street forked to the north a house had fallen under a bomb, and a young man, weeping aloud, was digging at the ruins with his hands.

"Was it your house?" Liu Ma bawled at him, and her old face wrinkled up with pity.

"My house, my silk shop, and all I had are buried underneath it," the man sobbed, "my wife and my old father and my little son!"

"How are you escaped?" she asked, and now she began to dig too, and Sheng looked about him for something to dig with.

"I went outside for a moment to see which way the enemy came, and they were there over my head," the man cried. At this moment he came upon a small piece of red flowered cloth. "It is my little son's jacket!" he screamed.

By now Sheng had seen a carrying pole lying beside a dead farmer. This man's baskets of rice on either end of the pole were as smooth and whole as when his hands had made them so, but a piece of metal flying through the air had caught him between the eyes, and had shaved off half his head as cleanly as a knife parts a melon. So Sheng took the pole and began to dig and Mayli when she saw the flowered cloth fell to her knees on the rubble stones and dug with her hands, too.

Soon the child was uncovered, and the young father lifted him up in his arms. But the child was dead. Not one of them spoke, and the young man lifted the child up and sobbed to the heavens over them, until none of them could keep back tears from his own eyes. Mayli wiped her eyes with her kerchief, and Liu Ma picked up her apron. But Sheng put down the pole.

"If this child is dead, be sure all the others of your house are dead," he said, "and you alone have been saved for some will of Heaven. Come with me. I will give you a gun for revenge."

Now the man could see easily that Sheng was a soldier and a leader of soldiers, and so he turned blindly, the tears still running down his face, and made as if to follow Sheng with the dead child lying in his two arms as though on a bed.

"Leave the child," Sheng ordered him.

But the young man looked piteously from one face to the other.

41

"I can leave the ones that are buried under the house," he said, "but how can I put down my little son? The dogs will eat him."

"Give him to me," Mayli said. "I will buy him a coffin and see that he is buried for you."

"Good," Sheng said, and his eyes fell warmly upon her when she said this.

So the young man gave her his dead boy, and Mayli took the child in her arms. In all her life it was the first time she had ever held a child so close. By some strange chance this girl had been near no child. Alone she had grown up in her father's house and in a foreign land where she had no cousins and cousins' cousins. She took this little creature and he crumpled in her arms and lay against her so helplessly that her heart swelled in her breast and she could not speak. She could only look at Sheng.

Over the dead child they looked at each other and though neither of them had ever seen him in life, this death of a child made them suddenly tender toward each other again.

"I will come to you as quickly as I can," Sheng said.

"I shall wait your coming," Mayli said. It was only a courteous sentence, such as any one uses for an expected guest, but she made her eyes speak it, too.

So he understood, and he went his way, the man following, and she went hers.

"Let me carry the burden," Liu Ma said.

But Mayli shook her head. "I am younger than you," she said, "and I am stronger."

And so she carried the child home, and there the house was as they had left it, though on the south side ten houses had fallen in a row, and a cloud of dust was everywhere. Inside the court her little dog stood trembling and waiting, and when she came in it smelled the dead child and lifted its head and whimpered. But she went on without speaking and laid the child on her own bed.

He was a fair little boy, about three years old, and his face was round and smooth. So far as eye could see there was nothing injured in him, and she took the little fat hand, wondering if by some chance there was still life in it. But no, she could feel the stiffening of death begun already in the delicate fingers, dimpled at the knuckles. So she laid it down again and sat there a while, not able to take her eyes from this child whom she had never seen alive. And for the first time it came to her what this war was and what it meant in the world when a child could be murdered and none could stay the murderer. Anger grew in her like a weed.

"I wish I could put out my hands and feel an enemy's throat," she muttered.

At this moment Liu Ma put aside the red satin door curtain and peered in because she heard nothing so long but silence. There she saw her young mistress sitting on the bed, gazing at the child.

"Shall I go and buy the coffin?" she asked.

"Yes," Mayli said.

"But where shall we put the grave?" Liu Ma asked.

"We will find a little land outside the city," Mayli said. "A farmer will sell me a few feet somewhere for the body of a child."

"To rent it will be enough," Liu Ma said. "A child's body does not last long, and this child is not even your own blood."

"Every child whom the enemy kills is my own blood!" Mayli cried with such passion that the old woman hid herself quickly behind the curtain.

So Liu Ma went away and after a while Mayli rose and drew the curtains about the bed and she went out into the court and lay down in a long rattan chair that she had bought and kept under the eaves of the house. She lay with her hands over her eyes and the dog came and curled beside her. The little dog was alive and the child was dead. There was no meaning to this. For the first time she understood something of Sheng's anger that she had valued a dog so much. If she had come back and found the dog dead she would have mourned for a pretty thing but she would not have wept. But the child was a life and now she, too, almost hated the dog.

She did not weep again, for she was not given to weeping, and when Liu Ma came back with the coffin in a riksha, she helped her to carry it in, and together they laid the child in it. The riksha man waited for his fee, and he found another man, and then they all went outside the city wall, Liu Ma and the coffin in one riksha and Mayli in the other.

A mile or two beyond the city they found a farmer, an old man whose sons had gone to war, and for some silver put in the palm of his hand first he dug a hole at the far end of a field and they laid the coffin into the earth.

"You are to guard it that the wild dogs do not dig it up," Liu Ma told him, but he chuckled at her.

"Do you think the dogs need to dig up graves nowadays? No, they are better fed than any of us!" He sighed and spat on his hands and lifted up his hoe and went back to his work.

And Mayli and Liu Ma stepped into their rikshas again and went back to the city.

IV

IN THE night she woke. For a moment she listened to hear what had wakened her. But there was only silence over the weary sleeping city. Nothing had waked her—nothing, that is, from without. She lay, listening and aware suddenly of everything, of her body and her breath, of the room and the bed she lay upon, where today she had laid the dead child. All was real and yet nothing was real. She had waked to the blackest melancholy she had ever known, a sadness so heavy that it stifled her.

"Did I dream an evil dream?" she asked herself. But no, her mind was empty of everything except this desperate sense of loss. Yet what had she lost? The child was not hers. Could his death alone have made this melancholy? She sat up in fear. Was there some one in the room and had she waked because she felt an evil presence near her? She leaped from her bed and lit the candle that stood on the table and she held it high and threw its light toward the door. But there was no one. She went to the door and opened it. There Liu Ma slept on a couch, and she was not awake. She lay sleeping with her mouth open, her old face the picture of peace. And yet everywhere in the house was this deep emptiness.

"What does this mean?" she asked herself. She went back to her room and closed the door and stood there, the candle in her hand.

Everything about her seemed suddenly foreign and she longed for some home she did not have, that she might escape the disaster that was everywhere around her. But what home? She had no one except her father far away.

At the thought of her father all her longing welled up. She thought with sudden sickness of longing of the cheerful room in the American city, where he lived. She thought of the clean bright curtains, the blue carpets on the floor. Why had she left him? Why had she left that good place?

She had left it because she wanted to share in the war in her own country.

"You will be sorry," her father had warned her. "You will wish you had not gone. You are not used to troubles."

"I cannot go back," she thought. The red line of her full lips grew straight. "I will not go back," she thought.

She blew out the candle and crept back into her bed and pulled the red flowered silk quilt over her head and cowered under it for shelter. But what shelter was it? Liu Ma had bought it made at a shop and it was cut for the usual small woman and not for a tall woman, and so when Mayli pulled it over her head it left her feet bare, and when she pulled it down over her feet, her head was out, and she could not curl herself small enough.

She grew impatient at last and got out of bed again. And all the time the knowledge of desolation did not leave her. She sat on the side of her bed with the quilt over her shoulders and gave herself up to the misery she did not understand. And now she thought that there was no place for her in her own country. There was no place here for such women as she was. Peasant women tilled the soil as the young men did, or if they had been to school they made themselves into nurses and caretakers of the wounded. But what could she do who had never done work of any kind? She had left her father to come back to her own country and he did not even know now where she was.

Of all the world she really knew only Sheng and in a few days he would be gone. Then what had she left except old Liu Ma and her dog? Her lips curled at the thinness of such a life. In these times, with all her wit and skill and cleverness, was this enough?

45

She threw off the quilt and lit the candle again and began to walk about the room to warm herself. And whether it was the blood beginning to warm her body and to flow hot into her brain or what it was, suddenly it came to her with clearness what she would do. She would go into the west, too. When Sheng went to fight, she would go to do—anything.

When this thought came it came as hard and true as though a voice decreed it. Her loneliness went away and with it the stupid sadness she could not understand. Yes, there it was, she would go with the armies. Well, but how?

There were no women in the soldiers' ranks of the armies that were being sent. They were the armies only of the best trained men. Often she had heard Sheng boast that the men with whom he marched were the picked and chosen, and he boasted what was true, that the One Above had himself examined every man to see that all were young and whole. It was the only time that Sheng had seen the One Above and he had talked for days of that grave thin face and those dark and piercing eyes.

"I went into his presence," he had told her, "and when I saw his eyes, my body prickled as though a thousand needles touched me." And then he had told her what the One Above had said, "Of all my men, you are the tallest and the best in body. Therefore be a better soldier than the others."

"And so I will," he told her.

Now she wished she had learned something of the care of wounded, but she had not. She knew nothing even of the sick. Well, then she must have another influence to let her go.

So as her brain went flaming on its thoughts, and as her will grew firm and stubborn, she was her old bold self. "Why should I not go to the One Above?" she asked herself. "I could go to him, and if he will not let me go, then his lady will. I daresay she is like me. We both grew up in the same foreign country. She will know what I want and how I feel. She is an impatient woman, too."

So she planned, and knowing that she would not tell Sheng, for she knew he would forbid her. He always said that men about to go into battle must not think of women or have women near them or remember there were women on the earth.

46

"And what of the girl soldiers?" she had asked him once when he said this.

"They are not girls when they become soldiers," he had told her gravely. "A soldier is not male nor female, he is all soldier—that is, will and steel and power and fight and fire."

If she told him what she planned he would shout at her, "And what can you do with your feet in satin shoes?"

"I will tell him nothing," she thought. "I will go and get my way. Whether he likes me to be there or not I shall not care."

When she had made up her mind thus she lay down on her bed again and fell asleep as sweetly as a child does.

. . . "Where has she gone?" Sheng asked Liu Ma two days later.

"How can I tell you when she did not tell me?" Liu Ma said. "When I asked her where she was going she laughed and said that she would not tell me because you would ask me and if it were in me you would pull it out. So I know nothing and there is nothing in me. All I know is what I saw, that she had her little box and she went with it in a riksha."

Sheng pawed the earth with his foot like an angry beast. "But what direction did she take?" he bellowed.

"Since our street is at an end three houses away," she said calmly, and with secret pleasure to see this big soldier teased, "she could only go one way and you know the street turns there and so beyond it I did not see."

"But she told you when she was coming back," he said.

"She put some money in my hand and told me to feed myself from it and that before I had eaten it all up she would be back," Liu Ma said.

"Let me see how much money she gave you," Sheng commanded her.

So the old woman put her hand in her bosom and brought out ten silver dollars wrapped up in brown paper.

"How many days will you eat from that?" he demanded of her.

"I can eat it up quickly if I eat well," she said. "Or I can eat poorly and make it feed me for a month."

He would like to have pushed her old face against the wall, it was

47

so calm, but if he did she would tell him nothing. So he only kicked the small dog that came smelling at him timidly, and the beast howled and fled.

"Kick the dog if you will," Liu Ma said. "I do not love that dog."

She pulled the silver ear-pick from her coil of hair and began slowly to pick her right ear. A look of dreamy pleasure came over her face and after a moment she yawned and put the ear-pick back into her hair.

"It is very quiet with her gone," she said. "I fall asleep without knowing it."

But he did not answer. He stared about the empty court and then thrust his hands into his girdle and turned away. But at the gate he paused to shout at Liu Ma.

"If she comes back, tell her I have gone away to war."

She had sat down and already her eyes were closed, and she opened them a little at this.

"Eh!" she murmured, and she folded her hands over her belly and closed her eyes contentedly as a cat does.

. . . At that moment Mayli was swinging high above the mountains in the General's own airplane, and the General was beside her.

She had gone straight to his headquarters, and because the guards knew her they had let her pass them. The General was at his breakfast when she came in, and she laughed when she saw his wry face. For what he ate was not the rice and dried fish, the sweetmeats and the dainty salted vegetables he liked. He ate a foreign gruel made of oats because he had heard it gave strength to men's bodies.

He rose when she came, being a courteous man with some knowledge of the new manners toward women, and then he said:

"I would ask you to eat some of this food, but I swear it would be no kindness in me. Now I know why the white men look so grim until noon, if this is what they eat when they get up."

She laughed and took a spoon and dipped it in the main bowl that stood in the middle of the table. Then she too made a wry face. "But it is burned bitter," she said, "and it has no salt, and it is meant to eat with sugar and with cream."

"What cream?" he asked.

48

"The cream of cows' milk," she said.

But he looked at her aghast. "Am I a calf, to eat milk from a cow?" he cried.

She laughed so much at this that her cheeks grew red and he was pleased with himself, for he was still a young man.

Then he grew solemn and he clapped his hands and a soldier came in and he shouted to him, "Bring in the cook!" and so the cook came in and he roared at him, "You have burned this foreign gruel and put no salt in it and no sugar and why did you not tell me it must be eaten with a cream made from cows? You told me you understood everything about it!"

The man turned pale under his skin, and he faltered. "But I knew you did not like the smell of milk, because you always say the white men stink."

"Is that what they smell of?" the General cried. "Well, I say that it is a good thing they smell so. I shall know my allies by their smell."

He laughed at his own talk, and then waved his hand at the dish. "Take it out," he said to the cook, "and throw the stuff away and bring me rice. And do not even give this to the dogs. Throw it in the ordure jar where it belongs."

So the cook took away the dish of oats and soon he brought back the rice the common soldiers ate, and the General took up his bowl and chopsticks and held his bowl to his mouth and ate down the good food with sighs of pleasure.

Now all this was quickly done, and yet it had seemed long to Mayli, but still she had let the time pass until the man was pleased again. Then she said, "I daresay you will be going back once more to see the One Above before you go west?"

He looked up from his bowl. "Who told you we go west?" he asked.

"I know," she said, smiling the least smile she could. "And I want to go, too."

He put down his bowl. "You!" he cried. "But what would you do?"

"You are taking women with you," she said, and she leaned her two arms on the table and would not let his eyes escape her.

49

"Well, only those to care for the wounded," he said. "We take some doctors and with the doctors are the nurses. It is not we who take them but the doctors."

"I can care for the wounded," she said.

But he shook his head. "It is not my affair," he said. "I will give no such permission. Why, if my men knew, do you think that they would believe why I took you? Would they not see how young you are, and how beautiful? And my wife—do you think she would not scratch out my eyes and pull out my hair? No, we go to win a war."

She seemed to yield to this, and at least she said nothing. But she sighed and then she said gently: "Perhaps you are right. Well, I will ask another kindness of you. Take me with you to the capital when you go to see the One Above."

"Whom have you there?" he asked sharply.

"I must do something," she said humbly. "I came here thinking I would join an army or be of use, but I am no use. If I go to the capital perhaps I can help the Ones Above. I can work in their orphanages, or use my foreign language for them. I know my father would be willing for that."

Now it happened that this General knew her father very well and the more he thought of what she said, the better it seemed to get this handsome, bold woman near to the Ones Above so that they could guard her. It would be a favor to her father, he told himself.

"That I will do," he said.

And this was how it came about that she went with him in his own plane. He had planned not to go before the next day at dawn, but when he found she would not go to her home again, he could not think what to do with her, especially now that the young captains made excuses to come in while he ate and tell him one thing and another and always to look at Mayli until his skin burned hot under his collar. What if one of them should tell another and he another, until mouth to ear his decent wife should know of it? And would she believe him when he said the girl was the daughter of a friend and as much forbidden to him as his own daughter? His wife was so jealous by nature that she always believed what she thought instead of what he told her.

So he had put off what he planned to do that day and in less than

50

two hours after he had filled himself with rice, they were in the sky.

Mayli sat behind him, and the little plane dipped and soared and fell into a pocket and came out again, and under them the clouds swelling upward. She felt the sweetest pleasure now in thinking that Sheng did not know where she was, nor would he dream of this. When would she see him, where would they meet and when she saw him what would be their first words again?

She smiled into the heavens, and the General turning at that moment caught the smile. "I feel I am a dragon," he shouted at her, "a dragon riding on the clouds!"

She laughed and the wind rushing through a hole where the cover was broken, tore the laughter from her lips.

V

Now these Ones Above were no strangers to Mayli. She had heard her father talk much of them. The lady was once her mother's friend, and the One Above was himself her father's friend, and the one, moreover, to whom her father looked for direction and command.

Therefore Mayli prepared herself for the meeting, not only in her looks and garments but in what she would say. The meeting was granted easily enough. Mayli sent a message and a message was returned. It was written in English by the lady herself, and it said, "Come and breakfast with us tomorrow."

So the next morning Mayli, having slept heartily in her hotel after the day's ride through the sky, put on her favorite gown of apple green and bound back her long black hair in its smooth knot and she added scarlet to her lips and a touch of black to the ends of her eyebrows and she hung plain gold rings in her ears. Then, going out of the hotel, she sat herself in a riksha which was waiting at the door.

"I go to the Chairman's house," she said, for the One Above was commonly called the Chairman, and all knew him by that name.

Without any astonishment, the riksha puller said, "The price is half a silver dollar to the ferry," and when Mayli nodded, he tightened the girdle of cloth about his middle and set off at the smooth running pace to which his brown legs were used.

The streets leading to the river were lines of ruin, and there was scarcely a whole house to be seen anywhere, so heavy had the summer's bombing been in this city of Chungking, but nobody seemed to see it. Indeed the war had gone on so long that there were now children able to talk and to run about and even to work at small matters to help their parents who had never seen a roof whole over their heads, and who looked on bombings as on thunderstorms and hurricanes, and no more unnatural. On these streets the people went about their business of buying and selling, and in some places houses were even being mended while business went on inside them, and children ran and played and fell under the feet of carriers and riksha runners, so that pleasant curses and laughter and the shouts of people at their everyday life filled the air, even so early. There was liveliness everywhere and no sign of fear or sadness, and Mayli found herself smiling out of simple satisfaction that she was alive too and here and on her way to have breakfast with the Ones Above. And as she liked to do, being so full of life herself, she fell into talk with the person nearest, who was the riksha puller.

"Are you one of those who have come up from under the feet?" the riksha puller asked in politeness.

Now Mayli knew that that this was the manner in which the people of this city asked whether one were a citizen here or not, and so she said, "I come from far away indeed." He was willing to talk as all his kind are and willingly told her that the times were good for men like him.

"I had rather pull a riksha than be a scholar in these days," he said laughing. "The truth is that so would scholars. Why, I know a learned man who has papers even from foreign schools, and yet he is pulling a riksha because he earns more so than he did being an official. Yes, in times like this a pair of good legs are worth more than a headful of brains and a bellyful of learning."

And he went on and told her that his family had escaped without death through two summers of bombings, and that even the smallest

52

child learned last summer to toddle toward the cave in the rocks when the signal went up for the enemy in the skies, and so that his wife would not have to walk so far with the children when he was busy with his trade he had built his hut near the mouth of the cave, and they were very comfortable there.

"Still, it is not a good life," Mayli said, "and there must come an end to it."

"There comes an end to all things," the man said cheerfully, "and our care should be only to be alive when it comes."

So saying, he drew up before the river, and Mayli paid him his fare, and something more, and then she stepped upon the ferry boat that was waiting for last passengers.

The boat left the shore as soon as she came, for the ferry man was awed by her looks and good garments, and as he rowed across the river, she stood and looked at the scarred city on the shore. It was like a battered brave creature, a dragon who has fought and been wounded and still holds up his head. The light on the muddy river made the water look pearly clear and the city still more dark and scarred.

The ferry had a few early passengers, and they all stared at Mayli, but she did not speak. On the other side of the river she found a car waiting which the Ones Above had sent to meet her, and the driver was a young soldier who saluted her and drove away over the rough road so quickly that the car shook and squeaked in every joint. When this was ended, she came down again and found a sedan chair, waiting for her to take her up a hill, and so by many vehicles she came near to a plain brick house, and surely it was no palace, and yet here was where the Chairman and his lady lived. A guard or two stood at the gate but they knew of her coming, and let her pass, and she walked across a small garden space and to the house. And in the house a serving man took her into a plain room, furnished half with Chinese goods and half with foreign, and in it nothing was rich or costly, and she sat down and waited.

She had not long to wait, for in a moment or two she heard footsteps soft and quick, and there was the lady herself, very fresh and pretty with the morning. She put out both her hands to Mayli and

Mayli felt those strong hands, small and slender and firm, and holding so much within them.

"So you are your mother's daughter!" the lady cried. "Let me look at you. Yes, you look like her, the same big eyes and the fortunate nose. I remember your mother was very beautiful." She sat down on the long foreign couch, all her movements quick and full of grace, and she pulled Mayli down with her.

For the first time in her life Mayli was shy and speechless, to her own dismay. Never before had she been so that words would not roll to the end of her tongue, but now she sat and only stared at the lady. The lady was dressed simply but very richly in a dark blue silk, the sleeves cut short. But over the robe she wore a little jacket of velvet of the same color, and this dark hue set off her clear skin and red lips. This was a very handsome face. The features were each handsome enough, but what made it most remarkable was the proud intelligence in the eyes, and the changefulness of the mouth and the fearlessness of the head carried high upon the slender and most graceful body. She was not a young woman, this lady, but she looked imperishably young. Of her temper Mayli had heard many stories, and now she could believe them, for there was too much power and passion here to mean an easy temper.

"And tell me about your father," the lady said smiling. "The Chairman thinks very highly of him, you know. Yes, it is true he listens sometimes to your father's advice, and then I grow jealous." She burst into clear laughter as she said this. "He will not always listen to me," she said, twisting her lovely mouth into pretended pouting. "Oh, what a disadvantage it is today to be a woman! Do you not feel it so?"

She put the question and looked so beautiful that Mayli was compelled to laughter, too. "I cannot think of any disadvantage it is to you to be a woman," she said.

"Oh, but it is," the lady said quickly. "You cannot imagine. I long to do this and that—anything and everything—I see so much to do, and then sooner or later it comes. The Chairman says, 'Remember that you are a woman, please.'"

She laughed again, willful, charming, impetuous laughter, and for the first time in her life Mayli had no wish to talk but only to listen

54

and watch the laughter and the earnestness play like light and shadow over this most lovely face.

Then suddenly the lady fell silent. They heard a footstep at the door. The lady rose. "It is he," she said. Mayli rose, too, and so they were standing when the door opened and into the room came the Chairman himself, with no guard or servant to announce him.

He was a slender figure, seeming taller than he was. He had the carriage of a soldier and such a face as Mayli had never seen before. First she saw the eyes. They shot their beams direct upon her and she felt him looking at her so clearly that it seemed she felt two shining dark blades pass through her brain. And yet she did not feel he saw her at all, but only what she was thinking. That she was young or a woman or beautiful meant nothing. What she was thinking meant everything.

"This is Mr. Wei's daughter, Mayli." The lady said to him. "Do you remember I have told you about her mother?"

The Chairman came forward. "I do remember," he said. Now his face was kind, and he took her hand. His hand was hard and thin and strong, sinewy like his face and body. But it seemed steel and not a man's hand and she felt her own soft warm flesh against that touch of steel. Even his voice was not like a man's voice. It had a high thin quality, steely too, and it sounded as though it came from far away in the man. He turned to the lady.

"We must breakfast," he said. "The generals are waiting for their orders. They must return at once to their posts."

He led the way and the lady followed, taking Mayli's hand again. How different were the hands of these two, the woman's so warm and soft and enclosing, and the man's so thin and hard, and yet both so strong!

They sat down to a small table and food was brought, half foreign, half Chinese. The lady ate bread and coffee and egg, and the man ate rice and salted foods. There was this division between the two. The man was of his own time and his own country and people, and the woman was herself, a creature speaking now in one language and then another, as easily in English as in Chinese, and thinking now on one side of the world and now on the other. Her thoughts flew from country to country and she seemed made of

55

them all. But the man was Chinese, and he spoke only Chinese and sometimes when she spoke too long in English, he fell into deep silence, as though he had forgotten her. Then quickly the woman, always seeing him and everything he did and how he looked, began to speak in Chinese again, and if he did not answer she would recall him by a touch, or a question.

He spoke very little and she spoke very much. She pressed Mayli with many questions, and then did not listen for the answers. And yet she seemed to pluck answers out of the air. From two or three words she comprehended all.

"Did the Americans think the enemy would attack them?" she asked, and then when Mayli began to answer she answered her swiftly. "Of course the Americans never think anything at all. They are so busy." She frowned and bit a crust of bread with her white teeth. "I need money for my war orphans. I have not enough. And it is absurd that we have not more planes. I tell the Chairman—"

He looked up, his face mild for the moment and kind. "The planes have been promised us," he said.

She made a pretty face of laughter at him. "Oh, you who always believe!"

"I believe our allies," he said.

"Those who ask receive," she retorted. "Does it not say so in the Bible?"

"We have asked," he said.

"There are many ways of asking," she answered him, "and we have only asked as gentlemen ask—with our words. Others are not so gentlemanly and they receive when we do not."

This it seemed was an old argument between them, for stubbornness settled between the man's brows. And stubbornness hardened the woman's beautiful mouth. Silence came down upon them both. And yet in spite of the quarrel and stubbornness and silence none could sit in this room with them and not know that the woman's uneasy world lay in the man, but that the man's heart was not wholly in the woman. Half hatred, half love, something flashed between them like lightning. In Mayli the thought of Sheng quickened. The Chairman, too, had once been a nameless young man, the son of a plain good family among the people such as Ling Tan's

56

was. He was not learned to this day nor had he risen by any power except his own. When he wed this woman there had been great wonder everywhere, Mayli had heard her father say, for the lady was the daughter of rich people, educated in many schools. Nor had he yielded to her imperiousness. There were stories all over the land of the quarrels of these two. This proud woman had married him as her equal and she would be equal to him, and yet time and again he made her take the place of a woman. There was the time when the governing council met, at which no women were allowed, and she would go, but guards had stopped her at the door, though she was his wife.

She had demanded of them, "By whose orders do you forbid me?"

They had answered, "By our Chairman's orders," and so she had yielded, though with anger. Who could know how furiously she had reproached the man? Of these things neither spoke.

And there had been the story of how once her anger overcame her and to revenge herself she wrote a letter to the one who had once loved her as his rival, and he came upon her as she wrote and she was afraid and hid the letter. When he commanded her to let him see what she wrote, she refused and then he cried in a terrible voice,

"I do not command you as your husband but as the head of this nation!" and he drew out his sword. Then she held out the letter to him and he read it and threw it back on the table.

"I do not care what you write to that fellow," he had said, all his anger turned to ice, "but I do care that you refuse to obey me when I speak."

Time and again, the stories said, when she was too proud to yield to him, she went away and left him and stayed away. There were those who were glad to see her go, because of her power over him. But though his anger could last for many days, and so could hers, the day always came and they knew it must come, that whether the quarrel were healed or not, he would send for her or she would come without his sending and their love and hatred would go on.

For the woman had this hold upon the man, that she held him by body and mind and soul, too, and he had never seen another human being who could hold him by all three. She was beautiful and she was learned and clever and full of guile and wisdom and she knew the world as he could never know it and she had words on her tongue to suit every need. And yet she divined in him his soul, that would not be satisfied unless it, too, were fed. He needed to believe that what he did was great and right because it was also good, and he was one who by his nature was compelled to believe that the self in him must be in the path of Tao. This need she satisfied in him. She could pray with him when he needed to pray, and where else was there a woman like her in the world who could satisfy a man both saint and soldier?

Mayli watched them and felt their power and their attraction that somehow drew her into the circle while it excluded her, for the man and the woman lived alone together wherever they were, and yet all the world drew around them.

And all this was shown in the lightest laughter and the gayest words, in the gravest declaration. Thus the lady told of some small thing a child had said in one of her orphanages. Yesterday a little boy had said, "Must I read, lady?"

"Yes, you must read, because all children must learn to read," she said.

"But I have no time to read," he had told her distressfully. "I have to fight the enemy. Please teach me first to shoot a gun, lady."

And after laughter the lady said gravely,

"They shall all be taught to shoot and read. In this world we have suffered because we have only learned to read and not to shoot." And then she said yet more gravely: "Some might have led the way in this war to a new world where we could trust them, but now we cannot trust them. They break their promise to us over and over again."

But the Chairman would not have this return to their quarrel. He rose, having finished his meal, and he took his teabowl in his hand for a last drink of the hot tea before he went away. "I shall not believe that yet," he said to her. "And because I will still believe in my allies, I am sending my best divisions to Burma. If we can fight side by side and win the campaign and keep the Great Road open, then I shall know you are wrong."

He nodded his head quickly to Mayli and went away, and so at the table the two women were left alone. For a moment there was

58

silence, as though when he went away energy went with him out of the woman. She sat with her round bare elbow on the table, her long eyes downcast, her mind gone with him. When she lifted her eyes, Mayli saw fear in them.

"I am afraid," she said, "I am very afraid."

"Why, lady?" Mayli asked.

"I am afraid of this campaign," she said. "He is sending our very best, our most highly trained, our seasoned fighters, the ones he ought to keep for our own country I tell him. What if the enemy advances upon us while these divisions are in Burma? He values them so much that it is like sending his sons away from him. And yet he says he must send his best."

She was speaking in English, as she did when he was not there. "I dread the effect upon him," she said, "if the campaign should not go well."

"Why should it not go well?" Mayli asked.

The lady shook her head. Her beautiful face was very sad now. "There are reasons," she said. "There are reasons. I wish I were a man and could lead the divisions myself, I would see that those reasons would not prevail." She sighed a great sigh. "I wish that I could know from day to day what happens, so that when the campaign is won—or lost—we might know the truth and be misled no more."

Mayli's heart leaped. "Send me," she said, "in your place. I will go and I will watch and I will tell you faithfully all I see and all that happens."

The lady lifted her head and fixed her beautiful powerful eyes upon Mayli's face. "It is too dangerous," she said. "I must think of your father and your mother." But she did not move her eyes from Mayli's face.

"You know that fathers and mothers matter nothing," Mayli said quietly. "You know that only one thing matters today—that each does his duty. If women can fight in the army beside men, if women can walk thousands of miles beside men, I also can do these things."

"Yes," the lady said, "you can. For if I were you, I could. But what will you be? There are no women in these divisions. Do you know medicine?"

"No," Mayli said. "But I could take care of those who do. Let me be the one who takes care of the women nurses. I will see to their food and their shelter and that what they need is given them and I will stay with them at night and see to their protection in the strange country."

"Yes," the lady said again slowly. "You could do that."

"And wherever I am," Mayli said quickly, "I will watch everything and tell you all. I will be your eyes and your ears."

"Yes," the lady said again, "you could be my eyes and my ears."

She sat reflecting upon this for moments without speech, and the sunlight coming through the window caught the clear green jade in her ring and made it gleam. It was a fabulous piece of jade and if it had been sold it could have fed all her orphans for many days, and yet it was part of this woman and not to be sold. For here was the woman's strength, that beauty belonged to her. Any who knew her would have cried out at the selling of any part of her beauty, for there is a beauty more necessary even than the life of another creature. And Mayli seeing such beauty felt her own devotion well up in her like loyalty to heaven itself.

The lady lifted her eyes as though she caught this warmth upon her own heart and she said. "I can trust you and you shall go. Now leave me and I will prepare your way."

VI

MAYLI did not see the two again. She returned to her hotel and, after waiting a day, she received a note written her by the lady, in which she said: "That which we planned is done. You will return to Kunming by a plane ready tonight. I hope your mother looks down and approves."

Mayli did not go out from her room all that day, but she slept and woke to eat and slept again. When at last near midnight she stood at a certain spot beside a small lonely plane she felt refreshed and ready for whatever was ahead of her.

Inside the plane there was one other passenger. He was an officer in a uniform she did not know, a young man with a large, plain face. He spoke to her and used her name, and she knew therefore that he had been told who she was. But he did not speak again. He wrapped himself in his cape and in silence the return was made.

When she entered her little house the next day she found nothing but stillness and peace. It was so quiet a spot after the speed of her journey, after the excitement of her visit, that she could scarcely believe it was there. In the court the bamboos were motionless and the little pool was clear and still under the blue sky of the fair day. And yet scarcely had she come near her door when the little dog heard her and began to bark wildly with joy that she had come back. In a moment Liu Ma came out of the kitchen, her rice bowl in her hand. She was eating, and she had not thought to see her young mistress.

"You are come," she cried, and put down her bowl and made haste to fetch tea and food. Soon the place was quiet no more, between the dog and Liu Ma and Mayli herself, who, being full of health and pleasure, could not keep from singing and calling out to Liu Ma. She made no secret to the old woman of her wish to know whether Sheng had come while she was gone.

"Did the Big Soldier plague you while I was gone?" she shouted to Liu Ma in the kitchen.

And Liu Ma shouted back, "Did he not? I am sorry for you, young mistress!"

"Why?" Mayli asked. She had put her porcelain basin of hot water at the window and there she stood washing herself, the steam coming off her lovely skin, and her lips red.

"He is roaring like a tiger," Liu Ma shouted back. "He bellowed north and south, east and west, because he did not know where you were."

"And you could tell him nothing!" Mayli cried gaily.

"Nothing, nothing!" the old woman cackled, coughing in the smoke behind the stove. Now that her young mistress was back she felt excited and alive again, and she made haste and dropped this and that and broke an egg on the floor and called in the dog to lap it up and tried to do everything at once.

61

As for Mayli she had never felt so filled with joy in all her being. Not so long as she lived would she forget the Ones Above and especially the lady whose eyes and ears she was to be. Nothing she could have been given to do could please her more than this, and she knew she could do it well, and she trusted in herself. She sat eating heartily of rice and egg and fish and tearing a strip of brown baked sesame bread apart with her hands, biting the tiny sesame seeds with her white sharp teeth, and throwing bits to the dog, and all the time her mind leaped across the miles of land and the mountains, to the battlefield.

"Surely we will succeed," she dreamed, "and the enemy will be stopped by our men and before all nations it will be seen that we are brave and we stopped them. When our allies see our success they will honor us for it and redeem their promises."

So her great thoughts went on, leaping from crag to crag of the mountains and making the hardships of the battlefield easy and the armies victorious, and in those armies would not . Sheng be the bravest and the best of all the young leaders? She and Sheng together, could not they be two like the Ones Above some day? Then since she was not a dreamer by nature, she laughed at herself and pulled the dog's ears.

"You will be ill if you eat any more bread, you mouse," she said, and she rose and paced about the court restlessly and thought whether or not she would tell Sheng that she was going or whether she would let him find out for himself. This she could not decide for nearly an hour. There would be pleasure in telling him, for how could he forbid what the lady had commanded? And yet she was a mischievous creature and she could not forbear the thought of her laughter when he saw her the first time on the march with him. The nurses would be taken in trucks as far as these vehicles could go, doubtless, and she imagined herself riding past him, and she imagined his face when he saw her. This so tempted her that she decided that she would not tell him. No, and she would not tell him even that she was come home.

Then she remembered the General. She knew he had come back before her, for the Chairman had said he was sending the generals quickly to prepare for battle. Would he not tell Sheng immediately when he saw her name upon the lists? Then she must go quickly to his headquarters herself and beg him to keep her secret.

This no sooner came to her mind than she did it. She combed her hair freshly and thrust red berries into the coil, and put on her red wool gown and her long black cape, and smoothed perfume into her cheeks and palms, and was ready to go.

"Where are you going now?" Liu Ma shouted to her through the kitchen window.

"I have business," Mayli replied, "and if that big soldier comes while I am gone, you are not to tell him I am here."

This comforted Liu Ma, who did not put it at all beyond her mistress's mischief that she would go to visit a man in his own rooms. Liu Ma often said aloud that once a woman steps over a broken wall she makes a road over it, and by this she meant that walls ought to be about women or they go anywhere and do anything without heed to decency.

So Mayli took a riksha and went to the General's headquarters, and she thought, "It will be my usual evil that Sheng is there, too," but no, he was not. When she gave her name to the guard at the gate, he took it in and the General who had come back the day before her ordered that she was to be brought in. He was alone, and he welcomed the thought of her company. Although he was a man who would never have looked at any woman except his wife with thoughts of intimacy, yet he relished a chance to talk to pretty young women, knowing his own inner safety.

So now he laid aside the paper plans he was studying and straightened his collar and looked at himself in the open window which was good as a mirror and smoothed his hair and rose when he heard her footsteps. She came in swiftly, not knowing she unconsciously imitated the lady in the way she walked and moved and in her warm quick smile.

He bowed when he saw her but she put out her hand in the foreign gesture which was natural to her. He hesitated and then put out his own hand and touched hers quickly. She laughed at his cool touch.

"I forgot that to shake hands is not natural to us," she said frankly. "I have been too long away from home."

"Sit down," he said and himself sat down.

The smell of her perfume was in his nostrils and he breathed it in deeply. His wife was a good woman and he loved her and she had borne him two sons, but his parents had chosen her and he never forgot that this was so. Now with vague longing he looked at the fresh beautiful face. She had sat down and thrown back her cape and she leaned her arms on the desk, and looked at him frankly. He was made shy by that frank gaze and yet he enjoyed it. "These new women," he thought, "though perhaps troublesome to a man, yet have their charm." He had no wish to marry one of them. A man did not want so much charm in a wife. But still it was pleasant to look at one like this so long as he had no responsibility for what she did or said.

"I come always to ask you to help me," Mayli said coaxingly. She never coaxed Sheng. With Sheng she was ruthless and teasing and she spoke out her mind, but her instinct taught her that she must not let this General think she knew herself his equal.

"I am always glad to help you," the General said smiling.

"Have you seen the lists of those nurses who are to accompany the three divisions to Burma?" she asked.

"I have not," the General replied. "I have been too busy with other parts of the campaign."

"Then I am in time," she said. She leaned forward a little more closely. "You know that I went to see the Ones Above," she said in a low voice. "Did they speak of me to you?"

"I did not see the lady," he said, "and with the Chairman I spoke only of military affairs."

"The lady has appointed me to go as the one in charge of the young nurses," Mayli said.

The General smiled. "The lady does what she likes," he said. "But are you not young to be put in such a place?"

Mayli smiled a most mischievous smile. "I am young, but very strong," she said. "I can walk for miles, I can endure heat and I can eat whatever there is to eat."

"A good soldier," he said. "Well, what else? Your work is not under my direct command, you know. You must report to another."

He began to search through the papers and he found one and read out the name, "Pao Chen is your superior."

She put the name into her mind securely. "Pao Chen," she repeated. "But that is not why I come to you."

He leaned back and looked at her, still smiling. "When will you tell me why you have come?" he asked. "Look at these papers on my desk. Each one must be made into an act. And how few days we have left! There has already been too much delay."

"I will speak quickly," she said. "It is a thing short and yet difficult for me to say. It is this—please tell no one that I am going."

Now that she came to her request she found it impossible to speak Sheng's name. She blushed brightly and winked her long lashed eyes as he looked at her.

"Why should your name be kept so secret?" he asked astonished.

She saw he had no knowledge of the reason, so she said bravely, "The young commander—the one you have newly promoted—of whom I spoke—"

"Ling Sheng," he said.

"Yes," she said, "it is he—I do not wish him to know that I go."

"Ah," he said.

"He has some silly thoughts of me," she went on, her cheeks burning again, "and—and—it is better if we do not meet—that is, we have a grave duty to do and I do not wish to—to—"

"You have no silly thoughts of him?" The General's smile was teasing.

"None, none," Mayli said quickly. "I must do my work well, and I do not want him thinking his thoughts. He has his work and I have mine and I do not want to know what he thinks. Moreover, if he finds I am going he will come and try to prevent me."

"He can scarcely do that if the lady has told you to go," the General said.

"You do not know him," Mayli said with earnestness. "He thinks he is the one who can say what I shall do and what I shall not do."

"In other words he loves you," the General said with mild laughter.

"But I do not wish to be loved," Mayli said hotly. "This is not the time for such things."

The General shook with silent laughter for a moment. Then he

65

wiped his eyes. "You shall have your own way," he said. "I have a campaign to undertake and I agree with you that it is better for him to know nothing about you. If he is wounded, he may discover your presence. If he is not, there is little reason why he should ever know you are with us."

"That is what I wish," Mayli said. Now that she had what she wanted she would not stay one moment longer, knowing that nothing makes a man sorrier that he has done a good deed to a woman than to have her linger on after he has done it, and this especially when he doubts himself wise to have yielded to her.

So she rose and leaned on her two hands on the desk, and smiled down at him. "How good you are—how kind," she said. "And I promise you I will do all my duty and if there is any need you ever have of me, call upon me."

He nodded at her, and felt warmth stirring in his belly as though he had drunk a draught of sweet hot wine.

Now just at this moment a soldier came in to say that the commanders of the divisions were waiting outside as the General had ordered them to be at this hour.

"Ah, yes," the General said. "I had forgotten—let them come in."

But Mayli put her hand to her lips at this. "No," she whispered. "Let me go out first."

"Ah, yes," the General said again. "I forgot—yes, he is one of them." So he said to the soldier. "Well, tell them to wait a moment."

The soldier went out, and after a minute to allow him time, Mayli said good-by and her thanks again and she went out, too. She was afraid that Sheng might be somewhere to see her, and she drew the collar of her cape high and bent her head and hurried her steps. But she did not see him anywhere and so she thought herself safe.

Now so she might have been safe, if the soldier had not been a dirty fellow who loved to joke about women and men, and so he went back sniggering and told the three commanders that they must wait a while because the General had a visitor whom they must not see.

They looked at each other and did not answer out of respect for their superior, but when the soldier was gone Sheng said plainly, "I did not think that he was such a one."

66

"He is not," the second commander said. "The minds of inferior men are always ready to make such accursed talk, especially about those who rule them."

Now the room in which they waited was a small room off the main court. A hallway passed between the court and the room, but there was a door into the hallway and this was open, and toward it the third one now stepped.

"I see a woman, nevertheless," he said unwillingly.

They all stepped to the door then, and they all saw the tall slender woman wrapped in a cape for one quick second, too quick to catch any of her looks. But Sheng knew the moment that he saw her who it was. Many women wore such capes, but he knew this tall woman, and for proof it chanced that his eye fell on her hand holding the collar of her cape about her and he saw on it the green gleam of jade.

Who can tell the rush of terror and fear and anger that now swept up his body? Was this where she was all these days, here in this house? Had she gone nowhere but here? Was his own general his rival with her?

The soldier was back again before he could think beyond his fears. "The General invites you," the man said.

There was no more time. Sheng was compelled to move forward with his fellows and he marched beside them into the room where the General was. There the General sat, his cheeks flushed and his eyes bright. They stood at attention side by side, and saluted and at that moment Sheng smelled in his nostrils the faint sweetness of perfume left upon the air.

. . . "The Big Soldier did not come," Liu Ma told Mayli as she came into the gate again.

"Ah, good," Mayli said carelessly. She felt happy and yet restless, and when she had taken off her cape and changed her robe to a softer one, she still felt restless. She walked in and out and then in and out again of the little court. If he came she would tell him nothing. They would play and quarrel and fend off their love, and she would tell him good-by when he went away and then let what happened happen. She was restless with secret laughter and gaiety, and she teased her little dog and played pranks on Liu Ma until that old woman lost her temper outright.

"You are not a child," the old woman scolded her, "I swear I wish you were though, so that I could beat your bottom. Heaven send you a husband soon, and I shall not care who he is. I have a mind to hunt for that Big Soldier myself and tell him he can have you for nothing and I shall only be glad to have some peace."

"You would have no peace," Mayli laughed. "You would have to come along to take care of me, and you know how we quarrel, he and I."

"At least it would be he and I against you, you naughty demon," the old woman said.

The truth was that now, slowly, the old woman had begun to grow fond of the tall young soldier, and she had today made up her mind that it would be better indeed if her young mistress married him, for who else but a soldier would marry so free and wild a thing? A decent man wanted a quiet and obedient woman, and would she ever be a good wife to any usual man? Liu Ma could not believe it. So she had made up her mind secretly that when Sheng came next time she would let him know that she had changed and that now she favored him. She waited for him with impatience, never doubting that he would come as he had come every day to ask if there were any word of Mayli.

He did not come. All that day he did not come, and the old woman grew anxious. "It cannot be that the Big Soldier has gone off to war somewhere?" she asked Mayli in the afternoon of the second day. "He has not stayed away so long as this before."

"What do we care if he is gone or not?" Mayli asked, pulling her dog's ears. "We do not care do we, little dog?"

"I am used to that long radish," Liu Ma said unwillingly.

"You like radishes better than I do, then," she said, still laughing.

But Mayli would not acknowledge even to herself that she, too, wondered why Sheng did not come.

From that day, Mayli spoke no more of Sheng. There was no time indeed, for early the next morning Mayli was summoned by messenger to come to her superior, Pao Chen, to receive her orders.

When that message came she deemed it time to tell Liu Ma what lay ahead, and so, when she had eaten and when the old woman came in to fetch away the bowls to wash, she lit a cigarette and said, "Liu Ma, I have something to tell you."

"Tell on, then," the old woman replied. She stood waiting with her hands folded under her apron upon her middle.

"I am going away," Mayli said abruptly. "I have received a command from the Ones Above to do a certain work I cannot tell of, but I must do it."

Liu Ma did not speak, but her jaw dropped and she stared at Mayli.

"What day I go is not yet known," Mayli said, "but that messenger who came this morning brought me the order from my superior and there I must go and see what is wanted of me. As for you, you will stay here until I return and keep the dog and this house. If you are lonely you may find another woman to stay with you."

Now Liu Ma was used enough to change in her long life and, hearing whence the commands came, she did not dream of crying out against that, but still she did not like what she heard and because she could not protest the larger she protested the smaller.

"Why should I want another woman here to be fed and spoken to and noticed all the time? I had rather stay alone with the dog whom I know."

"You shall do as you like," Mayli said with good humor. "All that I ask is that you keep the house for a home for me."

"I do not know whether it is well even for me to do that," the old woman said, wanting to feel peevish. "This is not my native earth and water and how shall I know whether you will come back or not? You may change your wish and here I shall be waiting for you until I die and die, perhaps, with nothing but a dog beside my bed."

"Now you are being troublesome," Mayli said laughing. "I say then that you are only to stay if you wish to stay and, when you go, lock the gates and take the dog or leave it, and in all things do only as you wish, good soul."

Thus she took away all cause for discontent, and this made the old woman more peevish still. She clattered the bowls as she picked

69

them up and she said, "Why is it you are being sent for a work? Even in a dream I could not guess."

"You must ask the lady that," Mayli said. "I too wonder why I am sent, but I am sent and so I must go."

"She does not know you," Liu Ma exclaimed. "A willful rootless man-woman sort of thing you are," Liu Ma went on, "and what will you do—hold a gun and march beside that big soldier?"

Now this pricked Mayli very deep and so she grew angry and leaning over she slapped Liu Ma's cheek. "Hold your jaws together," she cried. "I do not even know whether I am being sent where he goes or not. How evil an old mind that always runs upon lust and lechery!"

Liu Ma drew herself still at this. "I am a decent woman," she bawled, "and what my mind runs on is getting you wed and made decent, too, instead of running everywhere loose. The only decent woman is one wed to a man and behind walls and made the mother of his children."

"You dream, old woman," Mayli retorted. "Is this a time for marriage and having children and being locked behind walls?"

Now that she spoke so sternly Liu Ma was frightened and so she held her peace and went on about her work though she thrust out her lip in a most sulky fashion. And Mayli made ready to obey the summons she had been given, and her anger made her silent, too, and she felt righteously that she was not going westward because of Sheng but truly enough because she wanted to go for what use she could be.

So she went on foot to the place where she had been told to go, and when she reached the gate she saw other women going in, too, all young and strong and grave-faced. She joined them and went in with them to a large room where two men sat behind desks and took their names and sent them to the right and left to wait.

When her turn came she was not sent with the others but straight ahead through an open door and there she found the same man who had been the only other passenger in the plane with her a few days past. She wondered when she saw him that he had not spoken to her that day beyond the commonest greeting. But still it was so that he had not chosen to speak, and now she did not recall herself to him. She stood before him until he bade her sit down, and then she sat and waited while he looked at a paper before him. Then he put it down.

"You have been told your duties," he said.

"I have been told only part of them," she replied.

"Here is all your other responsibility written down," he said, and he took the sheet of paper and handed it to her. "Read it," he commanded, "and tell me what you do not understand."

She read it carefully, and there was nothing she could not understand. Indeed all was written down and numbered. He waited motionless while she read.

"Is all clear?" he asked.

"It is clear," she replied.

"It is your duty to see to each of these things," he said, "and if any fails to be done I shall look to you. Your co-worker will be the head doctor, Chung Liang-mo. Together you two will be responsible for all that concerns the sick and the wounded and the nurses will work under both of you. In this he will be responsible for the medical and surgical matters, but you will be responsible for all that concerns the nurses, the food, the quarters, the supplies. Where you disagree, you will come to me and I will decide between you. I do not expect disagreement."

She bowed her head in assent. He struck a bell on the table and a soldier came in.

"Invite Dr. Chung to come here," he said.

He sat silent and without moving until in a few minutes another man entered the room. Now Mayli waited with some impatience for this man, for this was the one with whom she must work side by side, and if she disliked him from the beginning the work would be the more difficult. But the moment he came in she liked him. Chung Liang-mo was a man short and strong in the body, and his head was round and his face round and he had a patient mouth and patient good eyes, and yet intelligence was the light behind the eyes. He was neither shy nor bold. He greeted Pao Chen as though they were friends and sat down, and Pao Chen seemed to wake into new interest and he said,

"This is your co-worker, Wei Mayli, of whom you have been

71

told. She has received her orders and you have received yours, and it would be well for you to draw apart and talk together awhile. Go into this next room while I proceed with what I have to do."

Dr. Chung rose and smiled his easy smile and he said to Mayli, "Shall we go apart?"

She rose, too, and followed him into the other room, and there he sat down and she also. Then he took out of his pocket a sheet like hers and gave it to her. "I will read yours and you mine," he said, "so that we may know all our work."

"Here is mine," she said, and so they studied the sheets for a moment.

"This Pao Chen," the doctor then said, "is a strange man. He will always write a thing down rather than speak it, but he has a head so clear and hard that his mistakes are very few. He is a man who had rather act than talk, and yet I do not know another better for his part of this campaign." He looked at Mayli kindly, examining her face. "You are very young, I think," he said. "Have you ever endured any hardships?"

"I have not," she confessed, "but I am ready to endure them."

"We shall have great hardships," he said gently. "This campaign must be a difficult one. The Chairman has laid down a very stern duty for the soldiers. We are not to yield. That is the only order. We may die, but we may not surrender."

"It would be the Chairman's order," Mayli said, remembering that soldier's face with the eyes of the saint burning in it.

"Many will be wounded," the doctor went on, "and we must be ready for day and night without sleep or rest, once the battle begins."

She bowed her head, "I can eat and sleep or I can go without," she said simply. "I have only one question—when do we go?"

"That one question no one can answer," he replied. "It is locked in the mind of the One Above. When he gives the sign we go. But all is ready. One division indeed is already gone. Two more go within the next few days. Then we will go, or perhaps we go with them."

She heard this and her heart immediately put another question of its own—was this Sheng's division which had gone and was that why he had not come near her? But who could answer a question her heart asked? She sat silent, her eyes upon the doctor's round patient face.

"We are not even sure where we are sent," the doctor said. "There are those who say we go to Indo-China. There are those who say we go to join the white men in Burma. Others say we go both ways. We shall not know until our feet begin the path."

Her heart cried out another question—"What if I go one way and Sheng another?"

But who could answer any question of the heart? She could not speak it aloud, and after a moment she rose.

"You will therefore be ready to leave at any moment," he said.

"I shall be ready," she said.

VII

THEN she chid herself. In such times as these, when the enemy threatened the life of the nation, when the artery of the Big Road into Burma was about to be cut, what right had she to think of herself or what her heart cried? These were not the times for love. She had said it often to Sheng without believing it for herself. Now in the presence of these grave men who were planning for the lives of many others, she did believe. For one moment she was afraid of herself. Had she the strength and the courage indeed to see wounded and dead, to travel by foot and by cart and by any way she could over hundreds of miles of rough road and roadless country and jungle? But it was too late to draw back now. And if she drew back could she endure the waiting and idleness? It seemed to her that the whole city would be empty if Sheng went on and she were left behind. Whether she met him or not, it would be something to know that she went westward when he did and that they were employed in the same great thrust against the enemy.

"What are your orders?" she asked Dr. Chung.

"I will ask you to come each day to my office," he said, "and help

73

me prepare the boxes of goods which must accompany us. There will be nothing except what we can take with us."

"I will come tomorrow morning," she said.

And so she went each morning thereafter for eleven mornings and came home late for eleven nights. She did not mention Sheng to Liu Ma except one day when the old woman wondered again where he was.

"That big soldier—where can he be?" Liu Ma asked.

"Doubtless he has been sent to Indo-China," Mayli replied calmly. "Many have been sent."

She felt Liu Ma's eyes upon her sharp and curious for a moment, as the old woman busied herself with her dusting, but she remained calm. Something about that calm held back Liu Ma's tongue and from that time on she, too, spoke no more of Sheng.

. . . All her life now began to fall into the pattern which was to govern it for many months ahead. She rose early in the morning, ready for the day's work. Never before had she had work to do every day, but these hours were filled from early until late. When she had eaten her breakfast she put on a dark robe, padded with silk, and she walked a mile or more to the house where the hospital supplies were gathered together. However early she went, the doctor was there before her, his stiff hair brushed up from his plain good face, and his hands, red with cold, piling goods into bundles and tying them himself if no one else came as early as he. But soon the long room made of boards and paper was full of men and women, nurses and soldiers and clerks, checking lists and putting aside drugs, wrapping them into oil cloth and oiled paper and nailing up boxes. At one end of the room these boxes began to grow into a great heap. Each must be weighed for none could be heavier than the back of a man could carry.

On the very first day Chung had assigned to Mayli the task of overseeing the goods which the nurses must use and he had thrust into her hands a sheaf of lists.

"Check them yourself, please," he said in English, "if there is anything missing, supply it."

He always spoke to her in English, for his own language was a

74

dialect of a remote region far in the depths of the province of Fukien, and English came to his tongue quickly, for he had spent more years abroad than he had in his own home, and French and German were as quick on his tongue as English. Yet his short squat figure was common looking enough. Only his hands were the fine hands of a surgeon. She did not know enough in those early days to protect his hands. But the time was to come when she had seen them explore the tendrils of a man's life so often that she ran to save them when he touched a coarse or heavy thing, lest their life-saving delicacy be harmed.

He spared himself nothing, this doctor. She saw him stoop and heave up a box as though he were a coolie, and test it on his back to see if its shape were hard to balance upon his shoulder. He pounded nails and he picked up the glass of broken bottles and cut himself often. In her own corner of the long room day after day as she checked off her lists and saw to the goods, he was everywhere, kind, silent, busy.

Slowly the mass of goods, the crowd of men and women grew into order and readiness. She came to know her nurses one by one. There were several score of them; some were dull and slow. But all went because they were glad to go, and all felt that what they did was a worthy necessary thing. Four she soon knew because they were always near, ready to take her commands. One of these was Han Siu-chen, a student whose family had been killed in a sack of Nanking, and she had escaped by being in an inland school. She was a round-faced girl, merry in spite of her sorrows, but she had plenty of hearty hate for the enemy, and she was eager to do her work for revenge. Her plump hands with their pointed fingers were always raw with chilblains, for she had a fine rosy skin, the blood very near the surface so that her lips were red and her cheeks scarlet and ready to burst with blood. These hands were what made Mayli notice her first, for she had called to the girl to fold some bandages that had come out of their wrapping, and she saw blood on the white cloth.

"Whose blood is this?" she asked.

Then the girl, shame-faced, held out her pretty hands, and they were cracked and bleeding.

75

"Come here and let me oil them and bind them," Mayli said. "What can you do with hands like that?"

Every day thereafter in the morning Mayli oiled and tied them with bandages, and so she came to know the girl, who was always blushing and laughing and crying out that it did not matter about her hands.

The second girl was a thin, pale, small one from Tientsin, a city girl accustomed to wealth, whose parents had escaped before the enemy, and her mother had died from hardship, and her two brothers had been killed in battle and she and her old father were left alone. He, having nothing else to give, and being old and feeble, besought her to go and in some way avenge herself for her brothers. When he found that she was unwilling because when she went he would have no one to care for him, he took a peaceful poison, and she found him dead one morning, and knew that now his command upon her could not be denied. This girl's name was Tao An-lan.

The third girl was a very pretty one and her name was Sung Hsieh-ying, and she had suffered no hardships of any kind, except when the city was bombed, for she belonged to this city and had grown up here, and her whole zeal was love of her country, unless perhaps she longed for change and travel, but she thought it was love of country.

The last girl was no girl at all but a young widow who had suffered from the enemy in ways she would not tell. But she had been a soldier in the army in the northwest, and had been captured and had escaped, and passing through many ways, she had come at last to this place and hearing that armies were being sent westward, she offered herself. Her name was Mao Chi-ling.

Each of these women had been taught, as all had, the care of wounded and sick men, and some knew more than others, but all knew something.

Besides these four, who attached themselves of their own will to Mayli as their head, there were all the others who from day to day began to look toward her as their head and the one between them and the others above, and this made a change in Mayli. She who all her life had thought of no one except herself now found these young women for whom she must think and plan. She worked all

76

day and in the night she woke to dark fear lest she had forgotten something, which when they were in the middle of the march in the jungle, would be needed perhaps to prevent death. There were no books to tell her anything of the march, and now she began to search out those who had traveled westward and she asked a truck driver or a bearer coolie, a soldier, or a traveling merchant, any and all who had been to the west.

"What is the climate there?" she asked.

"So hot that hot tea is cool," one said.

"So rainy that the clothes mildew and fall from your back," one said.

"The insects consider you a gift from heaven," one said.

"The snakes rise up in the middle of the path before you and greet you as their daily rice bowl," one said.

"The poisonous vines reach out their arms," one said.

"The sun peels off your scalp, hair and all," one said.

"Fever crawls into all your seven apertures and shakes your bones like dice in a cup," one said.

"The rivers lie smooth and small until you come and then they rise into seas and swallow you. The river gods there are very strong and evil, and they have all been bribed by the enemy," one old man said. He had fallen into a river somewhere and his leg had been bitten to a stump by a crocodile.

She listened to all they said, finding the truth in their several ways of telling her that the country through which they would march was dangerous difficult country, full of sickness and ill fortune. It would be her duty to guard as she could against these evils. Medicines Chung would take, but she bought extra leather shoes for her women, to each a pair more than they wore, and she rolled wide strips of the heavy cloth woven in the farmhouses of that region, and these were to wrap around the legs to prevent the insects, and she found yards of coarse linen and she tore them into veils, to keep away the poisonous flies and mosquitoes, and she devised and packed boxes of compressed extra foods, each woman to have such a small box of dried bean-curd and salted meat and rock sugar. Everything must be light and small, for if the carriers failed, all must carry their burdens and none must be heavy laden at any time, since to

77

breathe the very air in the jungles was a burden. There were tales enough everywhere of the foreign soldiers who had so much to carry to provide comfort for themselves that they could not march quickly enough to catch the enemy.

An old soldier who had come back from a battle in the south cursed and spat and laughed as he said one day, complaining against carrying a change of garments, "Shall I be like those foreign turtles who carry summer clothes and winter clothes and rain shoes and a rain cloak and bedding and food and a sun hat and a rain hat and everything but a house? A gun, all the bullets I can steal, a second pair of straw sandals, and it is enough. I can feed myself as I go, and why should I be afraid of rain?"

This indeed was the temper of all the soldiers. They were willing to carry only what would help them in the battle. Each man held his gun dearer than himself, and guarded his ammunition even from his comrades, for there were those who would steal bullets who would have considered it sinful to steal anything else.

The day came for which all waited. The General, who had waited with great anger and impatience for the command to come down from above, had declared himself ready for the past eleven days, and everywhere he was cursing and swearing that there must be some trick to delay their going, for why did they not go, seeing that the enemy was everyday growing more strong? In the islands to the south the white men had been defeated again and again, and now they were clinging to the sides of mountains in dens like beasts. Then suddenly one day the order came down, and within an hour he had sent it out, and all knew that the next morning at dawn the great march would begin.

That night in her little house Mayli could not sleep. Twice and three times she got out of bed and examined her garments. Everything lay upon the chair ready for her, the heavy shoes, the uniform that was like a soldier's, a pistol, her pack. Once she opened the pack, counting everything that was in it. She had a belt made with pockets for her money, to wear under her coat.

In the middle of the night the door opened and Liu Ma came stealing in. She had a small bag in her hand, not much bigger than her own palm, and she gave it to Mayli.

"What if a button tears off?" she whispered solemnly. "A small thing may cause great trouble."

Mayli took the bag and inside she found short Chinese needles, and yards of fine strong silk thread wound small about paper spools, a pair of small steel scissors very sharp, and there were two brass thimbles, some foreign bone buttons, six foreign closing pins, though where Liu Ma had found these luxuries who could tell?

"I had not thought of this," Mayli said. "But indeed it is what I might need very much."

"Why should you think of a small thing when I do all your sewing?" the old woman said. "But now who knows whether you will ever need me again?"

Saying this she burst into loud tears, and sobbed. "You are a troublesome child to me, but it will be more trouble to live without you!"

"I shall be back," Mayli promised her. "You must wait here for me and see—I will come back, I promise you."

"Only Heaven can fulfill promises," the old woman said and went away wiping her eyes on the corner of her jacket.

In the darkness Mayli lay down again upon her bed. Now that she was about to leave, and indeed perhaps forever, her mind seemed to be one vast confusion. Why was she going? The will to go had begun half idly as a wish partly made of loneliness, partly made of her reluctant love for Sheng, partly out of a true longing to be useful to her country. Now all of these parts had become a whole. She was going. She knew that Burma had become the single gate for China to the rest of the world. The gate must be kept open, for only through that gate could help come against the enemy.

. . . This purpose to hold open the gate of Burma was indeed the purpose of every man in those three divisions of soldiers, the purpose in every heart, man or woman, who set out the next day at dawn upon the march. The singleness of their purpose tied them together closer than a family, and they all felt their closeness. Yet who put it into words? The start was made like any other start, in a confusion of noise and bawling shouts, of complaints against loads too heavy, of small stubbornnesses and sudden quarrels. First the trucks

79

were loaded to go as far as they could go. Goods and women were loaded into trucks and then men crowded in where they could. To one man in each truck a plan was given of where the route lay and where all must wait for each other at the end of the road.

Mayli, in her stiff cloth uniform, her pack strapped to her shoulders, stood ready at the head of her young women. They were dressed alike, and as she was dressed, and in their gravity each young face looked strangely like the next. Next to her stood her four aides. Their hearts were like her own, beating with excitement and fear and will for victory. Siu-chen's round red-cheeked face was like a solemn child's, and An-lan was paler than usual. Chi-ling, the young widow, looked sad and a little weary, as though for her the march had already begun. But Hsieh-ying, the girl who had suffered no hardships yet, was smiling and gay and her eyes were black and shining and her lips red because she kept biting them.

"Watchers of the wounded!" a man's voice yelled. "Protectors of the sick! This way—this way!"

A little lieutenant waving a sheet of paper shouted at them and hastily Mayli stepped forward and with her all the others, and they marched forward to the trucks that had been set aside for them, and they began to climb in, the girls courteously waiting for Mayli to climb first into the seat beside the driver, who was a big common-faced fellow with small eyes set close under bristling brows of stiff black hairs.

A moment, a scream or two, some excited laughter, and they were ready to start. Now the truck where Mayli sat was the first in the four that carried them, and when the driver pushed a handle, it would not start. He stamped both feet and pushed another, and still it would not start. At that he cried out to heaven and beat the sides of his head with his palms and cursed his vehicle heartily.

"You who slept with your own mother!" he roared at the truck. "Have I not stuffed you full of foreign oils and poured water into your belly? Did I not burn incense for you to the gods yesterday? Now what more will you have?" He jumped down from his seat and kicked the truck well in its under parts and then leaping into his seat, pushed yet another handle.

All was of no use. The vehicle groaned and hissed and roared inside, but it did not move. Then Mayli who had often sat in foreign cars abroad saw a small handle and she pointed to it.

"Let that fly back," she told the man.

He grinned at her and let it fly back, and the truck moved at once. He was not in the least abashed that he had forgotten to do this one necessary thing, and he complained as the truck bounced and leaped along the rough road. "The trouble with these foreign inventions is that none go far enough, in my opinion. If these foreigners are so clever at such things, why not go something further and add a self-releasing brake, so that the vehicle can remember its own needs? This cursed brain of mine, how can it think for me and for a vehicle, too? Must everything rest upon me?"

Now at this moment Mayli saw that the hood of the truck had been removed, and that all the inner parts of the engine were open to the dust and the rain. "Is it not very unwise to have the cover off the engine?" she inquired. "If it rains, we may be stopped, or if the engine clogs with dust."

The driver pulled his little cap sidewise over his eye that was opposite her to leave his eye clear that was next her. "What am I that twenty times a day I must heave up a cover and put it down again?" he said. "I took the cursed thing off."

This he said in the gayest and most careless manner, and all the time he talked he drove that vehicle like a wild animal down the road. Soon Mayli was speechless, and all she could do was to cling to her seat and brace her feet against the floor, for she was thrown from side to side, and up and down, and the man said grinning at her, without staying in the least his fearful speed, "Lady, it would be better to put another soldier on the other side of you, so that you would have us both for cushions."

"Can you—can you—not go a little slower?" she gasped.

But he shook his head to this. "This accursed son of an obscene mother," he shouted at her above the din and rattle. "If I let him go slower than this he thinks it is time to rest. No, once I let him know it is time to go, I must keep him going until I myself am too hungry and must stop for food. Besides, in the afternoon he never goes as well as in the morning. Do foreigners not work in the afternoon?"

She shook her head and did not try to answer except with laughter for by now what breath she had was not for talking.

How welcome was noon of that day! Without a word to prepare her the driver stopped the vehicle suddenly ánd seized her by the shoulder to keep her from shooting out over upon the ground, for the glass was gone from the windshield. The stillness was dazing. She sat for a moment in it to collect herself, but the man had already leaped down and he was pushing his way into an inn and shouting for food. Then when she had rested a moment she was compelled to laugh again and so she climbed down.

"I feel I have already marched a hundred miles," she said to Hsieh-ying who ran forward to help her. They clustered around her and Hsieh-ying said:

"This afternoon I will change places with you, for I saw how your driver paid no heed to any clod in the road. Now the man in our truck was a student and he is very clever and escaped the ruts and the clods."

But the truth was that Hsieh-ying, being a hearty woman, had liked the heartiness of that soldier who had driven the truck. This Mayli divined and let pass with a smile.

So when they had eaten of what had been prepared for them, great bowls of rice and meat, and cabbage, nothing could prevent Hsieh-ying from climbing in beside the big-faced fellow and Mayli found herself beside a pale thin young man who nodded to her without smiling when she took her seat.

It was true that this was a very different fellow. He knew his vehicle like a brother, and he handled it with care and the vehicle moved along as smoothly as a cat. It was the same road and no better than it had been, but how different it was! Mayli said, "You drive this car as though you knew it."

"I do know," the young man said. "I am an engineer. I have a degree from an American college."

"Then why are you doing this?" she asked.

Without knowing it she spoke in English and in English he answered her. "I was studying in America—my last year—and then I couldn't go on. I had to come home and get into it. Well, I went to Chungking and waited and waited. Months. Nothing happened. This chance came and I took it."

"Nothing happened?" she repeated.

His lip curled. "I hadn't what it takes to get through to the big fellow," he said.

"What it takes?" she repeated.

"Pull—money to open the gates—politics—something."

"But it takes nothing," she said. "I have nothing and I went in and saw them both."

He shrugged his shoulders and kept his eyes on the road and was silent for a long time. Then, without moving his eyes from the road, he began suddenly to talk to her.

"Ours is the most beautiful country in the world. Look at those mountains! They are the most beautiful in the world. I was sick to get back home."

Indeed all around them was very beautiful. The hills, bare of trees but covered with ruddy winter grass, were purple in the evening, a rich purple against a gilded sky. In the valleys the farmhouses clustered in villages, which lay before the mountains, and the hills were terraced into fields. Blue-clad farming folk stood at their doors to watch the trucks go by, and little children ran to the roadsides to shout to them and wave their arms. Bamboos were still green in the hollows of the hills, and now and then a temple roof lifted its high pure curve.

"This is what I came back for," he told her, still in English. "I came back for this land and these people—not for any big men at the top."

"Are you a communist?" she asked out of a second's instinct.

"I don't know what you mean when you say communist," he retorted. "I'm a man of the people." He was silent again for a long time and then he said, "Of the people—by the people—for the people."

She recognized the familiar foreign words without knowing why he used them now. Nor did he explain them. They rode another half hour in silence, and he drew up smoothly outside the gates of a small town. "Here is where we camp tonight," he said and leaped out.

83

She climbed down then and saw him, before she turned away, examining the vehicle as tenderly as though it were a living creature that belonged to him.

"Tomorrow I must ask him his name," she thought, and she wondered that she had not asked it today. But she had not. Names seemed meaningless. They were all moving forward together and the name of any one was nothing.

VIII

SHE said to herself that certainly she could not sleep. Never in her life had she lain upon the ground to sleep. The four girls had piled some straw under her and when she had seen that all were in their places for the night, fed and cared for, she had lain herself down with her blankets wrapped about her. They slept in the back courtyard of a temple. The men were in the front, and this back room was very small so that half of the women slept outside, and she had chosen to be among these. The night was not cold and its silence was broken by the small waterfall of a brook which had been led through the court from the hillside above the temple. The tinkle of the water teased her ears for a while as she thought of the day.

"Certainly I cannot sleep," she thought, but it did not seem to matter whether she slept or not. What did anything matter that might happen to one person? She lay thinking that for the first time in her life it seemed of no meaning what happened to her, no, nor even what happened to Sheng, wherever he was. They were being swept along in the same great wave westward. They might meet and they might never meet, and this, too, was without meaning. To go on, to find the enemy, to defeat that enemy, for them all this had become the whole of life.

. . . In the morning she woke first. For an instant she could not find herself. Upon the gray morning air, now very chill and damp,

84

she heard the thin struggling crow of a young cockerel. Then she saw lights already lit in the temple and, lying a moment longer, she heard the deep droning chant of the priests at morning prayer. This was a Buddhist temple and the music, though so old that its source was far beyond the memory of any man now alive, still had foreignness in its cadence. It had come from India and India was in its sound. She had never seen India, nor ever thought of it except as a color upon the map at school. In this gray dawn, listening to the chant, she thought of India as the land toward which their faces were now turned. In ancient days men had gone from China to India to find a new and better god. An emperor had told his messengers, "I hear there is a god in India whom we do not have. Go and find him and bring him here to live with us." So they had gone and found Buddha.

Now they went toward India, soldiers and not priests. Thousands of soldiers went even on foot, dragging artillery behind them by ropes and straps across their shoulders. They were camping somewhere now on the road. Thirty miles was their day's march and they had set off two days earlier than the trucks, and the trucks had not caught up to them yesterday.

At her side Chi-ling lifted her head.

"Are you awake, captain?" she asked. For captain was the title that Pao Chen had given to Mayli.

"I am awake," Mayli replied.

She put back her blanket and sat up. All about her heads lifted. They had not been sleeping either, but waiting, and when they saw her awake one by one the young women rose and folded their blankets and packed their knapsacks and bundles, and almost in silence they all did this.

And Mayli was among the first and she went to the temple kitchen. There she found two old priests already behind the great earthen stoves feeding in grass, and there was a cauldron of water very hot.

"Dip in, lady," the old priest said, not looking at her because she was a woman. "That is water for washing."

She saw a tin basin there and she dipped a gourd dipper into the hot water and she took the full basin and in a corner behind some bamboos, she washed herself and combed her hair. She had kept her

85

hair long as it was, but at this moment combing it over her shoulders, she thought:

"What will I do with this hair? What can it be but a care to me?" For one moment she thought of Sheng and how he had liked her hair long.

"I like to know that a woman is a woman when I look at her," he had said once when she had teased him by saying she would cut off her hair as many women now did.

But she thought of him for only a moment. Then she seized the long twist in her hand and went to where she had slept and opened her pack and took out the little scissors that Liu Ma had put in her sewing bag. Holding her hair in her left hand she cut it off at her neck with the scissors. The women watched her, but no one said a word. She went with the long hair in her hand into the kitchen and she went behind the stove where the little old priest was crouched, and before his astonished eyes she thrust her hair into the fire like grass.

He chuckled and she saw his toothless gums. "I swear it is the first time priest's breakfast has been cooked by woman's hair," he said in the little high squeaking voice of a eunuch.

She smiled and went away again, and out in the court she shook her head, and the wind was cool in her short hair. She felt light and free, and from that day she held her head higher than before.

. . . On this day the Big Road, which had risen beneath them as they traveled it the day before rose still higher upon the mountains. They had come by small roads until a day ago, to escape the enemy's bombing. But as they had come near to the border, the order came down to move south on the Big Road. Who had not heard of this Road? They all knew how it had been made by men and women whose tools were the spades and hoes with which until now they had tilled only the fields. Those who had no tools had used their hands.

Mayli rode in the second truck in which she had been the day before, and she was glad of that, for now the young engineer made her see that which without him she might not have seen with understanding. He was in the truck when she came out, after she had been busy with all she was responsible for. It was her pride that not one

86

moment's delay should be caused by her women, and so she stood waiting at their head outside the temple when Chung came out. He smiled ruefully when he saw her there, for his own garments were hastily put on and his hair stood up unbrushed.

"To get up early," he groaned in pretended agony, "it is the curse put upon man."

"I thought you were always earlier than I am," she said.

He yawned loudly for answer and shook himself like a dog and took a piece of brown sesame bread out of his pocket and gnawed it while he found his place on the top of bales of goods. She took her own place when all her women were in their vehicles, and the young engineer sat waiting, his motor hot, and he very neat and clean and his hair smooth.

He looked at her with the smallest of smiles on his lips. "My name is Li Kuo-fan," he said. "Called Charlie by the Americans."

"Charlie?" she repeated. "It suits you better than Li Kuo-fan. Let it be Charlie. And I am Mayli, surnamed Wei."

He nodded without repeating her name and the truck started. She could see excitement in his long narrow eyes. "I've looked for this day," he said. "I have wanted to travel the Big Road since it was made. This is my first chance. Maybe this is why I came along."

The road rose ahead very rapidly, and yet its slope was clever and even. It clung to the sides of the steepening hills like a trail.

"See how it follows the footholds on the hills," he said. "It was made by men who had walked these hills so long that they knew where foot could cling."

So it had been. Generations of grass cutters had found the most hidden easy path for the feet, and generations of traders, following their pack mules on their way to the West, where they could sell their goods and find new goods to bring back, had searched out the possible ways, as they climbed the mountain ranges of the western wall.

"They asked foreign engineers how long it would take to make this Big Road," Charlie said. "They considered their tools and said 'Years.' But the Chairman said, 'It must be months. We will use our own tools.' So it was months." His eyes swept up the climbing agile

87

road. "I'm proud of it," he said, and she, looking at him, saw his eyes fill with tears and she was silent.

They passed in the middle of the morning a great hole in the road where yesterday the enemy had bombed it, and there they saw such men and women as had built the road. They were now mending the hole, and it was nearly ready for their vehicles. Who were these people? When the vehicle stopped she came down to rest herself and to tell her women that they too could come down since it would be awhile before they could go on. She saw the rugged blue-clad crowd busy at their task, and she went over to a woman who sat flat on the earth, pounding rock to pieces with a harder, larger rock. The woman was young, but the rock dust had made her face and hair gray, and it clung to her eyebrows, and it was thick on her shoulders. Near her in an old basket a little child slept, under a torn quilt. When Mayli came the woman looked up shyly not sure whether this was a foreigner or what. But Mayli spoke to her politely. "Have you eaten?" she asked. Now this was the salutation of the north, and the woman answered it as a question.

"I have worked all night," she said. "And I eat while I work."

Now that she perceived that Mayli spoke her own language a wide bright smile came over her dusty face and her teeth were very white and even.

"And the child?" Mayli asked, astonished.

"He sleeps here well enough," the woman said laughing.

"But your family?" Mayli asked.

"There is my man and me and the older two, and we all work here on the Big Road," the woman said with pride. "We helped to make it."

"Like this?" Mayli asked.

"I pound rock and my man carries earth," the woman answered. "The girl pounds rock over there, and the boy carries what we pound." She nodded to a girl child a few yards away, who had stopped to stare at Mayli.

"Which is your man?" Mayli asked.

The woman pointed with her chin at a man digging with his hoe in another place. He filled his bamboo baskets and lifted the pole on

88

his shoulder and carried them and emptied them where the earth had been blown away.

"We live not far from here," she said, pointing again with her chin, "and when they call for the road to be mended, we lock the door and all come together. Let the enemy blow their holes—we can mend them." She laughed and again her white teeth shone out of her gray and dusty face, and she began pounding. Men and women, they worked with the unhasting speed to which they were used and in less than an hour more there was a bridge of earth and rock, narrow but firm.

"These are the people to whom I belong," Charlie said when they went on again.

"Were your parents really like these?" she asked.

His thin lips grew more thin. "The people are my father and mother," he said shortly. It was all she was ever to know of his forebears.

This day was one like the many that came after it. If she had been timid or afraid, she would have been often afraid, for that road now soared so high that to travel upon it was more like flying than riding upon rock and earth. More than a few of her women were sick and they leaned over the side of the vehicles where they rode and vomited heartily. But they did not complain and they would allow no delay. Once when the road marched along the top of a high ridge between higher mountains, Mayli chanced to look back, and she saw An-lan, her pale face set in terror. Indeed it was a cause for fear to see how the ridge dropped down on both sides of the narrow rough road. She called back, "An-lan, An-lan, can you go on?"

The girl could not answer. Her lips were stiff and when she put out her tongue to wet them her tongue was dry. She could only nod her head.

"All right?" Charlie asked.

"An-lan is green with fear," Mayli said. "But this is no place to stop."

"It is not," he replied, and could not take his eyes for one instant away from the perilous trail.

It was indeed a dangerous spot. At the foot of the precipices on both sides of the road they saw the wrecks of trucks and cars which had slipped and fallen to one side or the other. But the wrecks were surrounded with men who were taking them to pieces and packing the metal into bundles which they could carry. Metal was precious, and at a certain town on one of the days, she found one place where this metal was very precious. This town had for hundreds of years been famous for the making of scissors, and today, in the midst of the war, the scissors makers went on with their trade.

Now they had all stopped here for their noonday meal, and Mayli and her women were very curious to see these scissors. They were wrought with skill and so delicately chased that each woman was anxious to buy a pair, and they were willing to go without their meal if only they could buy a pair of the scissors.

Mayli bought scissors, too. She found a small sharp shining pair upon which butterflies were chased, and though she had the pair Liu Ma had given her she could not resist these. The edges were sharp as little knives.

"How sharp the edges are," she said to the old man who sold them to her. He had a little wayside shop, open to the street, and he had nothing but scissors for sale.

"It is the foreign steel," he said. He put on his brass-rimmed spectacles and took up the scissors to explain them to her.

"But where do you get such steel?" she asked.

"How impatient are women!" he said, and he reproved her with his little solemn eyes. "I am about to tell you. The steel is from the trucks that slide over the side of the Big Road. You must know that these trucks are made in the Mei country. The steel there is mixed with many metals and it is very hard—harder than any iron we can make. I wish I knew the secret of those makers of steel. Now because of this we make the best scissors we have ever made, although for hundreds of years our scissors have been famous in these parts."

"I have been in the Mei country, America, they call it," she said smiling, "and I have seen the great steel furnaces where the metal is mixed."

Then to his hanging jaws and wide eyes she told him how she had gone to see great steel works as indeed once she had when she went home with a schoolmate who lived in Pittsburgh.

90

"That was a sight," she said. "The furnaces were bigger than a house and the metal poured out like living water, white hot, but what the alloys were I cannot tell you. I only thought what a wonderful and fine sight it was."

He wrapped the scissors for her in soft paper as he listened and then he shook his head gravely.

"Those foreigners," he said. "They know everything that has to do with metals and steels, and they can fly their airplanes as though each man had made his own. I see them sometimes fly over our heads. They come out of the mountains and their cloudships are enough to frighten any devil, with their grinning jaws. How the enemy shrieks and flies when they come! Who are these men who drive such monster machines? I thought, once, that such men must be ten feet tall and winged like eagles. But no, I see them now sometimes, for there is an airfield for them in a town not far from here. They are only young men, foreign, but full of temper and noise like any other young men. They come down out of the sky and bellow because they are hungry." He laughed silently and folded away his spectacles. "Children," he said gently, "children—playing with magic!"

He looked so wise in his age that she felt humble before this old man, who had done nothing but make scissors all his life, and she took her purchase and went away.

But she did not forget what he had said. On the afternoon of the next day when they were winding along a very hazardous part of the road, their hazard suddenly increased. Seventeen enemy planes appeared out of the sky behind the mountains. The day was clear and blue, and there was no hiding place anywhere. Below them the precipices fell away for a thousand feet and above them the mountain soared on. There was no cave nor rock big enough for them to creep under. Nor had they time. The enemy rushed out like dragons.

Who could decide whether to halt or to speed on?

"Even if we stopped and crawled under the trucks, what use would that be?" Charlie groaned and he pressed his foot and the truck darted forward, swaying over the edge of the narrow road.

Those vicious enemy planes dropped down and now the valleys

roared and the mountains crackled with their noise. Mayli gripped the side of her seat with her hand and braced her feet against the sloping floor. She knew instantly the full meaning of their peril. It might be that at any moment they would be fragments of steel and wood and human flesh flying down the precipices.

Then as swiftly as the enemy had appeared there came four other planes from heaven and they attacked the enemy so swiftly that eye could not follow them. She saw them close, now high, now low, now weaving in and out among the fire from the enemy guns. Such a battle went on as she could not have imagined. The enemy forgot its attack and turned against the four planes, but who could catch those skillful creatures of the sky? Six enemy planes crashed into the valleys, and without loosing a single bomb the others went away.

Now Charlie stopped his truck, for the four planes were driving the enemy beyond, and it was better to stay back, and the whole long line of vehicles stopped and they all watched.

"The Flying Tigers," Charlie said. His lips were quivering and his eyes were shining. He was panting as though he were running.

"Get 'em," he had muttered all through the battle. "Get that one —good boy—there goes another. Oh, you good boys—oh, you great fellows—"

It was over in less than ten minutes, but when the skies were clear again, her whole body ached, as though she had been hours in the one tense position. She felt her hand hurt her suddenly, and when she looked at it she saw she had pressed the metal side of the seat so hard that she had cut into her own flesh.

But before she could speak she forgot it. She heard a sudden roar of wings, and there at her side hanging over the emptiness which fell away to the plains below, she saw a small plane for one second very near her, and out of it leaned a laughing American face. She saw him wave his hand, then he flew upward again and on over the mountain's head. Then she remembered what the old man had said yesterday when he sold her his scissors. Children—playing with magic!

. . . And yet nothing was so strange as one more thing which happened on the last day of their journey on the Big Road. Their

92

eyes were filled now with the beauty of this journey into the height of mountains and the depth of valleys, with waterfalls flying hundreds of feet through the air. Their eyes were stretched with all they had seen. When night fell they camped in majestic sleeping places, in little towns caught high above crags, or in temples built in cuplike valleys upon mountain tops. They grew silent because of the grandeur of their days. A laugh could echo across ten valleys, a shout could shake the rocks of mighty cliffs. Without knowing it they spoke in soft voices and kept their laughter low. Then slowly as days passed the mountains sank to hills and the chill dry air softened. Bamboos grew again and lilies and ferns, and now they were coming down the mountain walls, into the lowlands which led to Burma.

Here was the strange thing. A certain town, scarcely more than a village, lay waiting for them at the end of a day. Mayli had settled her young women into their places as she always did and then she had a little time for herself, and, being eager to see strange things, she went to the gate of the temple which they had hired for a stopping place, the men this time being in tents outside the city, and as she stood there she saw a handful of young women come by who were not hers. Now she knew that there was another encampment in this city, for when she went to make her usual report to Chung, her superior, he said,

"There is a contingent of sick men here, left from the other army. They are men who have been struck down by the black malaria, and tonight I shall go there to the south of the city where they are encamped, and see how they are. I purposely directed our men to camp on the north, for there should be no coming and going between us."

"Black malaria?" she repeated.

Then he told her of that disease more swift than any human enemy which hides in the lowlands about the mountains and it is so hateful because it seizes men's brains as well as their bodies.

"How can I guard my women from it?" she asked in great alarm.

"They must not be bitten by mosquitoes," he told her, and so she had spent her evening telling her women this, and a certain old priest came by while she spoke, and he said, "Let them sleep near burning incense for the devils which bring the disease hate incense burned to the gods." So he went and brought back handfuls of incense and spills made of brown paper which he lit and blew upon to light the sticks of incense.

It was after all this that Mayli had gone to stand at the gate for a little while to watch the street and the people who came and went here. And thus she had seen the handful of young women who were not hers.

Now this was the thing which happened while she stood, and it was the sort of thing which men hearing it would say could not happen but it did. Among those young women she heard a voice she thought she knew and she looked and saw a face she did know, and who was it indeed but Sheng's younger sister, that little Pansiao whom she had left months before this in a school in the mountain caves where she had taught for a while?

She stared at the girl, and thought, "It is she, Pansiao," and then she thought, "It cannot be Pansiao, for she was so young and tender and how could she be here?"

The young women were passing very close now. They were all in uniforms and they were laughing and talking. As they came near, Mayli spoke in a low voice, but very clearly "Pansiao!"

The young girl whom she was watching stopped, turned, and stared at her with rounding eyes. It was Pansiao.

"Oh," she cried. "You!"

She sprang out from among her fellows and seized Mayli's hand in both hers and stared at her and laughed and pressed Mayli's hand to her breast. "Where did you go?" she cried. "Oh, how I missed you when you were gone! It was because of you that I ran away. Yes, because of all you said to us. Do you remember how you would not let me learn 'Paul Revere'?"

"I do remember," Mayli said laughing. "Come inside the gate."

"This is my friend," Pansiao said joyfully to the other girls, who were standing fixed with astonishment. "This is—she is my teacher —or she was."

"Come inside, all of you," Mayli said. So they came inside, and sat down on the marble steps in front of the temple, and there Pansiao told how she had run away from Miss Freem and the school in the caves.

"Six of us ran away," she said, "and some went one way and some another. Well, it was so easy. I just ran away one day, and the army was not far off and there were enough people moving southward and I went with them. They let me eat what they ate when they heard I went to join the army."

She looked so naive, so fresh, with her red cheeks and her soft brown eyes, so much a child, though thin and hard-fleshed with walking, that Mayli could not but smile her tenderness. And added to her natural tenderness was this, that Pansiao was Sheng's sister and it was Pansiao who had first told her about Sheng, and had wanted her, childlike, instantly to be his wife.

"Do you know your brother is somewhere on the way to Burma?" she now asked Pansiao.

Pansiao clapped her hands and then put her hands to her cheeks. "You mean my third brother?"

"I do mean that one," Mayli replied.

Pansiao leaned close. "You are not—are you?"

"I am not married," Mayli said, and could not prevent the heat rising to her face.

"Nor is he, yet?" Pansiao asked gently.

"No, he is not," Mayli said.

She felt her face very hot under the young girl's clear gaze, but what more could she say and what could she do but speak of something else?

"Where do you go now?" she asked Pansiao.

"I have not been told," the girl replied.

"Would you like to join us and go west?" she asked.

"Oh, I would like to go with you," Pansiao cried.

"Then I will see what I can do to bring it about," Mayli replied. It would be sweet to have this child with her who was Sheng's sister. She put out her hand and touched Pansiao's hand. "Go back," she said, "and come again tomorrow morning with your things. Tonight I shall talk to those who are above me and ask them to let you come with us—with me."

"Oh, what if they will not!" Pansiao cried.

Mayli smiled. "I think they will," she said. Her eyes and voice were those of one not used to being refused.

95

Pansiao jumped up. "I will go and pack my things now," she said. She dropped to her knees before Mayli.

"Let me come back tonight!" she pleaded.

Who could refuse such adoration? Certainly Mayli could not.

"Very well, tonight," she said. "It will be best, for we start the day at dawn."

IX

ALL during these days Sheng had been waiting, his men gathered grimly about him, on the border of Burma. They had climbed the wall of mountains, cold by night and hot by day even though their feet were in snow. They had walked a thousand miles and more, a steady march of thirty miles a day, each man carrying his rifle and bayonet, a rain hat of bamboo, a helmet, a packet of three days' food, a second pair of shoes, a water bottle, a spade, twenty bullets and two hand grenades. Carriers came with them, marching beside them. Although each carrier had his load of eighty pounds of rice, Sheng had not forced the march nor delayed it, knowing that his men had their own place in the long steady stream of strength coming out of China. This place was at the head and they were the vanguard, but there were others to the north and the south. As he went he made careful note of the path, the land and the people, remembering especially where food was plentiful and where it was not. If food was scarce it was never that it was withheld from them, for the people everywhere were welcoming and gave whatever they had.

He came near to the borders of Burma with his men on the exact day, lacking six hours, of the time which his General had set for him to be there. His men were mud-stained and weary, but they had fought the enemy many times in the past and now they were full of eagerness for this new battle they believed would be the greatest of all. Not one rifle had been lost or even wet with rain on the march. These rifles were new weapons which the One Above had ordered to be given them, and each man felt his rifle a personal gift and if his own head lay in mud while he slept at least his rifle was laid high and safe. They had dragged artillery behind them, too, over the high mountain gorges, and this they had kept ready oiled and quick for use.

They had another strength than that of weapons. On the day that this march had begun, secretly lest the enemy discover it, the General had told them that they were being sent to Burma not as any usual army might be sent.

"You are going," the young General had said, standing very slim and tall, "as a token of our leader's faith in the alliance with the nations now united against the enemy. Our leader is determined to throw all his strength into the struggle against tyranny in the world. We fight in our place in a world war."

This saying the men had never forgotten. They knew that they must stand for their country and for their leader before the foreigners who were to be their allies, and how proudly each man held himself and how carefully and courageously each did his duty was a sight which day after day struck Sheng's heart almost with pain.

For, though the General had spoken so clearly to the soldiers, yet Sheng knew very well the doubts in the secret place of the General's own mind. To Sheng the General had said, and at the last moment: "I wish I had our leader's faith! I wish I were sure that we are not betraying our own men!"

Sheng had carried all these sayings with him as he led his men through valleys and gorges and over mountainsides. He spoke to his men gravely each evening of the duty that lay upon them to fight beside their foreign allies in such a way that all those who heretofore had looked down upon them as inferior and weak should see how brave they were and how ready and resourceful. How often was he to remember those evenings! They stopped when night fell, wherever they happened to be upon some lonely mountainside, the gorges falling away beneath them into darkness, the sky pulsing with stars above them or bright with the moon. If luck came they found a temple, or a small village clinging to the rocks. Each night when his men had rested and eaten and before they slept they had gathered about him, and then in his simple abrupt way he spoke

97

of the day's march, what was good and what he wanted mended the next day, and he listened to any questions or complaints, and then at the last he said, each day, something of the same thing, in such words as these:

"You are not to think of yourselves as a common and usual kind of soldier. In the old days soldiers were held in low esteem and they were men of fortune, selling their courage for the highest price. But we are of a different make of man. Here am I, a farmer's son, and my father was once well-to-do and we were three brothers in his house, always with plenty to eat and wear, and the crops good on the rich river land which now the enemy holds. Here am I, owning nothing today, and I fought my way here, having been first a hill-man and then a soldier, but always with only one hope, to kill as many of the enemy as I could. I have risen to be your head only because luck has been with me and brought me here, and I am no better than you, be sure. We are all equals and brothers in this war, chosen because we are strong and young and because we are not afraid to die. We were chosen by the One Above because we are his best. He sends us to fight beside the white men, to show them what our best can be. Whatever happens no man is to think of retreat or of his own life."

"You do not need to say that to us," the men muttered. "Where you lead we follow."

"Even if I should be struck down," Sheng said gravely, "each man must think for himself as he has been taught to do, and behave as a leader behaves. On the way in which you fight hangs more than you know. Our foreign allies must see in us what our people are, and allow to us our equal place in the world."

So day after day with such high words, he taught his men that they were indeed no common army, but an army with one mission, to acquit themselves nobly in the eyes of their foreign allies, and to do their full share in defeating the enemy. And if it happened that they stopped at a temple or in a village, others came near and stood listening to his exhortation. Priests stood silent in their gray robes, and some in saffron robes, to hear what he said, and in villages the peasants and their sons stood listening, and more than once young men followed Sheng out of their villages in the morning because

98

the night before their hearts had been so moved by what he had said to his men. Nor did Sheng forbid them. He was once such a young man himself, and if an army like his had come through his village, be sure he would have followed it too, and he added the young men to the carrier corps, since they were not trained yet as soldiers. In this way they had come down out of the highest mountains and so drew near to the borders of Burma.

Now Sheng had dreamed of nothing but coming to Burma and marching straight into the battlefield. Often the men had asked him, "What is our plan when we reach the border?" and always he answered, "It will be told us when we reach the border. The foreign commander under whom we are to serve will tell us there. But certainly there will be no delay, for the enemy has persuaded Thailand and is already in the south. Be sure the man of Mei will send word what we are to do."

For so great had been the faith of the One Above in his foreign allies that he had given over these his best veteran troops to the leadership of a foreigner. Who did not know this man? Every man in Sheng's company knew that name, and though none had seen him, they asked Sheng often about him, but Sheng had not seen him either.

The General had only said, "We are to serve under a man of the country of Mei." This the General told him the last day, that day when Sheng had seen Mayli wrapped in her long cape, flitting through the General's court. His mind had been all mixed with his feelings and yet he heard this clearly enough to ask,

"Why has the Chairman put us under a foreign leader?"

"There are things not to be understood in this war," the General had replied. "Put it this way—the men of Ying will deal more easily with him than with us." His lips curved with bitter meaning. "The Ying men speak but one language and it is their own," he had added.

The young officers who had stood with Sheng before the General that day had not answered. Each was thinking that it seemed strange indeed if they must be led by a foreigner, and yet if their Chairman had so decreed what could any do? They could only accept.

"This white man," Sheng had asked after a moment, "is he a good heart?"

"I have seen him twice and I have talked with him," the General replied, "and it seems to me his heart is good. He is tall and thin, not young, and his temper is reasonable. Nor does he hold himself above his men nor above us. Those who know him say he takes off his coat and fights in the ranks. He is not like the men of Ying, who expect even a dying man to salute his officer—or so it is said."

"And how shall we understand this foreigner when he speaks?" a second officer had asked.

"He speaks our language," the General had replied. Then he had leaned over his desk and with his eyes piercing first one and then the other he had said: "Hark you, it is my belief that we can follow this one and trust him. But he is not the highest in command. They have put another over him, these islanders. He is in command of us but they are in command of him."

They had stared back at him, trying to drain the last drop of meaning from this warning, and they waited to see if he would say more. But he struck the desk with his palm. "I have prepared you for anything," he said, "and you have your orders." Upon that they had left the room, and Sheng had seen him no more.

Sheng was now exceedingly anxious to know how the war was in Burma. All during these days of march he had been cut off from any news. Where was the enemy now? Had the white men held? If they could hold Rangoon, then all would yet be well, for if the white men held that city upon the Bay of Bengal, the Chinese could hold the road from Lashio and the north, since the enemy would have to carry their war supplies hundreds of miles from Bangkok.

But when he reached the Burma border, there was no news. All was as peaceful as though war were nowhere in the world. He led his men into the suburbs of a small town and since his were the first vanguards, the people stared at them, astonished and fearful. It was a mixed place, made up of Chinese mixed with Burmese and tribesmen, and it was easy to see the mixture. The Burmese were darker of skin than the Chinese, lighter even of foot, and their ways were full of childlike gaiety and merriment. Chinese and Burmese lived together here well enough, and yet there was some impatience between them, too, for the truth was the people of China were shrewder and better at trade than the Burmese and this often made a Burmese angry, for although he knew the Chinese who was his neighbor worked harder than he did and so deserved to grow rich sooner, yet the Burmese did not love him better either because he worked harder or grew richer. So it came about that although the two peoples married each other's daughters and lived side by side and in the same houses even, there was often that secret anger in the Burmese man's heart, and in the Chinese hearts the small mild contempt because the Burmese loved pleasure too well.

This was easy to see and Sheng saw it the very first evening when he sauntered upon the street of this strange town and stopped at an outdoor inn to ask the price of a sweatmeat. He had eaten only rice and dried fish all these days with such vegetables as could be found and now he craved sweet on his tongue. The inkeeper was a Burmese and he scowled at Sheng and muttered the price so low that Sheng could not hear, and Sheng asked him outright, "Do you want to sell me your wares or not?"

The Burmese spoke Chinese well enough and he said, "What do I care who eats my sweets if he pays but how do I know you have the money? I have been cheated before by a Chinese."

At this Sheng grew angry and he threw down his coin on the counter.

Then the Burmese was good-tempered again, for it is not easy for those people to stay angry for long, and he wrapped the sweet in a twist of newspaper, and said as he gave it to Sheng: "Do not be angry with me. When a man is twice bitten by a dog he is a fool if he does not expect it the third time."

"How a dog?" Shen inquired, "and how a bite?"

The Burmese shrugged his graceful shoulders. "The further you go into the land the more you will see what I mean," he said. "Between the Chinese and the English, we Burmese are pinched as a beggar pinches a louse between his thumb and forefinger."

"English?" Sheng asked, not understanding the foreign word.

"You call them the men of Ying," the shopkeeper said. "The English! They govern us for their own good, and the Chinese steal away our business. The truth is we hate you all."

The man said this with a great burst of laughter and he spat freely on his own floor and rubbed his head and stamped his feet and felt better. And Sheng took his sweetmeats away and chewed them thoughtfully as he went, though the taste of them was foreign on his tongue.

It was true, as any eye could see, that behind the counters in the shops along the streets, if they were prosperous, the owners were nearly always Chinese. He stopped at one of these to buy himself some cotton socks, because his left heel was rubbed sore by walking, and behind the counter was an old man, but not too old, who was Chinese, and Sheng fell into talk with him. After greetings he found the man came from the other end of the Big Road and that he was new here, having only come a few months ago.

"You have prospered quickly," Sheng said looking about the shop, which though small was very well stocked.

"Any one can prosper here," the man said. "The people spend their money easily and they like bright toys and luxuries and they are lazy and love food and sleep and laughter. They are children."

But mischievous children, Sheng told himself. For when he reached his camp that night one of his men cried out, "Are you bleeding, Elder Brother?"

"No, certainly I am not," Sheng relied, "but why do you ask it?"

"You have a great spot of blood upon your coat in the back," the man said. Sheng took off his coat then, and there upon the back was indeed a big blood-red stain, but when he examined it he found it was only spittle stained scarlet with betel nut. Some one with his mouth full of betel had spat upon him in a crowd and Sheng, seeing it, cursed and swore but what could he do but wash it off as best he could? He had no second coat.

That night he spent studying the map of Burma which the General had given him as he had given one like it to all his officers. He had studied it often enough before, but tonight he studied it with new care. For this day or two had already taught him that when they entered Burma it would not be with welcome from the people of the land. "English and Chinese, we hate you all," the Burmese had told him. What would this mean? he asked himself soberly.

He sat far into the night pondering the map with its small, closely printed names. He had learned in the last year to read, and he read the words beneath the maps, too. It might have been two countries, so different were the two halves of Burma. In the north, where the great river Irrawaddy had its upper reaches, there were mountains and hills, and these hills ran like long lines north and south. These hills, the maps said, were filled with tribesmen and they lived there amid great forests. The tribesmen, what were they and would they be friend or foe? Sheng cursed maps and notes that told such things as that there was oil in the mountains of upper Burma and that gems were found there, great emeralds and rubies and the finest green jade, and yet did not tell what the men were who lived there and whether they were friend or foe.

And in the south where the Irrawaddy opened its wide mouth there was another country, filled with rich farmlands, and growing the whitest finest rice in the world. This southern country spread for a thousand miles along the sea, and flung out a thousand islands, but what were its people he had no way of knowing, for the maps did not speak of the people.

He folded the booklet away at last and in the darkness he lay down in his blanket, thinking of what he had read. This town was almost at the juncture of these two parts of Burma, and yet were they to go north or south, they would go into unknown country. A great weight of fear fell upon him out of the night. What would befall them in this unknown country where the jungles were deep and the roads few? They went in as allies of men who were hated by the people, men who had ruled here for years upon years, but what people can love foreign rulers? In his fear he longed for the coming of his General, and he made up his mind that he would go to him the moment he came and tell him of the dangers ahead. Yes, whatever the General had done, whether or not he had persuaded Mayli beyond what he ought, this was now no time for men to think of women.

He heard the loud whine of mosquitoes beginning to swing about his head and though the night was hot he covered his head with his blanket. He had heard that mosquitoes brought malaria, and though he doubted it, having all his life been bitten heartily by mosquitoes from spring until winter in his father's house, yet it might be true that these mosquitoes so far from home had poison in them.

He lay sweating under the blanket, sleepless, his mind sifting fragments from his past, himself in his father's house, his brothers, Jade and his mother and his sisters, and Orchid who was killed so mercilessly and Mayli, again and again Mayli in her little house in Kunming. There she was doubtless at this moment, playing with her dog. He remembered her as he had seen her that day at the window of her room, her long black hair hanging in the sun, and for a moment all his healthy young body sprang alive. He ached and suffered his ache, and then he put the thought of her out of his mind. He might never see her again, and it was better for him to reckon that he might never see her again. Well, let it be so. He had sworn that he would not think of a woman until the victory was won, and among his men almost all had taken a like vow. Those who had not were only a few and they were sheepish when the others found them near a woman.

Remembering his vow, he felt his body suddenly eased again. His longing passed, and he fell asleep.

With the next day word came that the General himself had arrived, and Sheng made haste to go and report to him all that happened. In the middle of the afternoon he had heard the news and he first spent an hour washing himself clean in a bath house. In this bath house the serving men were all Burmese, or men with mixed Burmese blood, and they were nearly all lively, beautiful boys, laughing and gay with each other, and heedless about their work. When Sheng came in a very young serving man came forward and a red flower of some kind that Sheng did not know was thrust behind his ear and his teeth were red with betel and his skin shining with oil. About his head he wore a striped silk turban of red and yellow, but when he went into the steaming air of the bath he took this turban off and to his surprise Sheng saw that the young man's hair was long and fell about his shoulders. When he saw Sheng stare at his hair he gave it a sharp twist and knotted it on his head.

"I belong to the brotherhood," the young man said in broken Chinese and Sheng let it pass at that. Next the man took off his

104

short cotton top garment, to be ready for his work, and then Sheng saw that his body was marked with tattoo marks. But he supposed this too was a sign of the brotherhood and so he said nothing of it. But the young man's slender smooth arms were strangely strong. They were almost like a girl's arms to see, yet he lifted the buckets of hot water as though they were nothing.

"Can it be inquired what is your brotherhood?" Sheng asked after he had been scrubbed with a brush and had sweat and shivered under hot water and cold.

The young man did not answer for a moment. Then he said, "Have you heard of Thakin?"

"I have heard of nothing," Sheng replied. "I am newly come here."

The young man said nothing more for a while. Then with a strange sort of bitterness he exclaimed to Sheng, "Why have you Chinese come here to help the English?"

At this Sheng was so taken back that he could not answer without thinking what to say. Was this bitterness even in the humblest of people? After a moment he said, "We have not come here for any other purpose except to drive out the East Ocean dwarfs and they are your enemies as well as ours."

At this the young man pressed his full lips closely together and there was no more talk. Sheng paid his fee and gave the lad some tea money and that one put on his turban again and thrust his red flower behind his ear and Sheng went to see his General.

The General was weary enough but he had taken no time to rest. He had busied himself with his men and with all those who came to report to him as Sheng did, and he sat now in a small room in the inn which he had rented for headquarters, and when he saw Sheng he motioned to him to wait for a moment while he read a letter he held open in his hand. Others were waiting too, but the General paid no heed to any of them while he read. Then he folded the letter and put it into his pocket.

"Which of you is first?" he asked those who waited.

"I will be last, Elder Brother," Sheng said.

"Sit down, then," the General told him, and so Sheng sat down and waited while one by one the others asked their questions and made report. In something over an hour it came to Sheng's turn, and the General, being now very weary, threw himself back in his chair and sighed.

"Close the door," he told Sheng, "but first send some one for fresh tea. I am thirsty."

So Sheng called a soldier and the man went away and came back in a moment with a pot of hot tea and then the General poured out two bowls and motioned to Sheng to drink and filled his own bowl twice and drank it down, while Sheng waited for the General to ask him his business. But the General did not ask, even when he had drunk his fill. Instead he unbuttoned the collar of his uniform and he sat there, his face very distraught, and he was silent as though his mind were full of secret troubles. Then he took the letter out of his bosom. "I cannot understand this," he said to Sheng.

He threw the letter to Sheng and there Sheng saw a letter from the American. It was written in Chinese, not by the American but by some one writing for him, and at his command, and the letter said that the General was to hold all the divisions at the border until further word.

"I cannot understand this," the General said. "I came here expecting to find my orders to march tomorrow. Instead I find the command to wait until further word. What word—whose word?"

They looked at each other. "I suppose, if I can guess, the word of those above the American," Sheng said very slowly.

"That," the General said clearly, "is what I also guess."

X

WHO can know the hardship of holding in leash angry impatient men when they are eager to be gone and cannot understand why they are held? That night Sheng did not talk long with his General, for he soon found that he knew as much as the General did and neither of them knew anything. He went away troubled and doubtful, and left the General sitting as though he were made of stone.

In the next few days there was scarcely an hour when some of the men did not come to Sheng and ask him when they were to march again. They came courteously making one excuse and another, but the burden of their coming was always the same, "When do we fight?"

What could Sheng say but the truth, that he did not know? His men stared at him and one of the boldest said bluntly, "Why do you not find out, Elder Brother? Ask the General."

"He does not know," Sheng said plainly.

The men went away staring and muttering, for these men had not been taught to be silent beasts before their leaders. Each man respected himself and was able to take care of himself in battle, and the price for this sort of soldier is not the same price as the enemy paid for their silent obedient creatures. These men of Sheng's fought well only when they knew why they fought and where and whom. They talked together and when they thought another way better than the one their leaders chose, they said so, for they were free men and fought as free men.

But, being free, they felt themselves worthy now to be angry and to curse heaven for all this delay, and to cry out against the waiting of their leaders. They were all for sallying into Burma without any foolishness of courtesy or lingering for invitation from the English.

"What cursed this and that keeps us here?" Sheng heard one of his men bawl one day to his fellows, and when they did not know him near. It was noon and the men had eaten their meal and were idling in the sun around their barracks. Some were mending their straw sandals and some were shaving others and some were smoking cigarettes and most were doing nothing. The place was full of noise and laughter and rough voices, but above them all rose this one voice. A murmur began when they saw Sheng, but the young man stood his ground sturdily. Sheng stopped to look at him. He was a heavy-set tall fellow with the burr of the north on his tongue.

"You are not more impatient than I am," Sheng said quietly.

"I am a small fellow and you are a big one, Elder Brother," the man replied. "If I were as big as you I would not wait."

His brown face crinkled with a smile and in his black eyes, sharp and shining, were mingled impatience and laughter.

107

"I am not big enough to do what I like," Sheng replied, and went on.

But how could anything quiet the restless young men? They fell into quarrels with each other and with the townsfolk, and looked at women too boldly and broke their vows, and the prostitutes raised their prices, and all complained day and night. None of this was made better by the news leaking in from the south, for there were always those who came in from the south for trade or to escape the war or to travel upon the Big Road, and their words were the same. The foreigners, the Englishmen, were massed along the Salween River, but the enemy had already crossed that river below and had taken the town of Martaban. At Paan the Englishmen still held and fired without mercy upon the enemy ships, but could they go on holding? Did they mean to hold?

Sheng listened to these travelers as gravely as his men did.

"It is not that Martaban is important," a peddler of small goods said to him one day, from whom he had bought a towel. "But Martaban is a bridge for the enemy coming from Thailand. Over that bridge the two enemy forces can join as one."

Then Sheng put questions to this man who was a man from India by birth, a man of low caste who because of his many travels had become so mongrel that he took the color of the country where he was. But he was quick and clever, too, and he knew the people everywhere he went.

"Why do the English not let us come in?" Sheng asked frankly of this stranger.

The man leaned forward, his dark hands outspread on his dark bare knees. "The English do not want the people of Burma to see you armed with foreign weapons and fighting under your own leaders," he said. His face changed and became a quivering mask of hatred. "The English will lose Burma," he hissed. "The people of Burma will turn against them. It is our chance everywhere to rid ourselves of the English." Spittle flew in a fine froth from between his clenched teeth and Sheng drew back.

"You are not of Burma," he said, "why do you hiss and hate like this?"

"If the people of Burma do not hate the English enough then

108

come to India and see how we hate them there!" the man said. His hands were clenching his knees. It was a sight very distasteful to Sheng.

"But the men of Burma do not like the men of India, either, I have heard," he said. "They wished to be separated from you, too."

The peddler shrugged his shoulders violently and his dark eyes rolled under their long curly black lashes.

"They remember Saya San," he declared.

"Saya San?" Sheng inquired, who had never heard this name.

The peddler tossed off Saya San with a flicker of his thumb and forefinger. "He was nothing—nobody," he declared, "an ignorant man of Tharrawaddy, though he began well enough. He killed an official—well, but his ignorant followers turned against my people somehow and since then—it is all reasonless—"

He untied his turban and twisted it again with long deft fingers. "You understand, the people of Burma are very ignorant. They read, they write, but they are ignorant. Laughter means more to them than freedom. Also—" he grinned and his white teeth glittered, "they hate the Chinese. Why? The gods themselves do not know anything about the people of Burma. Yes, but I know this one thing. The people here will not help the Englishman."

His face was smooth again and he put his anger away inside of himself somewhere. It was there burning out of his eyes and muttering in his voice when he said, "Englishman," but he did not let it out beyond that again, and in a few moments more he had lifted up his pack and gone on his way.

Be sure such words as these found their way among the men, too, and the General heard of it and one day he called his officers to him.

"We can be defeated by our own selves, if we allow it," he told them. It was an evening in February, but the air was as hot here as it would have been at home in June. On the wall of the room where they were gathered a lizard ran out from a rafter under the roof, and licked its delicate quick tongue at mosquitoes. Sheng watched it as he listened to the General. There was a new officer here among them, a young man whom Sheng had never seen before.

"I have asked our brother to come," the General now went on,

109

"and to bring us some direct news of our foreign allies, and to tell us of what we do not know, so that we can wait more patiently."

Upon this the young officer rose. He was an exceedingly handsome man, his face smooth and his features delicate. It was hard to imagine him a soldier until one saw the thin set of his lips. He had slight delicate hands, and these hands he moved now and then as he spoke.

"I am your younger brother from Kwangsi," he said. His voice was low and unexpectedly firm. "We came, my men and I, on foot. We had no truck, nor even so much as a mule. We carried our mountain guns and dragged what artillery we had. We crossed into the Shan states and we took with us our Chairman's command. We went to the Englishmen there and told the one in command that we had come. I gave him our Chairman's greetings, and I said, what our Chairman has said, 'If Burma wishes help from us, we will send thousands of soldiers here at once.'"

"What did the Englishman say?" the General inquired.

"He spoke very courteously through his interpreter," the young officer replied. "He said there were already many Chinese forces waiting in Burma, and he was glad to know that more could come —if necessary."

"Is that all?" the General asked.

"It is all," the young officer replied. "Except that he assigned us to the mountain territory then, for which he said our guns are well suited. There we wait."

They all sat immobile, listening. When this word "wait," fell upon them, the same fleet look passed over their faces. They were all hard young men, seasoned soldiers, and to wait was torture.

"But the fighting is very severe in the south," the General said. "Do the English plan to fight alone?"

"There are Indian troops also, but under English command," the young officer replied.

"South Burma will be lost while we wait," the General said.

"They have told me that Rangoon would be defended to the last," the young officer replied.

"But North Burma must be held at any cost," the General said, "and not only until the last. Even if South Burma falls, North Burma must not fall, lest our country be surrounded on all sides by the enemy."

There was a long silence in the room. The men sat gloomily, staring at nothing. The lizard fell flat to the floor with a slap of its full belly on the tiles and scuttled away, frightened by its own noise.

The young officer had sat down again and now he began to speak from his seat, his eyes fixed on his tightly clasped hands on his crossed knees.

"I asked the Englishman why they did not invite us to come in quickly, seeing that all plans had been made for our coming by the Two Above when they went home from India. He said that we would be invited in when all was ready. He said that his brothers were fighting a delaying war in the south in order to give time for the ground bases and the airfields to be prepared for us, and that the main war would doubtless be fought in the central plains."

The General gave a sharp loud laugh. "We can fight without these mighty preparations," he shouted. "We are used to fighting without any preparations!" He struck both palms on the table in front of him and rose and began to pace the room. Without knowing he had looked and walked like the Chairman himself.

Suddenly he stopped and looked at them. "I have this news," he said. "Our men have met the enemy in the northernmost tip of Thailand, where they were trying to cross the river west of Chiengmai, but that is still not inside Burma. I know this, too, that the enemy is gathering forces at Chiengmai."

"Is the enemy still gathering there?" Sheng asked.

"Yes," the General said. "It is we who ought to prevent them, but they are not being prevented."

He stopped suddenly and looked at them with impatience. "I have nothing beyond that to tell you," he said abruptly. "Nothing at all, for I know nothing. But if news does not come within a few days, I shall tell the One Above that I must be relieved of my command here. I must protest this waiting. Are we to sit waiting like hatching hens while Rangoon falls?" He motioned dismissal with outflung hands and they rose and went away, all faces grave, for where was there a commander to equal this one whom the Chairman had put over them? Young and yet the veteran of many wars, skilled in hill fighting and the bravest among his men, there was none like him.

Sheng went back very gloomy to his own place, and he looked so surly that none of his men, seeing him pass, dared to speak to him.

The General watched the young officers as they went out of the room. Each of them walked with the long easy step of soldiers trained to walk but not to march. They were slender, graceful, their very skeletons resilient under the spare smooth flesh. He was a hard man and he could be cruel but his heart was soft as a woman's toward his men. They were precious to him and he knew them, men as well as officers. Name and face went together in his mind, and though he risked his men resolutely to gain ground against his enemy, when he lost men needlessly he went aside alone and wept in secret, not for anger but because the hearts he trusted had ceased to beat and the bodies he had taken pride in were mangled and destroyed. Thus it was his passion not to lose his men without exacting the full price from the enemy.

He sat drinking tea thirstily, for in this climate it seemed to him he could never put in water as fast as it poured out of him in sweat, and then he went to the door and locked it and, having done this, he unlocked a closet in the wall, and took out a small radio. It was his most precious possession for it needed no wires or machinery to link it to the air. He had not known there was such a thing until it had been brought to him in some booty taken from the enemy in one of their battles, and he had not known how to use it until he had seen one like it in the house of the Chairman. He had struggled with himself for a moment as to whether he ought not to tell that one about it, so rare were these machines, but he had downed his conscience. He would need it sorely when he made this campaign.

Now he set it on the desk, and turned the knobs on its face, and set it to this wind and that. This magic thing could make him forget every worry and ill. It was as though his soul could leave his body and go wandering out on the winds and the clouds. Music came to his ears, sweet and wild, voices speaking languages he did not understand, moans and sobs and stammerings not human. But now and again there came words he could understand either in his own language or in the language of the enemy. He understood the enemy very well, for as a boy he had been in Japan for five years, studying. Because he knew the people there so well he could fear them and hate them. And it had stood him well to be able to know what they said.

Now over the evening air, as he faced the instrument south toward Thailand, there came a harsh brassy voice, shouting abrupt syllables.

"Rangoon burns! The defenders are defeated, and they put the torch to their own city. Today our forces bombed the city without mercy and those fires also burn. The British locked thousands of coolies upon the docks, fearing they would run away under our bombs. They perished a cruel death, unable to escape. The British officers and residents are safe in the hills. In the city their offices are being held by natives. The British care nothing for the lives of natives. But we come to liberate the slaves. Our forces are eighteen miles only from Rangoon. Do not flee, people of Rangoon! You are about to be saved."

He turned the voice off. Could these things be true? He turned the knobs again, this way and that, but there was no other voice, nothing but that enemy voice, shouting into the skies.

"We are building roads through to the north of Burma. North and south we attack. The enemy is caught between our two hands. Take heart, people of Burma! You will be delivered from your tyrants. We are your brothers, men of one race. Will the white men ever give you equality? They do not allow one of us to enter their sacred countries. Asia for the Asiatics!"

He turned it off again. It was impossible to endure the voice, lest there be even a fragment of truth in it. This was the fear that kept him sleepless at night. Could it be that when they had fought and won their war even then freedom would not be theirs?

He sat heavily by the table, his two hands clenched and lying on the top, motionless.

Who could tell? Had the Japanese not been so cruel, had they not invaded, had they used other means than death and destruction, they might have been right. But now, whom could his people trust? There was nothing to do but to fight on, one war at a time. When

113

this war was won, if another war waited, then that war too must be fought. But today Japan was the enemy.

He rose after a moment of such thought and locked the instrument away again, opened the door and shouted. A soldier came running and he asked, "Does any man wait to speak with me?"

It was late and he was tired, but at night there came to him often his spies who spread over the country everywhere, before and behind them as the men marched.

"Two men wait, General," the soldier replied, saluting.

"Tell them to come," the General commanded.

Almost immediately two men came into the room and closed the door behind them. He recognized them as two of his own men whom he had sent into Burma weeks ago. They wore the dress of Burmese farmers, and their skins were stained dark and their heads wrapped in cotton cloth turbans.

He greeted them with smiles, while they stood waiting to speak.

"You have chosen your coming very well," he said. "If you have come from the south, is it true that Rangoon is burning?"

"Doubtless it is true," the elder replied. "For any eye could see what must come there. We left there days ago, and we came here by foot and by cart, but we could see that the city must fall. There is no preparation made to hold it, our General. It was never meant to hold. Ships of the enemy come in from the sea, and the enemy is bearing down on it from everywhere, in spite of the heat and their thirst. They suffer from great thirst, and they fear the wells are poisoned and they dare not drink, yet they march on."

He listened, his eyes fixed upon them. Yes, he knew that terrible courage of the enemy. Their courage was whole, like a rock without a seam. It could not be cracked, the indomitable courage of the enemy.

"The enemy comes laughing to Rangoon," the younger man said sadly. "Now that Malaya is lost, all those forces can join them here."

"You must not say that all is lost," the General said in a low voice. "All is not lost when we are here waiting."

"You are waiting indeed, Elder Brother," the older man said. He was lean and dark and his skin stuck to his bones. "And sir, you will

114

wait and wait, until the city falls." He turned to the other. "Shall we not tell him what we saw?"

"Is it not our duty?" the other replied.

"Why should anything be hid from me?" the General asked.

So they told him, now one and now the other, that on the road from Rangoon to Mandalay so sure had their own people been of the enemy's victory that upon a hundred miles of roadway they had destroyed foreign-made trucks and cars and vehicles.

At this the General struck the sides of his head with his hands. "And my men walking a thousand miles and dragging their weapons behind them!" he groaned.

The two men looked at each other and the younger said quickly, "Yet it is better to have burned those vehicles than to have left them for the enemy to bring their men into Burma."

"How did they burn them?" the General asked. He had rubbed his hands through his hair until it stood up on all ends, and his face was haggard with weariness.

"They poured foreign gasoline over them," the older man said slowly.

"Gasoline!" the General yelled. "Oh my mother!"

The two men looked as guiltily at each other as if they had done the deed, for gasoline was dearer than silver since it was not to be had except at great cost of the distance from foreign lands from which it was brought.

"How many vehicles?" the General cried.

"At least two hundred," the older man said.

"All new," the other man said mournfully, "and each had six wheels and in one single town I saw twenty-three burned together and they were loaded with foreign machinery and rubber tires."

The General gnashed his teeth and tore at his hair again, and cursed the mothers and grandmothers of all those who had set torch to the vehicles. "They could have run them away, curse them and all their female parents!" he roared.

"But the enemy was between them and home," the older spy said.

"Have we not been told that nothing must fall into the hands of the enemy?" the other said. "We have been commanded not to let so much as a bowl full of rice or a stick of steel or a wheel or a rivet or a weapon of the smallest sort, be left for the enemy. Be sure those who burned the vehicles felt it sorely. I saw the tears running down their faces and the villagers who watched the fires wept with them."

But the General would not yield. "If it had been I, the vehicles would have been saved," he said stubbornly, and the two men seeing that he would not let his wrath be cooled, excused themselves and went away.

Late that night when the General could not sleep in his room because his anger burned in him still, he heard a commotion in the inn yard, and being still full of impatience, he leaped from his bed. He had lain naked, for he had drawn the grass-linen curtain of his bed close because of the mosquitoes, and he chose the heat instead of them. Now he stopped only to pull on his under garments as he went, and he burst out of the door impetuous with rage at this new noise.

"Mother of my mother of my mother—" he bawled and then he stopped short. The inn yard was full of women, and they stood there astonished to stare at him. He saw their eyes all turned upon him in the light of the great torch which the innkeeper held, and at their head and nearest to him was Mayli. Her face quivered with instant laughter, and so dismayed was he that he clutched his garment to him, and for a second stood his ground, forgetful of himself in what he saw.

And Mayli, her lips curving and her eyes dancing, although a moment before she had been too weary to draw her breath, saluted him and said, "We have only just arrived, Sir, and where are we to be billeted?"

Then he came to himself and he choked and in one leap and two steps he was in his room again and pulling on his uniform and buckling his belt around him. A moment more and he opened the door as though he had seen none of them before.

He looked very stern and he shouted, "Have you come? Where is your superior?"

"The doctor lost himself, I think," Mayli said gently. "He must have turned the wrong way. We were following him until about fifteen miles back, and then we could not find him and came on alone."

116

"Ha!" the General shouted and his aide came to his side.

"Take these women to the Confucian temple which was set aside for them," he said.

The General stood waiting, very straight and firm on his legs, while the girls fell in behind Mayli. She led them proudly but at the gate he saw her turn and her eyes met his, under the lamp over the gate, and he saw them shining with laughter. Then she was gone.

And he went back into his room and stood still in the middle of the room, and then it came to him how he had looked bouncing into the inn yard full of rage, naked except for the little cloth about his middle—he the General! And suddenly he began to laugh and he sat down to laugh and laughed a long while. When at last he went to bed again he felt eased and ready to sleep, and he was about to sleep until something came into his mind to wake him for yet one more moment, and this was the thought that waked him. Here were Sheng and Mayli, and Mayli had told the General that Sheng was not to know where she was. Would he tell Sheng or not that she had come? He pondered this for a moment and weighed the pleasure of surprising Sheng so joyfully and of teasing Mayli because she had laughed at him when she passed through the gate.

Then he thought, "No, this is war, and I must not forget it even for a moment. It is better that they do not meet, lest each forget their duty and think of love and it be my fault."

This he decided and he yawned two or three times loudly and shook himself so that the dust fell down out of the grass cloth canopy above him and he cursed once or twice more at all that the day had brought and so he fell asleep.

XI

IN THAT part of the town where the women were quartered Mayli was busy. She who had never had to work in her life was now finding it was pleasure to have to work, though more than half her pleasure was in feeling upon her the ordering of all these other lives. She liked to tell others what to do, and laughed at herself secretly because she knew she liked it, and so partly to excuse her own pleasure she saw to it that none could complain against her because she only told others what to do and did nothing herself.

Therefore if there were a filthy room to clean or a courtyard fouled by animals before they could use it, she commanded her women, "Fall to, every one of you, and clean away this filth!"

But even as she commanded it, she led the way, and from morning until night she did not take off the cotton uniform she wore. And somewhere, always close beside her, was Pansiao, who was happy and complained of nothing if she could be near Mayli.

This Pansiao was one of those who would never be anything but a child. What the war was for she did not know and she cared nothing. She had almost forgotten her old home and her parents, and when Mayli discovered this, she took care to speak sometimes of Ling Tan and Ling Sao, of the brothers and of Jade and the little children. Pansiao's round pretty face lit itself with smiles whenever Mayli spoke of these whom she knew were her own, but soon the smiles gave way to a strange listening gravity.

"Do you remember," Mayli said one day as they stooped together beside a pond to wash their clothes, "how there is a pond near your father's house? They told me it was made by a bomb, but when I saw it, there were already fish in it."

"Was there a pond?" Pansiao asked, puzzling. "Did I see it?"

"Ah well, perhaps you did not," Mayli said quickly. "But do you remember the little pool in the court where there are goldfish?"

Pansiao did not answer. She stopped beating out her coat on the stone where she had folded it and looked quietly at Mayli.

"Do you not remember the court and the table there under the reed mats and how cool it is in summer?" Mayli asked her.

"Of course I remember," Pansiao said slowly. Then a look of pain stole out of her eyes. "I cannot remember their faces," she said in a low voice. "I remember my third brother's face because we used to ride the buffalo together when we took it to the hills for grass, but my father's face—I try to think how it looks. I know my mother is a strong thin woman and she has a loud voice. But I cannot remember her face. It seems to me I cannot remember anything before

118

we ran out of our house that night and took shelter with the foreign woman."

The young girl's eyes strained through the distance, as she forced her memory, and then Mayli knew that indeed Pansiao's memory had broken itself off at that certain moment. "Do not try to remember," she said gently. "Some day you will see them all again and then it will come to you."

Pansiao laughed with sudden childlike laughter. "Of course it will," she said, and she fell to beating the garment again so that little droplets of water fell everywhere, and glistened on her pretty eyebrows and hung on her cheeks like tears. "But my third brother— Sheng, you know. Now I remember him so well. He had a bad temper when he was little and we all gave in to him. I was afraid of him, too, and yet when we were on the hills alone, he found red wine-berries and gave them to me. He used to tell me that one day he would run away from home."

Mayli swirled her wet blue coat through the pond water to rinse it. "Run away and do what?" she asked.

"That he would not tell me," Pansiao said, laughing. "I think he didn't know—I think he pretended he had some plan and he had none."

"It is just as well," Mayli replied. "Since all young men now must have the same work to do—to fight until the enemy is driven off our land."

"Yes," Pansiao said gaily, and by her look and voice showed she had no feeling or knowledge of the war.

For this young girl had learned to escape what she hated and feared, which was this war, and she escaped by willfully not knowing what happened around her. She busied herself cheerfully and with full content in whatever Mayli told her to do. She helped the cooks and she washed and mended and she took most faithful care of any who were sick, and soon all loved her and laughed at her, but let the war be mentioned, and blankness came over her face like sleep and her eyes stole away to one side or another.

She had one more strangeness. This floating mind of hers knew no difference any more between right or wrong. If she saw some small thing she liked she took it for herself. The first time Mayli discovered this was one day when she and three out of her four aides and Pansiao went out on the streets together to buy thread and new cotton socks and such small useful things. In a little wayside shop they paused to look at paper flowers for the hair—not to buy, for what use had they for such ornaments now in their life? But they looked for a moment, being women, and indeed the ornaments were very cleverly made, and there were butterflies hovering over the flowers, twisted out of gold wire and blue kingfisher's feathers. Then, when they had admired them enough, they went on their way. In a moment they heard a great outcry behind them and they turned and saw the woman who had been in the shop running after them and screaming and pointing at Pansiao.

"What now?" Mayli demanded of the woman. But how could she understand what the woman said, who spoke only her own language? Nevertheless the woman pulled and jerked at Pansiao and tore at the buttons of her coat, so that they all sprang to defend the girl. But at that moment the woman pulled off a button of Pansiao's coat, and there in the pocket underneath there peeped out two of the ornaments.

"Pansiao!" Mayli cried sternly. "How is this? I did not see you pay for these."

Pansiao's red lips trembled. "But I have no money," she said, opening her eyes very wide. "Nobody has given me any money!"

"Then how could you take these ornaments and shame us all?" Mayli asked her. The three aides were very grave, too, for the strongest command had come down from the General to all, men and women alike, that none was to take anything without paying for it, since they were in a strange city, whose citizens were not their own people. Only the young widow, Chi-ling, put out her hand and took Pansiao's.

"Tell us why you took them," she coaxed the young girl.

Now Pansiao began to cry. "They are so pretty!" she gasped, "and I have nothing pretty—no one little pretty thing of my own!"

"Who wants pretty things now?" An-lan asked bitterly.

But Hsieh-ying burst out at them. "Why shall she not have the miserable small things if she wants them? Here!" She turned to the woman. "What do they cost, accursed?"

She took some coins from her pocket and the woman pointed out a small bit of silver, and Hsieh-ying gave it to her, scowling at her hugely as she did so, and she had heavy black brows which contradicted her red-cheeked merry face. So the woman, being quieted by the scowl went away, and Pansiao sobbed softly and Hsieh-ying took the ornaments and put them in her hair and soothed her. "Never mind, you have them now, and they look very pretty," and in a moment Pansiao put her hand up and felt them and stopped crying, and so they went on again.

All this time Mayli had said nothing more, but after this she watched Pansiao and more than once she saw the girl take some small thing that did not belong to her, a comb or a bit of thread, and once Mayli missed her own little sewing bag that Liu Ma had made for her and went to Pansiao and asked her, "Will you give me back my sewing bag since I need it to mend my coat?"

At that Pansiao gave it back to her so promptly and innocently, taking it out of her knapsack, that Mayli saw indeed the young girl had no knowledge of wrong in taking what was not hers and thereafter she told all who had to do with Pansiao that none was to blame her but only pity her and put back secretly what she took, for some are wounded in body by war, but this one was wounded in her mind.

And Pansiao when she found no one blamed her was happy and full of willingness to do anything she was told, and only when she heard talk of war did the look of sleep come into her eyes.

In such small ways the days slipped past, one after another, and the women were not near the men, and not once did Sheng and Mayli meet or know where the other was. But each in his own place dreamed of the other, though not with any longing. For war is to the heart like pepper upon the tongue and it dulls every other feeling. The sour, the sweet alike are lost in the mere sharpness. So neither Mayli nor Sheng knew that within a mile or two the other was.

. . . Now though it is easier for women to wait than men, the restlessness of the armies began to filter through even to the women. Chung, the doctor, was restless and to while away the waiting days he began to see the sick and diseased about him in the city, and there were many. Since he came every morning to inspect the nurses, and it was part of his duty to see that all the living places of both soldiers and nurses were cleaned and healthy, he saw Mayli as part of his duty, and it was to him that she made report if any nurse were ill. To her he said one day:

"It chafes me very much to have so little to do, and I see around us here in this city many children with bad eyes and scrofulous persons and beggars with ulcers. We have no right to take the medicines we may need for the wounded when the battle begins, but we could brew some medicines from herbs and at least wash the sores we see."

"It would be a good thing," Mayli answered.

Thereafter each morning for three or four hours she opened the gate and let in the sick, and Chung came and said what their diseases were, and what could be done was done. The diseases were for the most dysenteries and malaria, eye troubles and sores, and these could be healed without too much medicine. Sometimes a man came with a leg that needed cutting off, or he had a cancerous bag hanging from him, or a woman had a torn womb, or childbirth delayed or some such thing, and then the doctor was tempted to use what he had for the soldiers and save a life. But he was saved from his temptation, for none was willing to be cut.

"Cut this off?" a man with a rotten leg shouted. "I come to be healed and not to lose a leg!" And all agreed that they could not enter into their tombs with a member gone, for how then would their ancestors recognize them?

And from Chung, too, Mayli caught the deep restlessness because the battle did not begin.

"This is not my work," he said gloomily each day when he had washed sore eyes and scraped out ulcers. "I could do this at home. I came here to take part in a war."

"Why do we not march?" Mayli asked wondering.

"Why not, indeed?" he asked and shook his head.

As for Pao Chen, he neither spoke nor heard. From morning until night he sat in the small room where he had a table and bed and he wrote down his complaints which he sent to the General and to the Chairman and to the American, and to the newspapers and to whatever he could, and since he sat cross-legged on the bed, and pulled the table near him, to write, men called him the Scribbling Buddha.

But it was Li Kuo-fan, called Charlie, who came to Mayli one night and said, "Tomorrow I shall be gone, but I shall be back in seventeen days or so."

"What if we march before you come back?" Mayli asked.

"There is no danger," he said grimly. "I think we are stuck here like camels in a snowstorm."

Now these two had kept a sort of rough friendship ever since the days when Mayli had sat in his truck to come over the mountains, and once in every two or three days he sauntered in and sat down near Mayli, and talked while she went on with what she did.

"Where are you going?" she demanded of him now.

He put his hands together and whispered through them. "I am sent," he said.

Mayli lifted her brows and he went on.

"The General is angry with waiting," he said. "Yesterday he sent for fifty of us to go out and see what is to be seen."

Then the red came up in his face and he said suddenly in English. "Keep an eye on that little sister of yours."

"Little sister?" Mayli repeated, wondering. Then she saw his eyes go to Pansiao, who sat on a bench sewing, and she made a little face at him. "So that is why you come here!" she said saucily, "and I thought it was to see me!"

"I would not dare to come and see you," he said impudently. "You are a lady and what have I, who am a son of common people, to do with ladies?"

At this she kicked up the dust from the ground at him with her right foot and took the apron she wore and shook it at him and he went away laughing. But after he was gone she thought over what he had said, and knew that he went because he, too, was restless. She stood thinking, and her eyes fell on Pansiao, and as though Pansiao felt the look she lifted her long-lashed eyes, and blushed.

"Do you see Charlie Li when he comes here?" Mayli asked her.

"Sometimes I see him," Pansiao said, and blushed more deeply still.

"Ah ha!" Mayli cried softly, and going over to Pansiao she struck her lightly on one cheek and then the other and laughed at her.

123

"But he looks a little like my third brother, I think," Pansiao whispered, to excuse what she had said.

Mayli stopped and stared down at the young pleading face. "No, he does not," she said quickly. "He does not look at all like him. Sheng is much better looking than Charlie."

"Is he?" Pansiao murmured. "Then I have forgotten him, too," and she sighed. But Mayli only pulled Pansiao's little nose gently between her thumb and forefinger and laughed again.

. . . Seventeen days later Charlie Li came creeping through the border post where an English sentry stood on guard. To deceive this man was easy enough. No Englishman, he had discovered in these seventeen days, knew the difference between Chinese, Burmese or Japanese, if their clothing was the same. Englishmen had bade him take off his shoes so that they could see his feet and because his big toe did not stand out from the others they let him pass, since he wore Burmese garments. But the enemy had already mended this defect, and had found ways of pulling their toes together. Four times Charlie had found such an enemy and out of the four times he had killed two of them. He had disguised himself well enough to pass any Englishmen, for he had darkened his skin, because the men of Burma are darker than Chinese, and he wore a priest's saffron robe. He was about to pass when the Englishman stopped him and pointed his gun at his breast.

"Take your bloody hand out of your chest!" he said. "What's that you've got there?"

Charlie brought out the alms bowl with which he had begged his way.

"Thabeit," he said with a false smile, for that was the name of the begging bowl in Burma.

"Get on, you beggar," the Englishman said, and let him pass.

And so Charlie went on his way over the border, his heart swelling with anger. How easily he could have passed had he been an enemy —how stupid were these white men who would trust none but themselves and they so ignorant that they did not know friend from foe! The old foreboding fell upon him. With such allies, could they win?

So brooding, he walked into the border town by the time it was

124

midnight and went straight to the General. He had decided that he would rouse that one if he were sleeping, but now he saw a light streaming out of the window and he saw the General bent over a map on the table and around him were his young commanders, Sheng and Pao Chen and Yao Yung and Chen Yu, their heads in a black knot together.

"Halt!" the soldier at the door cried when Charlie came near.

"Do not halt me," Charlie said, "I have news."

"Give the password!" the soldier demanded.

Now this password was changed from day to day and how could Charlie know what it was today? Instead he lifted up his voice and roared out the General's own private name, and at the noise the General came to the door himself.

"What is this noise?" he shouted into the darkness, and then the light fell on Charlie and he knew him and told him to come in and so Charlie went in and stood there before them. A cry of laughter went up from all who saw him, for indeed he looked like any traveling young priest of Burma, with his begging bowl in his hand.

"It is like a play," Sheng said grinning. "They come in, these spies, first one and then another."

"You are the sixteenth to come back out of the fifty," the General said. "Now let me hear what you have that is new."

He sat down behind the table as he spoke and he bade the young men sit down where they could, and so looking from one face to another Charlie told his tale.

"I went to Rangoon," he said, "because there is the heart of the battle."

The General nodded, and lit a cigarette. His smooth face tightened under the skin.

"Sir, you must know that Rangoon is a city owned by the white men," Charlie said. His voice was gentle, and his eyes were fierce. "There are many great houses of business but they are all the white men's. There are many schools, but they are for those who would be tellers and clerks and servants of the white men."

"Go on," the General said.

"But the white men are not there now," Charlie said, looking from face to face. "They have left the city and they are in the hills, safe

—waiting, they have told their servants, for a few weeks until the war is over."

His voice was singing smooth and quiet. A loud laugh·went up from the young men at these words.

"A few weeks, until the war is over!" Chen Yu repeated with scorn.

"Go on," the General said.

"There is a great golden shrine in that city, where there are two hairs from Buddha's head." Charlie went on. "The pilgrims go up and down the steps without let, all day long. They take off their shoes, for even the steps are sacred. But they say there are not above half as many pilgrims now as before."

"Leave off about the shrine," the General said. His cigarette was already gone and he lit another. "Tell us about the harbor. Is it well defended?"

"It is scarcely defended at all," Charlie said. "There are but poor defenses ever built or planned. Yet it is a very great harbor. I was told that when the rice harvest is ripe more people come in and out of that harbor from India than go in and out of the American port of New York in a year. Indeed that whole region is very precious to the white men for its rice and oil and metal and fine woods, teak and—"

"Is there no defense at the city?" the General demanded again.

"None," Charlie said. "And I heard many other things not good. Along the docks I saw barbed wire barricades with gates and great locks upon the gates. I supposed that these were defenses against the landing of the enemy, and yet I wondered, for surely even the white men know the enemy will not come by sea but by land. Then I was told that these barricades are not against the enemy but against the coolies who carry the cargoes off the ships. The white men feared that when the city was bombed these ignorant working men would flee into the hills and there would be no one left to carry the goods. So they ordered these barricades made and when the enemy came over the city they ordered the gates locked, so that the coolies who were on the docks could not escape."

"Were they not killed?" Sheng cried.

"Are not their bodies flesh and blood like ours?" Charlie replied.

126

No one spoke for a moment.

"Go on," the General said at last.

"They are a miserable people in that region," Charlie said slowly, "and they die often of lung sickness. I was told that more people in the city of Rangoon die of rotting lungs than die by bombs, although in one day's bombing in the twelfth month more than a thousand were killed."

"Go on," the General said, "go on! Can we talk of men dying in these days? Tell me, did you see goods piled up for our men on the airfields?"

"Hundreds of tons," Charlie said, "goods from America, planes packed and waiting to be sent up the Big Road."

The General lit another cigarette and this time his right hand trembled. "It will never get there," he muttered. "It must all be lost —that precious stuff we have been waiting for all these months! The enemy will take Rangoon first. Of course they will take Rangoon first, where all their airships circle like crows around the carcass of a cow. It is the heart of Burma."

"It will cease to be in a few days," Charlie said in a low voice. "In a few days it must be lost. They will not hold."

The General's cigarette glowed crimson and burst into a tiny flame as he sucked in his cheeks. "How—they will not hold?" he asked.

"The white men will not hold," Charlie said. His voice suddenly broke and lost its smoothness. "They will retreat!" he cried.

Groans and curses broke from the listening young men. The General crushed out his cigarette in the palm of his left hand.

"It is what I said would happen," he said shortly. "We are not surprised. Let us not be surprised."

"But do we go on?" Yao Kung asked. He was a thin young man and at home he had a young wife whom he loved and three little sons.

"Wait," the General said. His voice was suddenly so thick that they all looked at him. "These white men," he said to Charlie. "Is there not one left in the city?"

"There are a few," Charlie said. "I heard of one who stays at the docks with his men. He has a young wife, and she has two small children. They are there. So long as he is with his men they still unload such ships as come in."

"Are the white men cowards?" the General demanded.

"They are not cowards," Charlie said slowly, "not cowards, but are they fools? They have prepared nothing—the people they have left in confusion thus—" He leaned forward, his hands upon his knees. "The enemy sent their messages over the air in the language of the people of Burma, telling them that they come to free them from the white men's rule, telling them not to be afraid. What did the white men do against this evil? They sent out their messages, too, to reassure the people and tell them not to listen to rumors— but these messages were in English, which the people could not understand!"

Rueful wry laughter went up from the young men. "I had rather they were cowards than fools," Sheng said. "Cowards only run away but fools stay to do their folly."

The General did not speak. He was sitting now with his head between his hands.

"Go away," he said, "go away all of you, and leave me to think what I must do. Pao Chen, you shall stay and write down a message to the One Above. I will beseech him once more to—to think what he does."

The young men rose and saluted and went away. Charlie followed them, and the General let him go until he had reached the door. Then he called him back.

"I shall not forget you," he said with meaning.

"Then send me out again," Charlie said gaily and he saluted again, his priest robes fluttering in rags.

The General laughed. "Get on your soldier's uniform," he said. "You deceive no one who knows the difference between a priest and a soldier!"

XII

THE General was uneasy and the more because for many days he had not been able to ask the Chairman for advice. The small radio set he had brought to Burma was broken beyond mending. So one day he called Pao-Chen to him and he said, "Write something which will move the Chairman's heart and make him see what he asks us to do. Tell him the radio machine broke itself and I have no way of hearing his commands. Tell him I am not afraid. Tell him I will fight where he tells me to fight, but in the name of all our people, tell him to give me freedom to fight our own war and not go into battle tied to an ally who retreats before we can get there. Ask him if we shall go in when Rangoon is already doomed. Tell him it is he who must decide and not I, whether these, our best troops, are to be lost in the jungles trying to save the white men, or whether we shall fight for our own reasons. Put your strength into words, Chen, and let them eat their way through the paper. Tell him the white men will not let us buy rice. Ask him where the American is. Tell him we sit here on our tails like treed monkeys, waiting while the enemy takes what he will. Nearly sixty thousand of the enemy are in the wilderness on the border of Thailand, ready to attack. That wilderness is the harshest battlefield in the world, and are we to fight upon it, not to defend our homeland but to hold the empire for the white men? Tell him twenty thousand of the enemy are just over the other border of Thailand and between the two enemy armies is a vanguard of their men. The Shan mountains lie there and their tops rise six thousand feet and their valleys are full of jungles. That is our battlefield, tell him. Tell him our spies say the white men are leaving the oil fields untouched—nothing destroyed, or so slightly destroyed that a few months will give them to the enemy, a few weeks, even. Tell him—"

Pao Chen's pen was rushing across the paper, and the sweat was pouring down his face.

"Make it as black as you can and you cannot make it black enough," the General said passionately.

"I make it black," Pao Chen muttered.

In silence the two sat for a while, and the only sound in silence was Pao Chen's foreign pen, scratching out the bold characters.

"Shall I read it?" he asked when he was through to the end of his paper.

"Read it," the General replied.

He sat with his head in his hands to listen, but at that moment the door opened and a seventeenth spy came running in. His garments were torn and his feet bleeding, and he had been wounded in his left hand and he had wrapped it in a sleeve torn from his coat.

"Rangoon!" he gasped. "Rangoon has fallen!"

The General leaped to his feet. "Put that on the letter!" he shouted. "Rangoon has fallen—tell him we are not yet allowed to cross the border, though Rangoon has fallen!"

And he stood there gnawing his underlip while Pao Chen set these words down. Then he snatched the letter and shouted for his aide.

"Let me!" Pao Chen cried. "Let me takè it to the One Above! I will carry the letter for you and I will speak for you."

The General paused for one second, his face purpling and his brows working above his angry eyes. "Well enough," he said shortly, "then take the small plane and go. I will wait long enough for you to come back but no longer. We march, one way or the other."

. . . The Chairman put down the letter which Pao Chen had written for the General. He had read it carefully and without haste, and his lady had stood behind him, reading as he read. She was very beautiful this night. She wore an apple green robe, made of silk and cut very long and close to her slender body, and over it she wore a sleeveless coat of black velvet, cut short to her waist and close, too. The collar of the robe was high and its green made even more clear her exceedingly fair skin and red lips, and the black of her soft hair, brushed back from her brow. Pao Chen saw all this beauty as every man who looked at her saw it, and acknowledged it without thought of himself.

Neither of them spoke, the Chairman or his lady. She who could be voluble as a child over small matters when she liked, could be very silent when it was wiser not to speak. She sat down and clasped her hands together. Upon her finger was the fabulous ring of jade which seemed part of her and in the lobes of her ears were small rings of jade. She fixed her great black eyes upon her husband's face. These eyes were the light of her beauty. They were so clearly defined in their black and white, so direct and energetic in their gaze, so fearless that all who saw her spoke afterwards of her eyes.

The Chairman lifted his head and the two exchanged a long look. Then he said to Pao Chen who stood waiting: "Do not think I am ignorant of what you have told me. I know and I have known. But I have had to think of more than this one battle. I think of our future as well as our present, and this war is a war in which we are only one among others."

At this the lady put up her hand impetuously. "We fought it alone for the others all these years. Are we to go on fighting it alone?"

He silenced her with a look. "I know what I do," he said.

She rose at that, her eyes very bright, and with a proud grace she left the room. The Chairman watched her go. His eyes were soft, but he kept his silence, and when she was gone he turned to Pao Chen.

"Go back to your post," he said. "I will come and see for myself."

. . . Thus it was that in a very few days after that the whole waiting encampment of the armies was thrown into turmoil.

"The Chairman is here," mouth whispered to ear. In less than an hour all knew that at noon of that day a plane had descended on the level ground outside the city bearing the Two Above, and with them the American. With what care each made the best of what he had, every soldier furbishing up his uniform and polishing his gun and washing his face and ears and smoothing his hair, and the women, how they gossiped among themselves about the lady and wondered if she were as beautiful as men said she was!

"Is she as beautiful?" Hsieh-ying asked Mayli.

"I think she is," Mayli said smiling.

"But no more beautiful than you!" Pansiao cried jealously.

"Much more beautiful," Mayli said, still smiling.

"I have seen her once," Siu-chen said proudly. "She came long ago, before the war, to our school and talked about keeping ourselves

131

clean and our garments buttoned and what she called New Life. She was very beautiful, it is true. I remember she saw my hands that day—chapped, you know, Elder Sister, as they always are in winter —and she spoke to the principal and told her to buy a foreign cream for me. But we never did. It cost too much."

In the mid-afternoon all were ready for inspection, and Mayli stood very straight before her lines of young women, and the Chairman and his lady came by with the American, thin and lean and gray-haired, and with them was the General. They all saluted the four and all kept their faces grave as the great ones passed by. But the lady stopped and said in her easy way,

"You all look beautiful, and never more beautiful than you are now, ready to serve your country." And to Mayli, she said, "Are you happy?"

"Yes, Lady," Mayli replied, not moving.

But still the lady lingered, and she put two delicate fingers on Mayli's sleeve and she said in a low voice, "You may come to me in half an hour."

But be sure the women heard, and they were envious of her, some gently who loved her and some not so gently. And after half an hour Mayli went to the house which was headquarters and there for nearly an hour the lady kept her. She was alone, for the Chairman was busy with his commanders, and because she was alone that lady put free and piercing questions to Mayli.

"I told you to be my eyes and ears," she began, "and so tell me all you have seen and heard."

She listened while Mayli talked, and every now and again she thrust in a barbed question.

When the hour was nearly spent she put her hands before her eyes and sighed deeply. Mayli waited for her to speak, but she only said, "Go back to your bed. You have been faithful eyes and faithful ears, but you have told me heavy news, heavier than you meant to tell."

At this moment the Chairman came in, and as soon as he saw the lady he said quickly, "You are not well!"

"Indeed, I feel I am ill," she said.

132

The Chairman bent over her, and he waved his hand toward Mayli.

"Go—go," he said, "bid the doctor to come here."

She was about to hasten away when the lady protested willfully, "No, only take me home. Let us go home at once. Tell them to prepare the plane instantly."

She rose and walked about as though she were in pain, and so the Chairman gave the order to the guard who was always at the door, and Mayli came away.

In only a little while they all heard the plane soar over their heads and turn eastward and after they were gone and Mayli had dismissed her women, the courts were full of talking and wondering and laughter and admiration for the two who were more than leaders to these simple girls. They saw in the two all the dream of love between man and woman, which they themselves might never have.

Even Mayli dreamed a little that night and she thought of Sheng with something more than she had thought of him for a long time. Had the Chairman been uncouth when he was young like Sheng? She remembered, as she always did, how he, too, had been the son of plain people, not much schooled, speaking no foreign tongue, accustomed to hardship and work. There were rumors enough that told of his mischievous youth. He had not always been this grave high man he was today. She sighed and wondered where Sheng was now and she rose from her bed and went to the window and stood looking out into the small piece of starry sky above the roofs and, feeling without thinking, she felt him suddenly very near.

And not too far away Sheng lay flat on his back on a pallet on the floor of the barracks, one in a long row of men. Behind the shut lids of his eyes he was seeing her face. He, too, had stood at the head of his own men without speaking while the Two Above had passed, but when the lady passed she gave him a full deep look and that look had lit his being because it made him think of Mayli.

He would not turn or toss and why should he let himself be restless? He might never see her again.

For after the inspection was over the Chairman had called all the young commanders to him.

133

"Tomorrow," he had said, "you shall lead your men across the border. We will wait no more."

And then his profound eyes had singled out Sheng. "You tall fellow," he said kindly, "here you are. I remember you, your name and your home. I sent you here because you are one of my best men. I have told your General that if there is any task too hard, he is to choose you for it."

At these words Sheng's pride rose in him like a banner. "And I will do it," he said.

. . . Mayli walked across the border at the head of her young women.

"We are on foreign soil," she thought, and felt a dread rise through her bones and marrow. On this soil who knew what would happen to all these she led?

It was a morning without cloud or shadow of any kind, and all were on foot, since the roads of this region of Burma were narrow and winding and not fit for vehicles. Ahead of them were the carriers, bearing weapons and food. Ahead of those were soldiers. She could see them winding like a huge long beast, the men in their blue uniforms packed together. She wore the same uniform and so did her young women. So too did the General himself, who had nothing to tell he was different from the soldiers, save his badge of blue enamel upon which was the white star of China. Behind them were more soldiers, winding as far as eye could see.

She smiled at her women. They looked fresh and strong under the morning sun, their skins were brown and their eyes clear. Not one had paint nowadays on her lips or cheeks. Such things were forgotten. She had put away her own foreign lipstick and powder and she washed her face with hot water and soap as they all did. Sometimes at night they rubbed a little mutton fat into their windburned cheeks and hands and that was all. Yet never had she felt so strong nor looked so well and that she knew. Even An-lan was beginning to lose her paleness. The slender girl smiled no more than she ever did, but the look of misery had left her eyes.

Now as she caught Mayli's glance she said seriously, "It is the first time our armies have ever marched on foreign soil."

134

"It is indeed," Mayli answered, surprised and suddenly grave. Yes, this was the first time that Chinese men and women had ever left their own land to fight. She marched on, thinking of this as she went. Behind them lay China, and all around them and ahead of them was Burma. She lifted her eyes and looked at the green hills. Had a knife cut through here, it would have divided Burma into Upper and Lower. To the right of them the land rose rougher, even as they could see, than it did to the left. Northward it would break into uneven hills that grew quickly into mountains, but southward the land leveled toward the sea. The road wound itself, reasonlessly, it seemed, doubled and crooked, as human feet had found the easiest way to walk, century upon century. It was rich country. The rice fields were green even now, and she saw the farmers bent over them. Sometimes like a lamp across the green they saw the saffron of a priest's robe. There were many priests here, many of them young.

Priests and all, wherever she saw a human face, it was merry and ready to laugh. The people looked up as they marched past, farmers stood to stare and children sucked their fingers. When they passed through villages of houses built upon posts, the people stopped where they were to watch them. At noon they halted but not in a village, for they had their own food. No one, the General had commanded, was to take so much as an egg from these people. Food would be bought and they were not to put a hand on anything that was not theirs; even when it was given them as a gift it must be refused.

"Remember you honor your country by what you are, or you disgrace your ancestors by what you are not," the General had said.

Therefore, at noon when the word came to halt, they sat down in open country along the road and ate the fried rice that was their ration and washed it down with the pale tea that filled their bottles.

The sun was hot and the road dusty, and as they sat a horde of small children came running across the fields and stood at some twenty feet from them and stared at them. Once, Mayli held out a handful of rice to them and they fled backward.

"How pretty they are," Chi-ling sighed. "I had a little boy once—" she rose and tightened her belt, and stood with her back to the

135

children. But no one spoke or answered her. In these days none asked another a question. Who had not lost one dearly loved?

Then the order came to march again and they all rose and fell into the long swinging step that carried them twenty miles a day and twenty-five and then to thirty. The afternoon wore on and the sun fell before their eyes as they marched southward toward the Sittang River. All knew that the allies had withdrawn from the enemy and that the Chinese armies were to meet them upon the left flank, and engage the enemy.

Engage the enemy! These words were said as easily as though one went to a rendezvous, a party, an outing, but Mayli dreaded the certain hour ahead and kept her dread secret.

That night, their first upon alien soil, a deep uneasiness swept over them all. They encamped at sunset in a shallow valley between low hills, and yet weary as they were none could sleep. Above them the sky was pearl and pink for an hour, both east and west, and then the color changed to purple. Around them the lights of villages shone flickering and small as fireflies. Mayli and her women were gathered together, their blankets spread, but none was ready to sleep. The uneasiness of the men had spread to them, too, and they sat silent, a few with their heads sunk in their arms upon their knees. But others rose and stood or walked here and there, stumbling over those that sat. The mosquitoes hummed in the night air, and now and then one heard a slap and a curse, and soon other slaps and curses.

"Why are we restless?" Mayli wondered to herself. Only Pansiao was asleep. She had brought her blanket and put it down next to Mayli and curled herself into it, head and all against the insects, and Mayli could hear her breath deep and regular as a child's.

Then suddenly she heard her own name murmured, and the women near her pointed toward some one standing at the outside of their circle, and Mayli rose and went toward the man. It was Pao Chen.

"The General sends me to you," he said, whispering. "He says, can you and your women not come out and amuse the men—sing, perhaps? Or talk to us? Or make a little play? The men are disturbed. They say the air here is full of strange spirits."

136

This command was so astonishing to her that she must think a moment. "Yes, we can," she said quickly. "Siu-chen can sing some foreign songs, and Hsieh-ying dances with a sword very well—and—yes, we will think of something. Give us half an hour, say to the General."

He nodded and went away, and she went into the midst of the circle and clapped her hands for them to listen to her, and then she called out what the command was and in her clear crisp voice that carried more powerfully than a man's voice through the twilight, she said,

"Who can do any small clever thing? Let none be shy! Think of the men, who must be eased of their weariness and made to laugh and so to sleep. Step out, each one—this also is for our country."

Then as though they longed for laughter, too, such a giggling and chatter rose that Mayli had to smile—these girls, these women, how young they were! Were there no war most of them would now have been in schools and homes, and here they were, part of an army, going out to engage the fiercest enemy their country had ever known! She who was so impatient of all tears suddenly felt her throat tighten at their laughter and her lips trembled as she smiled.

"Come, come!" she called. "Am I to wait all night?"

So one by one they came forward.

"I do know some foreign songs," Siu-chen said.

"And I have a sword dance," Hsieh-ying said.

"I know a juggler's trick my brother taught me once," An-lan said.

"I will tell a story," Chi-ling said.

And so, one by one, some twenty came forward, each with a thing she could do, and these followed Mayli toward the ranks of the men and there they found a hollow center ready for them. Pao Chen had waited for them and when he saw them coming he began to clap his hands and all the men clapped their hands, but softly and only for a moment.

There in the brilliant light of the moon Pao Chen spoke and spoke very well, as though he read writing aloud.

"Brothers," he said, "tonight we are far from home and the earth we call our own. It is true that no ancestor of ours has ever done what today we do. We carry the battle into the land of other peoples. This is foreign to us and because it is foreign we feel restless and not sure that what we do is right. Therefore let us reassure ourselves. We go at the command of the One Above and him we must obey. And the enemy is the same enemy, the one who even today let loose his bombs upon our own homes, who killed today his hundreds and his thousands. Though we are on foreign earth, it is not this earth we want. When the enemy is vanquished, we will go home again, taking nothing that we did not bring with us. Therefore we can be confident, knowing that what we do is right.

"Now, so that our hearts can be free and so that we can sleep our sisters will sing to us, play before us and speak to us for an hour or two. What their names are does not matter. They are our sisters, and it is enough."

So saying, he bowed, and stood aside, and Mayli came forward and in simple short words, she told what they would do. She, too, spoke no name, not even her own, for what indeed did their names matter? Before her in that bright moonlight she saw the faces of many men, and they had no names either.

"One of us will sing to you," she said, "and some of us will speak. And six of us will make a little play for you that these six played often in the villages of home, when they traveled from place to place to tell the people what this war is and how it must be fought by us all, here and at home."

Now, when she began to speak, Sheng was sitting far toward the back. He gave a great start and stood up on his feet. Could two voices be so same as this girl's and Mayli's, he asked himself? He stood listening, catching not every word she said because he was too far away, and because the mosquitoes whined so loudly about his ears. But how could he see her face in the moonlight? She wore the uniform they all did, and looked, from where he stared at her, like a boy. The breeze lifted her short hair and blew it back from her face, and he could see no feature clear.

He sat down again. Of course it was not she. How could it be she when he had left her many hundred miles away in a little house at Kunming?

Then he remembered when he had last seen her. He had not seen

138

her face, but only her hand wearing the jade ring. She had been leaving the General's room, and he and the other young commanders had been waiting while the guard flung them his ribald words.

"It will be a long time yet, elder brothers," he had told them, snickering. "The General has a beauty in there."

And when at last she came out it had been Mayli! He had led his men out at dawn the next day, and he would not go near her to ask her anything. A man about to go to battle must not ask a woman anything.

Now the girl stopped speaking and instead he heard her begin to sing a foreign song, her voice high and sweet. He had never heard foreign music in his life except sometimes out of the wireless machines in cities. But Charlie sat near him, and he knew Charlie understood all foreign things and he leaned toward him.

"What is she singing?" he asked.

"Some song she learned in school," Charlie said. He translated it after a moment. "Drink to me only with thine eyes," he said.

"Drink to me only with thine eyes," Sheng repeated astonished. "What does that mean?"

"It means," Charlie said, "that when a woman's eyes look into yours you need no wine."

Sheng did not speak again. He listened to the strange words and the clear high voice. The tune was painful to him. It twisted itself into him and made him tremble. "It is true," he thought, remembering Mayli, "when I looked into her eyes it was as though I drank wine. I felt my veins grow hot."

He rose when the girl stopped singing.

"Where are you going?" Charlie asked him.

"Upon my own business," Sheng said shortly, and he wound his way among the men, sitting and lying upon the ground as they listened. He went beyond the outermost edge of them. Then under a little tree he took the blanket he had with him and rolled himself up in it, head and all, and lay stolidly enduring his inner loneliness.

139

XIII

E WAS awakened by some one stumbling over his body. Before he could rise another fell over him and another. He sat up with a roar.

"You big turnip!" he bellowed and flung his arms out and grasped a leg. The man fell on him and they fought for an instant and then together staggered to their feet.

"Your mother!" the man cursed. They glared at each other. "You an officer!" the man shouted when he saw Sheng's shoulder signs. "Asleep, when the command has come down to march instantly! Our allies are in a trap, you sleeper! Where are your men?"

Sheng's jaw went slack and he rubbed his face with both hands. Then without a further word he put out his two elbows and made a battering ram for himself and so he charged his way through the running crowd of men.

How long had he slept? Not surely for more than an hour. The sky was glittering with stars, and the silence of night was deep over the valley. He seemed still to hear the echoes of music in his ears.

"I am an ox," he thought, in shame. "How was it I fell asleep?"

He caught sight of one of his own men and pushed his way to him.

"You, Little Crab!" he shouted. This man was called Little Crab because he was one of two brothers and because he had once received a wound in battle which had shortened his left leg so that he walked as though he were going sidewise.

"What is all this noise?" Sheng went on. He pulled Little Crab aside and they left the others and went a rounder way to their tent which was still shorter because it was out of the crowd.

"How do I know?" Little Crab retorted. "I am only a small soldier and nobody tells me anything. But when the women were making a play about how a girl student was captured—how she killed six of the enemy by poison upon her lips before it was discovered—in the midst of this a messenger came running from the General to say that we were marching within the hour, for the white men are trapped southward beyond the river, and there they are, all mixed together, advance and rear and troops, and the dwarf-devils are attacking on all sides. The white men have no food and no water, and unless we can reach them in time they will die like beasts."

Sheng's answer to this was to push ahead and leave Little Crab to limp on. In a few minutes he had reached the General's own headquarters and there he found the other commanders gathered already and waiting. If there was any doubt in the General's mind now he showed no shadow of it on his face. He stood behind his desk, in his hands papers which he read as he gave his commands in a low sharp voice.

"You, Pao Chen," he said, "are to form your men into the middle ranks. Yao Yung and Chan Yu, your men are to be the two wings."

He looked up and his darting eyes caught sight of Sheng, and a flicker of laughter shone in them for a moment.

"You, Sheng, look as thought you had been asleep in a briary bush," he said, in exactly the same voice.

Sheng put his hands to his head. In his haste he had left his officer's cap on the ground where he had fallen asleep, and he felt dried bamboo leaves in his hair. He combed them out hastily with his fingers, and his face was scarlet.

"I am a water-buffalo," he muttered. "Let there be quiet around me and I fall asleep like a beast."

"There will be no quiet for the next days," the General said grimly. "You are to be the vanguard. Your men must leave within this hour. You are to lead south and then bear west. You will cross the next river at the first ford, and that must be as soon as you can, for it is not trustworthy that the bridges further down still hold. The enemy is in a circle, or so it is said, around the white men."

"I am willing enough to obey you," Sheng replied and saluting, his hair still on end, he turned and walked quickly from the room. When he had reached the door he broke into a run, and nearly overturned the doctor who was hurrying toward the General. Chung's face was as pale as the handful of papers that fluttered in his hands.

"Is the General there?" he shouted as Sheng ran past him.

"Where else?" Sheng bellowed back over his shoulder. In the darkness a woman stepped quickly and lightly along behind the doctor, but Sheng did not turn to look at her.

As for the woman, it was Mayli, and at the sound of that voice

141

she stopped and stared after the young man's hurrying figure. A flickering lamp swung over the doorway of the General's door, but its light was lost here. Upon the threshold Chung turned and called back to her, "Don't delay—there's no time! We cannot start until we have our orders clear."

She pulled back her wondering mind. There was no time indeed, and indeed why should she wonder? There were thousands of young men with loud voices in the army, and why should she think of Sheng?

"I do not delay," she said firmly, and entered the General's room.

. . . Before midnight the march was begun. Whether or not the white men could be succored before it was too late was now the question, but every small old enmity was put aside and each man and woman thought only of the honor of his own people, that now it was they who went to rescue those who had always behaved as lords and masters to them.

"They look to us for once," the General had said brusquely to them all. A scornful pride had glittered out of his eyes and made his voice harsh. "We have never been fit for anything before, but now that they are trapped on all sides by the East Ocean dwarfs, they need us. Well, let us show them what we are!"

In this spirit every man did his duty and so the march began. It was not to be made in one day or even two or three. The terrain was their enemy, and the roads were few, for the white men had built few great roads through this land in the days of their rule. Small old country roads had now to be followed, roads rough with dried mud and broken ancient cobbles and rutted with the wheels of rude farm carts. Sometimes there were only paths, so that they had to walk singly, and twice they struck through the jungles with no paths, but this at least was in full daylight because of the snakes and the leeches and such hateful creatures. And it was not enough to watch what crawled under their feet. The skies must be watched for the enemy planes that went to and fro among the clouds, trying to discover just such aid as this to the beleaguered white men.

"We are safer in the jungle with the snakes," Sheng told those men who followed him.

142

Now all put on their green coats and wound branches of trees about their heads so that from above they would be the color of the earth and so less easily seen. And Mayli, walking with her women, bade them, too, wind branches about their hair. They were very pretty, she thought, watching them, and so young that they made a game even of this trick against death, laughing at each other, and one bending to twist another's crown of green more gracefully, and some were careful what leaves they chose, and Pansiao found scarlet jungle flowers on a vine and twisted them into her crown, and her round merry face under the flowers made them all look at her and smile.

And Sheng was in the vanguard, pushing on ahead of all the others, and Mayli and her women were in the rear, and still those two did not meet or know that they were part of the same battle. Across the grave business of the day and the night, even through the weariness of the march, each thought for seconds, for a moment, of the voice and the look that had been like, and yet how could they be one another's? And still the war carried them on, a part of itself, and separating them with the heavy duties each had to do, so that there was no time for thought or dreaming.

Each night when the company halted, Mayli must make sure that her women were fed and that they were safe for the night, and Sheng, when his men had eaten their rice cakes and dried beancurd and dipped up whatever water could be found to drink, must pore over his maps and send out his spies to see what could be learned about the enemy and about the trapped white men.

By now the whole countryside knew that the white men were encircled and a sort of glee was upon every face. It was an evil merriment, and Sheng took it as an enemy thing, for it was against them, too, because they went to the aid of the white man. Especially it was against every hapless man of India, who lived in these parts, for the people of Burma hated the people of India heartily, for they thought those Indians had come into Burma and had taken work and rice that belonged not to them but to the people of the land. Everywhere Sheng found this hatred as he pushed the spearhead westward and southward, and Sheng three or four times saved an Indian or even a family of them from the hatred of the people of

143

Burma. One of these left his comrades out of gratitude and followed Sheng for a whole day. But at the end of the day Sheng felt his devotion a burden and he called Little Crab to take the dark fellow away and let him live among the men.

"I am not easy with his eyes always on me and his leaping forward to help me wherever I move," Sheng said.

For so the Indian did, Sheng having saved him when some Burmese had drenched him with oil and set him on fire. So from that day on Little Crab took care of the man and somehow told him what to do, and the man obeyed him like a dog.

Now the General had appointed Charlie Li to come with Sheng, for Sheng was still a man of the hills to some degree and not used to being far from home. But Charlie was a man of any country where he set his foot, and he read people as farmers read the clouds and winds and he caught the thoughts of people like the breath from their mouths. So in the nights that they were upon this march he came back each night to Sheng and told him what he had found, for by day, in his beggar's garb, he wound in and out of the people on both sides of the march and ahead of it, and now he had enough of their language to know half what they said and to guess the rest.

"A generation will not undo the hatred we are making for ourselves, that we side with the white men in this war and not with our own," he told Sheng sadly. "It is we, they all say, who are betraying our side of the world. The enemy is spreading it everywhere that it is only we who help those who have ruled us. If it were not for us, and this is what I hear everywhere, the war would be won by now, they say, and the white men gone."

Sheng sat apart from his men at night to talk with Charlie, and tonight he sat on a rotted stump near the edge of a jungle where they had encamped well away from a village, so that if any came near they could see him coming. All around the encampment soldiers were awake and watching, for well they knew their danger. He sat there, his big slender hands clenched on his knees, his knees apart, and his head up and his eyes watching. He did not cease to turn his eyes here and there as he answered Charlie.

"If I had not suffered what I have suffered at the hands of these East-Ocean dwarfs, and what I suffered I will tell no man, if I had not seen what I saw in the city near my father's house and if I had not seen what happened in the village of my ancestors, then I might have said that these people do well to say we have betrayed our own. But I have seen and I never forget. White men I do not know. I never spoke to one since I was born. But the East-Ocean dwarfs I do know and I have seen them, and they are my enemies until I die, and after I am dead I will not forget."

His voice came out of the night like low thunder and he went on. "Do I love the white men whom I have never seen? Am I a fool? No, it is not to save the white men that I sit here tonight, my feet on this earth that is not mine, whose sands and winds are strange to me. But if the white man is the enemy of my enemy, then the white man is my friend."

"The country is rotten with spies," Charlie said. He pulled his ear restlessly. "Among the priests nine out of ten are for the Japanese. Among the people not one will lift his hand against them."

"Then these people are my enemy, too," Sheng replied heavily. He rose and looked out over the dark alien land spread around him. He sniffed the night wind. "Even the winds smell evil," he said. "There is a rotten smell to them."

"It is the jungles," Charlie said. "The jungles are rotting."

They were silent for a long moment, each unwilling to speak out his fear to the other.

"I am going to sleep," Sheng said at last, his voice as hard and dry as a dog's bark.

"Well, I will sleep an hour or two and then be on my way," Charlie replied. "I shall meet you somewhere or other. Do not look for me, but before night falls again I shall fit my footstep to yours."

"By the third dawn from this we should be there, unless the white men have retreated still farther," Sheng said.

"Retreat!" Charlie repeated. "They cannot retreat. They have not a single road open to them now. And they do not know how to travel without roads for their machines."

The two young men laughed without mirth and so parted.

. . . In silence the march went through the last day. By now the General knew to the third of a mile where the white men were waiting for rescue. He had communication by messenger with the American but he did not rely on it. The American was even more strange here than he was himself. No, he thought through that last long day, he must lean only on himself. To fight this war was beyond the white man who knew well only his own kind. He was filled with a strong scorn of these white men, all of them, who had left their countries to come here to fight among people whom they could not tell one from the other. He smiled bitterly many times as he marched that day, on foot like his men, his face spotted with shadows from the tree twigs around his hat.

"These white men!" he thought in mingled fear and scorn. "They cannot tell one brown face from another. Let an enemy stand before him and say he is a friend and the white man does not know the difference."

For his spies had brought back hundreds of stories. The enemy did not wear a uniform but went in a pair of drawers and on their feet were only sandals or rubber-soled shoes and they mingled with the people of the country who clothed themselves thus, and the white men took them all for one, not knowing the language of any of them. Here they had ruled for hundreds of years, and yet they knew not one face from another nor one tongue from the next.

"And we go to rescue these," the General groaned, and his scorn grew so high that when the American commander sent through his orders again in the afternoon where he was to go and what he was to do, the General crushed the papers into the palm of his hand and threw them away.

"I must trust to what wisdom I have of my own," he told himself.

Be sure that his scorn filtered through his voice and eyes and words, so that all of those whom he commanded felt it and breathed it in without knowing it. They went to join their allies, and yet they put no trust in those allies, even with all good will to do so. For some had a good will, and even those who had none knew that at least they had no choice. They must fight beside the white men or against them and to be against them was to join the enemy and this they could not do.

Then, too, who did not remember the Chairman as he had stood

146

before them the last time? His high voice had cut through the air like a whip above their heads.

"You bear our honor like a flag," the Chairman had cried. "Now let the white men see what we Chinese can do. If we acquit ourselves well I do not doubt that they will accept us at last as full allies in this war against the East-Ocean enemies. Where else shall we look for allies against these who would take our country for theirs, except to the men of Ying and Mei? I still put my faith in their victory. Obey that one, therefore, whom I have put over you. Not that you need a white man to be your leader, but he is to stand between you and the men of Ying, who are harsher and less friendly to us. And yet we must all be allies. Show that one what soldiers you are. Our whole people look to you. Men! I command you!"

Behind them as he spoke had stood that lady, and as the Chairman shouted these words she had raised her small clenched fist over her head.

The General remembered her as she stood there, a beautiful creature, but was she too not foreign? Often men had talked among themselves that it was she who kept the Chairman the ally of the white men. For she had spent the years of her childhood abroad and she had been nourished by the earth and wind of a country not her own. It was said she spoke their language better than she did her own. Certainly she spoke her own with a foreign curl to the words— book words, too, she used, long ancient words that came out of classics now dead, and she seemed not to know the sharp new short words of today. But then she lived apart from common folk indeed, being a lady, her ears jeweled and rings upon her hands.

He lifted his head to free himself of all these useless thoughts. He was a soldier and he had a soldier's duty ahead, clear and simple. He knew his enemy, at least, whether or not he knew his friends. He looked at the watch upon his wrist. By dawn tomorrow they should be over the river and in sight of the white men—if those men were still alive.

. . . As for Mayli, she was that night entirely sleepless and with more than weariness. The smell of battle was in the air. All knew that tomorrow there would be battle. But for her it was the first.

147

Now for the first time there would be men bleeding and dying and having to be cared for. Could she do her duty? She felt ashamed of all the uselessness of her life until now. She had lived softly and easily, apart from her own people. She had been a child abroad, and there among foreign people she had grown up. Yes, and even now she had not become a part of her own people. They were something of hers—a blood she shared, a nation whose citizen she was, but she was not a part of them as they were a part of one another. She longed at this moment not to be able to speak any other language except the one that her own people spoke. She wished she had not foreign memories.

"If ever I have time," she thought, "I shall read and read again, but not foreign books this time, and only the books of my own people—the old poetry and the old philosophy. I want to find my roots."

And then it came to her that perhaps she never would have this time, for she might be killed, and she wept a little, secretly, in the night, putting her hands to her mouth to still herself, for she lay among her women and they could have heard her. As it was, Pansiao did hear her, for this young girl still waited to see where Mayli laid herself down and she came and put her pallet there. She woke and lay still for a moment and then she put out her hand in the darkness and touched Mayli's cheek and found it wet. So startled was she to find that this one, too, could weep that she burst into her own tears, and then Mayli had to speak sharply to her, knowing that only sharpness could stop a sort of reasonless weeping like this, which might indeed sweep over all the women like a panic.

She sat up at once and took Pansiao by the braid of her hair and shook her a little. "Stop!" she whispered, "stop or I shall punish you like a child!"

And Pansiao did stop, terrified by fierceness in the voice she loved, and then Mayli lay down again cured of her own sadness.

"What is there for me," she thought, "except the one duty I see clear ahead?"

XIV

IN THIS mood did all those men and women rise the next morning long before the dawn broke, and they ate their cold rations and gathered themselves together and began to creep onward. Now the enemy was thick around them and every foot fell softly and not a voice spoke, even though the air hissed and split with the sound of guns not far away. The General had sent down warnings to them that the enemy might be perched like monkeys in the trees above them or hiding like beasts in the jungle, and for this reason he kept as much as he could to open country.

"Let each watch for himself and for all," were the words he had sent down. "Remember that here we have no friends among man or beast."

The truth was that none of them felt at ease here in war. They were men and women who could fight forever upon their own earth but they were not used to walking upon the earth of others. Upon their own land strength came up into their bodies, but upon this land they felt no strength coming up. It was an enemy under their feet.

They marched forward to certain battle then with their hearts silent, and because their hearts were silent they were afraid. They had for courage only the commands of those above them, and one of these was an American, and when had they found courage before only in commands laid upon them from above, as though they were hirelings? And the women felt the anxiety of the men and followed in dumb silence and Mayli could not cheer them by anything she did, though with great effort she had coaxed two soldiers to get some wood together and she had made a fire and given them hot tea before they started. But they had given her only wan smiles, and each brooded on some private sorrow that when she was at ease she could forget, but which when other fears pressed, she took out again. Thus Chi-ling remembered her dead children and An-lan her old father, and so it was with each one, and even the few who had no great sorrow felt that this was a dreary day for women, without home or shelter, in a foreign land.

Yet as the day came nearer to sunrise their spirits did lift somewhat, for so far they had gone without attack from the enemy and if they could join their allies before the enemy found them from the sky there was some hope that together they could form their lines anew and find a base for attack instead of the eternal retreat.

As for Sheng, marching steadily with the long steps of a farmer, he was eager to come upon the white men and see what they had for weapons and machines. So long had he fought with nothing but his rifle that it seemed to him if they could have even a few of those war weapons of which the white man had so many, then surely they could use them well and attack instead of retreat. How often had he hoped for a mortar only! But these white men had some tanks and planes even, and surely with these could the tide not be turned?

It was with this hope, therefore, that he paused at the place where the General had told him to wait, and he and his men waited above an hour, while the others gathered, and in talking he could not but show his hope, and his men caught it from him, and grew hopeful, too. They could hear clearly the sound of guns, and they listened. There were no great guns and they wondered at this. Had the white men no great guns?

Then by great luck Charlie Li came limping it. He had been scouting the countryside since three o'clock or so, and though he had a stone bruise in the sole of his foot, he had found exactly where the white men were.

"The enemy attacked them in the night," he told Sheng, "but the white men are still fighting."

"Do they have their machines?" Sheng asked eagerly.

"They have some machines," Charlie replied. "I could even see them. They are all gathered together, men and machines, in a shallow valley not above two miles from this spot. But they are hard pressed. A few are escaping. I saw here and there a handful of white men breaking away in their own cars."

"Then they have lost this battle, too," Sheng said soberly, "for men do not desert in victory."

But still he would not give up hope and soon the General came up with his men, and slowly all the forces gathered, and they were ready to go on as soon as the General had considered all the news.

The enemy, he now knew, was advancing on three sides up the valleys of the three great rivers. But these were only the main roads. Weaving in and out between them the enemy had made a net, blocking every road. And roads were necessary to the white men. Their great machine weapons were a curse to them for they must run upon roads. They lost their power from their very size when there was no road. The roads were few, and the enemy slipping among the people were hidden as they worked. And the people helped them and soon every road was blocked and all those great weapons were like leviathans cast upon a shore out of the sea, dead hulks, a vast burden upon the men who could not use them and yet were loath to leave them. Trees felled and lying across a road confounded those machines, for while the white men struggled to push aside the trees, the enemy came down on them from the skies and they shot at them from the jungles and the white men died by the score and the hundred at a single spot, trying to save machines.

All this the General knew and had heard from his spies, and he told himself he must press on, though every instinct in his brain told him it was a war already lost. But no one could read his inner hopelessness that day at dawn when he stood on a little hillock above the gathered crowd of men who were to obey him.

"Men!" he cried, and his young full voice rang over their lifted heads. "You have your duty to do. We will not ask what is to become of us. We are here to rescue our allies and to turn defeat into attack. Men! Do not forget that this is the same war we have fought for five years upon our own earth. The enemy is the same enemy and when he is defeated here he is defeated on our own earth. Men! We must defeat our enemy and restore the Great Road into our own country. Fight, then, for your own!"

A low cry went up from the men, subdued, restrained, but deep. Immediately all began to move as a single body westward and Charlie Li went only a little behind the General to point the way. But not once did the General speak except to answer when Charlie pointed out a way more short or a footpath more hidden toward the valley of the white men. So they went and the dawn broke and the sun blazed out with its sudden heat. The air had been hot and still before, but now the sun seemed to set it afire and what had been heat before was coolness to remember. Fresh sweat broke out upon every face, yet the General did not stay his steps.

"They are westward of the next hills," Charlie said at last in a low voice. The sound of guns was very near, now, cracking the hot air about them.

The General nodded and went on. But the soldier behind caught the words and passed them backward and from mouth to mouth they went and every heart tightened with hope and dread.

Then the General led them up a hill and then he began the slight descent. The column moved behind him down the slope. Ahead of him not far the General saw a motor car, then two. The motor cars stopped in the road and he lifted his glasses to his eyes and he saw white men, stiff with terror, their faces swollen huge through the lens.

"They are afraid," he said to Charlie in vast surprise. "Why are they afraid of us?"

He handed the glasses to Charlie, and Charlie stared through them. Then he began to laugh. "Doubtless they think we are the enemy," he said. "The enemy wears green uniforms—when they wear uniforms. But who but fools would wear another color in this green country?"

"Let them sweat and see what we are," the General said drily. "Luckily we have the white sun upon blue on our caps. If they cannot tell by our faces let them tell by that."

So he marched on and true enough it was that in a few moments when they came nearer the faces of those white men changed and what had been terror was now joy, and they stood up and waved their arms and shouted out and what they shouted, as the General could hear now, was the Chinese war cry.

"Chung kuo wan shui!"

Who can tell what small thing will free the spirit in men? But so it was those white men shouting the war cry which his men had carried into a hundred battles moved the General and he felt his spirit come out of his heart like a bird from a cage and he shouted in a mighty voice, *"Chung kuo wan shui!"* and all his men caught the shout and they shouted, too, until the cry went up to heaven itself. Not once did the General let his feet grow slow.

"Ask them where the enemy is," he commanded Charlie as they came up to the cars.

"Where is the enemy?" Charlie asked the white men in their own language.

"There—there!" the white men roared, pointing with their hands to the rear. Now they could see that these men were not soldiers for they carried no weapons. They were civilians of some sort. "The enemy is there and our men are still fighting," they shouted.

This the General heard and he listened while Charlie made it into his own language, and all the time he marched on, the column following him, still toward the west.

And behind him, as he passed them, Sheng stared at the faces of these new allies. He had never seen a white man close before. What faces were these—bearded, haggard, bony, the noses huge, the eyes sunken. White? They were dark with filth and burned by the sun to the color of his mother's red clay teapot!

And far behind Sheng, Mayli still trudged ahead of her women. The spring was gone from her step and her hair was wet with her sweat. But when she saw the men standing in the car and caught their grins she waved her hand at them and called out to them, "Hello, there!"

She knew well enough what power these words would have on those foreign men. Grimed and filthy as they were, their garments ragged and their hairy arms bare, they leaned toward her and shouted at her joyously, "Hello, hello, hello yourself! God! It's a pretty girl!"

She could not stop, for the General led on, but something young and laughing stirred in her heart. Oh, what good times she had had in America, dancing and talking and flirting with such young men! What good times the young could have together whatever their country! But not in times like these.

"Are they not very fierce, those hairy young men?" Pansiao asked anxiously at her side.

"No," she said shortly. "They are not fierce at all. But they are hungry and tired, and have just escaped death, perhaps."

She was hungry and tired herself and she sighed and suddenly wished with all her heart that the war was over.

153

Where was the glory of battle? When the General surveyed the scattered weary men who were his allies he wished himself unborn. Not one word came out of his lips, but his heart turned to a stone. These were not allies but burdens to add to all the other burdens of a strange country and alien people and an enemy superior to them in every weapon and way of war. He had hoped that at least by joining his own men to these something stronger might come of the union than either was apart. But he knew as he looked at them that when he allied himself to these he was adding weakness, not strength.

Nevertheless he marched through their ranks steadfastly, paying no heed to their few feeble cheers. At his side now there was Charlie Li, for the General could speak only his own language and he knew that he must report himself to the one whom the Chairman had put over him, the American.

He turned to his men. "You may be at your ease," he told them, and this word went down the line. "Rest," he told them, "and eat. We do not know when we must take up the battle again."

For there was this fortune that after fighting all night the enemy had ceased battle for the moment, and there were not even planes in the afternoon sky. In this short peace men had thrown themselves on the ground in whatever shade they could find, and some lay on their faces, some on their backs with their hats over their eyes, and some sat with their heads down upon their knees, their guns thrown down. The newly come Chinese stood staring and silent, looking doubtfully at their allies. Some of the white men, seeing them stand, lifted weary arms in salute, some smiled, some shouted out hoarse greetings, but for the most part they simply sat or lay in silence, as though their weariness were too deep for cheer.

Through them the General went his way, and soon he saw coming toward him the lean figure whom he knew to be the American. The two stopped short and each saluted the other, and then to the General's surprise, he heard the American begin to speak in his language. Now he had heard that the American did speak Chinese, but he had not believed it fully, and yet he understood well enough what it was he was saying. It was not perfect speech, and it was learned from common men, but the meaning was clear.

154

"I greet you," the American said. "But I fear you are too late," he added curtly.

"It is not my fault if we are late," the General replied coldly. "We were kept waiting on the border for many days."

"They could not easily find rice for so many men as you have," the American said.

"We could have found our own rice," the General said, "and we told them so."

"Whatever mistakes have been," the American said, "it is better to remember that we are allies, and the only hope we have is to work together and not against each other. Are you prepared for attack?"

"We have nothing else in mind," the General retorted.

By now he knew that he and this American would not like each other, and be sure the American knew it too. The knowledge showed in his shrewd blue eyes and dry voice. He looked past the General.

"Your men look fit," he said calmly. "It is pleasant to see somebody looking fit."

"My men are accustomed to hardships," the General said proudly. "They can travel thirty miles a day carrying all they need and find their own food."

"Then," the American said slowly, "I advise you as soon as you can to attack to the west. The enemy is entrenched in the city whose pagoda you see over those hills. Under cover of your attack we can reorganize and straighten the lines with the English."

He hesitated and then went on unwillingly. "I suggest that you quarter your men a little apart from these others—say, over beyond that stream. It is better to avoid quarrels among weary men."

"Quarrels!" the General said haughtily. "My men will make no quarreling."

But now Charlie interposed with a smile upon his lips. "What the American means is that the white men will not welcome us too near them. By all means let us remember that we are not white and let us keep to ourselves."

The General turned a sudden red under his sweat. "It will please us better also," he said.

The American looked grave and he put pleading into his voice and he said, "We have a fearful duty ahead of us if we are not all to be killed. Let us accept what is a fact and forget each other's faults. I will grant you whatever you are thinking, but in God's name forget it and help us. Afterwards—when the battle is won—take your revenge. But now," he flung out his hand and turned away, and then he took out his handkerchief which was wet and soiled and wiped his forehead and lifted his hat and wiped his bald head. "We may have only minutes," he said, "before the attack begins again."

"He is right," Charlie said to the General.

The General stood his ground a moment longer, motionless, struggling with himself. Then he saluted sharply, turned on his heel and shouted to his waiting men,

"Men! Fall in, to the left—march!"

They fell in, turned and marched toward the little stream and splashed across it, waist deep, and then climbed out on the bank beyond.

And the American stood watching them, sadness upon his exhausted face. His shoulder bones stuck out under his wet shirt and his hands hung at his sides like weights. Who knew what he was thinking?

Sheng, marching past him with his men, stared at him curiously. So this was the American! He looked old, too old for this life. So old a man should be at home among his children. Were there no young men in America? He was very thin, too, and his leather belt was wrapped nearly twice about his narrow waist. The muscles stood out on his lean neck and his face was so thin that his ears looked big. But big ears were a good sign of a kindly wise man, or so Sheng's mother had always said.

The American, catching Sheng's bold young eyes, smiled suddenly.

"Have you eaten?" he asked.

"How is it I understand your talk?" Sheng asked astonished, stopping where he stoood.

"Why not, when I speak your language?" the American asked. "I have lived in your country for twenty years."

"Almost as long as I have," Sheng said with his own great grin.

"You are young—a boy," the American said. "I could be your grandfather."

Sheng suddenly liked this American greatly. "It is true you are too old," he said politely, "you should be resting in your home."

But at that word "home" a flicker went over the bright blue eyes under the tattered sun helmet which the American wore. "It is better not to talk or think of home," he said in his dry voice. "Who has a home now?"

"My father's house still stands," Sheng said proudly.

"Where?" the American asked.

"Near the city of Nanking," Sheng said.

Then Sheng went on and the American stood there watching the long line of men and he let them all go until the very last, which were the carriers of goods and the hospital supplies and then the doctor and the women. These he stopped.

"You might stay, doctor," he said to Chung. "I would take it kindly if you could tend our wounded before the flies eat the flesh off their bones."

So Mayli, when they came to their allies, saw only a horde of hungry filthy weary men. Their faces were black with grime and streaked with sweat and their beards were unshaven and their eyes sunken in their sockets. The wounded lay in the small shadows cast by bushes and some were dying and many were dead. Her heart beat in her throat as she commanded her women quietly,

"Here is our work. We will lift those wounded but still living into the shade of that one great tree yonder. Then let each of you dip up water from that pond. We will not stop to boil it but I will pour disinfectant into it, and then each of you tend those who seem the weakest. Hsieh-ying, you are so strong. Gather some fuel together and we will build a fire and heat food for them. Ten of you will care for the wounded and two will help Hsieh-ying. Pansiao will stay by me."

So quietly she set each to her task while Chung smoothed a place under the tree and spread down a clean oiled sheet that he took out of his tin box of tools and he put on his surgeon's garments and prepared to cut out bullets and sew up gaps in the bodies of those who lay wounded. And now for the first time Mayli found herself quarreling with him, for she could not bear to leave any man who still drew his breath. But Chung said, pointing to this one and an-

157

other, "Let that one die, he is doomed. That one's eyes are glazed. We must save only those who have the chance of life."

"How can you tell who will live and who will not?" she cried.

But he was ruthless and pointed his finger at this one and at that one, signifying which ones were to live and which to die. And she felt tears come into her eyes while she worked without stop, but she took the time, nevertheless, to hold a cup of water for a dying man to drink and she took time to stop for the stained letters and pictures they held out to her of their wives and mothers and their children and those whom they loved. Even as they drew their last breath they summoned strength to search into some hidden place in their soiled garments and take out sweat-stained, bloody bits of paper like these and give them into her hands, murmuring and gasping their last hopes, "Tell them—tell them—" and before he could say what must be told, man after man died.

And without knowing it she began to sob, not aloud, but with deep inward sobs, and her throat was as tight as though an iron band were about it, and her hands trembled, and she saved all the poor bits of paper which had served to those men as symbols of what they loved best on earth.

She would not weep aloud, for well she knew this was only the first day of many days that would be like this, but she was new and untried and for this day at least there was no glory worth such sorrow. Her women were far more calm than she, for they had done these same tasks before and for men of their own kind, and these were strangers. But Mayli had seen young men like these living and full of merriment and noise, and she had seen them in their own countries, careless, well beloved in comfortable homes. She had danced with such young men and let them make a little love to her and they were not strange to her. It was piteous to see them here, outwitted and betrayed, cut off and trapped, and she felt no scorn for them but only sorrow. Most piteous of all was to see their gratitude when they heard her speak to them in their own tongue.

"I haven't heard—a woman—speak English—in a thousand years," a blond young lad sighed. He closed his blue eyes and clutched her hand. "Couldn't you—sing?" he whispered. "Just—something?"

And she, her throat still so tight that she could scarcely breathe

158

enough to sing, nevertheless forced herself and sang the first song that came to her lips, the song she had been singing a few nights ago,

> "*Drink to me only with thine eyes*
> *And I will pledge with mine."*

She sang it low at first but the singing eased her throat and in a moment her voice came more clear and the dying boy smiled.

"Why—it's an English—song," he whispered "How did you—"

His voice ceased and his hand loosened and yet she held it, her tears streaming down her face as she sang, until the song was ended. And then she put the heavy hand down, such a young hand, still bony and thin with youth, the nails worn down and blackened and the grime black in the fair skin. And then she put her head on her knees and wept indeed, careless of who saw or heard her, for it seemed to her that there was only misery and woe in such a world as this.

At that moment she felt herself lifted up. Two hands upon her arms grasped her and pulled her to her feet and she turned.

"Sheng!" she whispered.

"It was you, then," he said. "It was you I heard the other night—singing that same song!"

XV

THUS beside the body of the dead English boy did Sheng and Mayli meet. Had these been other days they might have taken time for surprise, but surprise of some sort came to them every day in this strange land. When anything could happen and none could foretell what he would be doing or where he would be an hour ahead, not Mayli nor Sheng felt surprise beyond the first outcry. Each took the other's two hands, and they stood, their hands thus strongly clasped, their eyes searching each other's faces, and each felt now what the other felt, a comfort that was beyond speech.

Gladness there could not be, for they stood in the midst of defeat and death, but courage poured through their hands to their hearts and in that instant he forgot his jealousy and his doubt of her.

He saw her face streaming with sweat, her hair hanging wet upon her forehead and at her neck. She had on a rough straw hat such as farmers wear and the fading green twigs were twisted about the crown. She was bone-thin, he saw, and her blue cotton uniform clung to her thinness, wet, too, with her sweat. Her feet were bare in straw shoes, and her sleeves were rolled above her elbows.

And she saw a tall gaunt young man, hard as leather, in a dirty uniform. Down that dark face of his the sweat poured in lines like rain and dripped from his chin. Indeed the sun was merciless upon them both. There were no trees except the squat growth of the jungle and the wounded had crawled to these small spots of shade and lay panting for water. Near them a shadow-faced Indian began to moan softly for water,

"Pani-pani—" he moaned.

They turned at the sound of his voice, and saw that his shoulder was torn away and that he was bleeding to death. Now Sheng even before he spoke to Mayli, dropped her hands and went over to the dying man and opened his own bottle of precious water and put it to the man's lips, and he lifted the man's head upon his right hand so that he might drink more easily.

"Oh, he will die anyway," Mayli cried in a low voice. "Save the water for yourself—"

But Sheng let the man drink and drink until the last was gone. Then he put down the man's head into the hot earth, and even as he did so the man died.

"The water is wasted," Mayli said in the same low voice.

"It would have choked me had I refused it to him," Sheng replied. He corked the empty bottle and slung it to its place and then he turned to her again and took her one hand and held it in his.

"Where have you been?" he asked.

"Here," she said, "with my women."

"And I have been dreaming of you in that little house with the foolish small dog you love better than you do me," he said.

"And I thought you were anywhere but near me," she said, her cracked lips smiling.

"It was you I heard singing that night we marched," he said, "and I thought it could not be you."

These few words they said to each other in the midst of the men who lay wounded and dying and sunstruck, and each knew that even this moment must end because of their duty to these others. Indeed the women were stealing curious looks at them already and so they unclasped their hands.

"I will seek you out tonight," Sheng said.

"I shall be watching for you," she said. And then it seemed to her she could not wait until night of such a day as this, for who knew at the end of the day who would be living and who dead?

"Take care of your life," she said to him and her eyes pleaded. "Be sure that the night finds you safe."

His hot dark face seemed suddenly to flame. "Do you think I could die? Tonight, after the sun sets."

He turned and strode off among the men who strewed the ground and she watched the tall thin figure for seconds, until she felt a small hand creep into hers.

"Who is that tall man, sister?" She heard Pansiao's voice whisper this at her shoulder. For now Pansiao had begun to call her sister, and this Mayli allowed, knowing how lonely the young girl was. She turned her head and stared down into Pansiao's wondering eyes. Then she began to laugh.

"How could I have forgotten you!" she cried. "Well, I did forget you, you little thing. Why, that is your brother, child—your third brother! We have found each other."

Now Pansiao did stare after the young man but he was already gone among the men. "Shall I run after him?" she asked.

But Mayli shook her head. "There is no time now," she said. "We have our work to do. But tonight he will come back, after sunset," she said, "and you must help me to watch for him."

She drew Pansiao with her as she spoke, and together they stooped over an Englishman who was crawling on hands and knees to find the small shadow of a wrecked truck. His head was hanging so she could not see his face.

"How can I help you?" she asked.

With mighty effort he lifted his head at the sound of her voice and at her English words. Then she saw that which put out of her mind everything except the man's misery. The lower part of his face was gone. He had no mouth to speak with, no jaw nor nose. Only his frightful eyes stared up at her in agony.

She bent and Pansiao helped her and they took the man under the shoulders and dragged him to the hot shade of the truck. She laid him down so that at least his head was in the shade and she took a hypodermic from her little case she carried with her and she shot the needle into his arm, and let him clutch her other hand. Then when she felt his hold weaken and saw his blazing eyes grow dim and dull, she put his hand down upon the dry earth and left him. There were others whom perhaps she could save.

. . . Here was the misery of that day, that while they did their work the great retreat went on. Living and dying, they had to move and move again. She knew that battle was roaring about her, but she gave no heed to it and worked steadily on with her women helping her and the doctor operating in a truck under an awning. Yet even so the order would be cried out over their heads that they must move still farther to the rear. For a battle is not a thing which can be seen whole. It is made of many small movements and many men and women and each is a part of a whole which he cannot see or understand. He must move when the order is cried at him, and he moves in the direction he is told, but why he does not know nor can he ask.

All through that hot day Mayli turned from wounded men to wounded men and new ones were brought continually to die or to struggle on with life. When she grew faint with weariness she looked at Chung and knew that still she must not rest because he did not. He had tied a towel around his head to keep the sweat out of his eyes, but the sweat poured down his cheeks and down his bare arms and it dripped off his fingers as he cut and sliced human flesh and tied veins and arteries and as they followed to bind where he had cut, bandages were wet with the women's sweat, but who could dry himself in this most pitiless heat? They drank whatever water they

162

saw, and into buckets that were brought from some drying filthy stream Chung poured a bottle or two of stuff and some salt and let them drink. Only with recklessness could life be lived now in the midst of death and when at any moment death might come out of the skies or out of the bush about them, why hold back from water for which they were famished?

Mayli watched her women narrowly to see how they bore the day and they bore it well, or so she thought. Pansiao, whom she had feared for most, bore it best of all. In the midst of all the heat and blood and dead, Pansiao came and went, fetching and carrying this and that, her small face cheerful however hot. Once she came near to Mayli and Mayli saw her smile.

"I keep thinking of tonight," Pansiao whispered.

She was a child indeed, and Mayli smiled back without speaking. In all this horror Pansiao could think of her own joy tonight. Her little mind had chosen to see no meaning in horror any more. She watched a man die and could feel nothing because she had seen it too often before, and death was part of life for her now. Blood and wounds and stench she let pass by her and she fixed her mind on something of her own. Today it was the thought of her brother, but yesterday it was a bit of sweet stuff she had found in a shop and bought for a penny and the day before that a kitten lost on the roadside. Tomorrow it would be something else.

Siu-chen, the young girl who had been a student in an inland school, and who was an orphan since the attack on Nanking, was crying as she worked. Now and again she lifted her hands all soiled with blood and dirt and wiped her eyes and her face, always ruddy, was splotched with blood not her own. But Mayli did not fear for her so long as she could weep. Nor did she fear for Hsieh-ying who cursed and swore as she lifted the heavy bodies of men to her back and carried them across the battlefield, or took the light ones in her arms like children. Mayli could hear her cursing and swearing to herself as she came and went.

"Oh my mother and my mother's mother, and look at all this waste of good men! Oh, these devils and may their fathers be turtles and their mothers' private parts rot away." Then she screamed, "Why, I know him, this one with his legs gone! Captain!" she cried

163

to Mayli, "he is the man who drove the truck—do you remember? He was such a hearty good man. Come here, my poor one, and let me get you to the doctor—"

Chung shouted at her not to bring him such men as this for how could he put two legs on a body? But Hsieh-ying bawled back at him that though her own mother were cursed she would pick up any man that looked at her with living eyes, were his skin white or black, and did he have legs or not, and the only ones she left were the ones already dead and would she leave this one whom she knew? But the man died as she spoke.

It was a strange thing that in this dreadful day when the enemy did not cease for one moment to harass them from the sky and from the jungles, in their frantic weariness they took time and strength to quarrel together, now Chung and Hsieh-ying and now bitterly any two who must come together as they worked. As often as the enemy weapons burst upon them, so often men's tempers, or women's, burst out in too much fear and weariness and heat and hunger. And worse than anything was the pitiless glare of the angry sun that grew steadily more fierce as the day went on.

But so long as they could shout and swear at each other or weep Mayli felt her women safe. Only when they were silent did she keep watch of them, and the two silent ones were An-lan and Chi-ling. These two worked without let all day, and when at late noon a little food was sent around, Chi-ling shook her head and would not eat.

Mayli went to her. "Eat," she said to Chi-ling, "I command it."

Chi-ling shook her head. "I cannot," she said, "even though you command me. I would vomit it up."

At that Mayli let her alone, and only watched her sharply as she and An-lan worked side by side, for between these two had grown up a sort of friendship, as though in their silence they found comfort.

So the long day drew on, and always more heavily, for by mid-afternoon all knew that the battle was being lost. Defeat was in the smell of the air, in the dust, in the heat. None spoke the word, but all knew, and the mounting of that knowledge swept through them like an evil wind.

164

The General knew it without waiting for his messengers to tell him. He had led his own men that day, endeavoring with all his heart to clear the road for their retreat. But so evil was the enemy, and so clever in his evil, that whenever a road was cleared in one place it was blocked again in another, and it was this endless blocking that held them constantly in trap. Now the General cursed the foreign machines indeed, for these machines were useless when their engines stopped, and like the heart in a human body, it was the engine which was most delicate and vulnerable in them. Again and again the enemy dragged the dead machines together across a road and made a fort behind them and sprayed the road of retreat with fire.

"We are tied to these machines!" the General roared to his commanders. "Would that we could trust to our own legs and leave the cursed things here to rust and rot!"

Yet how could they leave these instruments and vehicles in which their allies trusted? Because of machines men must follow roads and upon those roads the enemy rained down fire from heaven and sent out fire from the jungles, and everywhere and always the enemy found them because they could not take shelter and leave the roads.

When night came at last, they halted, knowing that in the night the enemy would block the road they must travel tomorrow and that the people of the land, who were their enemies, would help them and hide them and by the side of the enemy send out their bullets.

These bullets, Sheng discovered, were anything the people could find. The enemy had good bullets, newly made and of a sort that burst quickly and with a spray of fine metal that tore the flesh in twenty places. But late in the day, before the halt was called for the night, Sheng felt a sting in his left upper arm. He was at that moment in a narrow fork of road that led out from the main road, and the hour being late he was looking for a place of encampment for his men. He put his hand to his arm but before he could find the cause of the sting a rain of metal points fell upon the handful of men who were with him and they bent their heads and ran from that place. When he was somewhat safe again in the main road and well away from the danger of trees near by, he felt his arm and to his own amazement he found the head of a nail as neatly in his arm

165

as though a carpenter had hammered it in. He jerked it out by the head and found a nail between two and three inches in length, and he gave some good curses as he held it up between his thumb and forefinger.

"See this," he said to his men. "This is what they fell us with now."

"That nail," his aide said, "is from no enemy, be sure, but from one of the men of Burma who join the enemy against us. These Burmese have no good weapons yet, having been long forbidden by law of the white men to carry arms at any time, and so what they have are old weapons they have stolen or kept hidden against this day, and having no bullets for them they shoot out nails or scraps of any metal they can find."

Slow dark blood now was dripping out of the nail hole, and Sheng let it run awhile to cleanse the wound and then he tore a strip from the tail of his coat and bound it up and went on with his work. That night they encamped in no bypath but in the middle of the main road, whence they could watch on all sides whoever came near, and he spread his men out fanwise through the near-by jungle, the outer ones on guard all night, while the inner ones were to sleep until midnight, when it was their time to stand guard.

When all was ready for the night and the weary men had eaten the poor food that was all they had until new supplies could be sent up from the far rear, Sheng bade his next officer take his place for awhile and then alone he went down the road a mile and more to where the wounded were, to keep his tryst.

Now as he came near, his heart beating and leaping in his breast, he saw instead of the one he expected to be waiting for him at the edge of the encampment, the figures of two. In the moonlight that shone hard and as clear, almost, as sunshine upon that jungle road he saw Mayli's head lifted and listening, but clinging to her hand with both hands was a shorter younger figure. His ardent heart chilled. Why had she brought a stranger to their first meeting? Was she to begin again that fencing, playing and delay which had held him off so long? He grew angry at the thought.

"There is no time for such delay any more," he thought. "She must have done with it. I will have her deal with me now as truly as though she were man instead of woman."

He strode forward, quickening his step with anger, and so she saw his face surly when he came near. She did not speak. She gazed at him and waited.

"Who is this you have brought with you?" he asked shortly.

Then she understood the cause of his anger and she laughed. "Sheng!" she said, "you know her."

He cast a look or two at Pansiao but carelessly, so eager was he to be alone with Mayli. As for Pansiao, she lifted her little face timidly and looked with wonder at this tall harsh-voiced fellow. Was this indeed her third brother? She remembered him as a reedy, sullen boy who had been like a storm in his father's house. And yet she remembered, too, that sometimes when she was very small he had let her ride the waterbuffalo to the grasslands with him and there upon the peaceful sunny hills he had not been surly, but kind. He had pulled the sweet grass that had its tender silvery tassels folded inside green sheaths and drawing them out one by one he had held them before her open mouth and she had licked them in with her tongue while they laughed. And she could remember that sometimes he had sung to her.

"Do you remember the song you used to sing about farmers hoeing in the spring?" she now asked him suddenly.

And she lifted her voice and sang a snatch of it in a clear quavering trill.

"Why, how do you know that song?" he asked her. "It is a song of my native hills."

"Because I am Pansiao," she said, faltering under his stern dark gaze.

He stared down at her and drew in his breath and pulled his right ear. "What a thing I am," he said, "that I do not know my own sister—if you are my sister," he added, "being here in this evil hole and how you are here I could not think if I should think the rest of my life."

Now his surly looks were gone and he was all eager and amazed, and he gazed into Pansiao's face and the more he looked the more he saw it was she.

"What is the name of my sister-in-law?" he asked.

"Jade," she said, quickly.

"And what is the number of my brothers?" he asked.

"Two," she said happily, "Lao Ta and Lao Er, and you are Lao San, and our house is built around a court with a small pond in the middle and there are goldfish in it, and in the summer there is matting over the court and we eat there, all of us together, and my elder brothers' little boys run to and fro and—and—" she put her hand to her mouth. "Oh poor Orchid," she whispered, "I have not remembered you for so long and you are dead!"

"The two boys also are dead," Sheng said shortly.

Pansiao gave a wail of sorrow. "Oh, but they were so pretty, those two little boys!" she wept, "and I remember that the smallest one was so fat and soft when I held him and he always smelled of his mother's milk, like a little calf!"

There in that strange and lonely place, in a short hour of peace in the middle of the night, with the soldiers sleeping about them and the moans of the wounded in their ears, the brother and sister drew near to each other in longing for the home where they had been born.

"Let us find somewhere to sit down," Mayli said gently.

But where was there to sit in this evil place?

"We must not go near the edge of the wood," Sheng said. "The snakes are very swift here and deadly. We must stay where we can see the ground clear about us."

There was a broken truck near them, turned on its side and blasted partly away by an enemy shell, and upon this they sat, Pansiao between Mayli and Sheng. The mosquitoes sang shrilly about their ears and out of the night there came the sounds of the jungle on either side of them, those sharp sounds of restless small beasts, moving through the night, and sometimes they heard the stealthy crackle of twigs bent under the foot of some larger creature. There they sat in the hot moonlight and the memory of that farmhouse so many thousands of miles from here crept into them like a sickness.

Now they both fell silent for a while, and Pansiao stretched her memory and Sheng sat dreaming, forgetting all except his home,

168

and those from whom he had sprung. Who knows the paths of the mind?

. . . It so happened that at that very moment Ling Sao, too, was thinking of her third son and she lay sleepless upon her bed. She who at night always fell upon her bed and into sleep at the same instant was now uneasy because of new evil that had befallen the house that day.

Ling Tan could not sleep because of it and he lay at her side, still but wakeful. On this day he had heard from his two elder sons, who had heard it in the city where they had gone to sell new radishes, that the war was lost in Burma. From there, how many thousands of miles away, had the evil news come. It came by secret voices in the air, it came by whispers spoken behind hands and into waiting ears, and now many knew that Burma would be lost and because of this, years must pass before they could be free again.

So Ling Tan that day saw his sons come back gloomy from the city, though their baskets were empty. "What are the devils doing now?" he had asked them. In these days he himself went no more to the city, but used what strength he had upon the fields.

"It is not the devils this time but the white men in Burma," Lao Ta told him, and he sat down on a bench at the door and sighed and let his baskets drop, and took out his little bamboo pipe and stuffed it with a dried weed they used instead of tobacco nowadays.

Now this Lao Ta since he married the woman he found in his trap had grown sleeker and more fat than he had ever been in his lean life and this was because his new wife made him secret dainties and slipped into his bowl all the little best meats she could without being seen. She had made him give up his traps, too, and she had done this by persuading him that he must help his old father more.

"This you should do being so good an elder son," she had said, and she praised him always and coaxed him with her praise and without any force she had him little by little doing what she wanted.

But indeed this was the woman's power in the house that she could coax so sweetly and with so much love that it was a pleasure to yield to her. All she did was without any wish for herself, and her love poured out for them all and all loved her. With Jade she

169

never took an elder's place but she cried out with wonder at Jade's learning and her prettiness and she worshiped Jade's three sons and especially the two she had delivered at a single birth. Lao Er she served and praised and let him think he should have been the eldest son with so much wisdom as he had, and Ling Sao she studied how to spare and Ling Tan she spoke to as her master. Only to her own husband, Lao Ta, did she show her one great constant wish that she might have a son before it was too late, but of this too she spoke with only such anxious love for him that he was moved to comfort her instead of blaming her. "Leave off fretting for a child," he told her often, "I am pleased with you, though you are barren. These are ill times for children anyway." But still the woman prayed to Kwan-yin night and morning with her beads between her fingers, and still she hoped.

Therefore Lao Ta was cheerful enough these days so that gloom showed on him when he felt it, and all had shared his gloom when he told them what he and his brother had heard that day. They sat late in the evening talking of it and planning what should be done if Burma fell.

"Those white men," Ling Tan said again and yet again, "I never dreamed it that those white men could fail. Why, their guns—their weapons—how could it be?" And he thought sadly how little worth their promise was if Burma fell.

"Years it will be for us if we are shut off," Lao Er said sadly and his eyes sought Jade's.

"Are our children to be brought up as slaves?" Jade cried out. Now Jade had sat silent all this while, and at her sudden cry they all turned to stare at her. At this she burst into tears and ran out from the room.

Ling Tan looked at his second son's grave face. "What does she mean?" he asked.

"It is her great fear that our children will not know what freedom is," Lao Er answered. "So far she has been hoping beyond reason that the white men would vanquish the enemy quickly, and she knows that for this Burma is our last hope."

"She always knows too much," Ling Sao sighed. "That wife of yours, my son, she knows as much as any man."

170

Ling Tan spoke again to Lao Er. "If you want your sons to grow up free then you must leave this house."

"What?" Ling Sao cried at this. "Am I to let my grandsons go out and be lost like my third son?" And she put her blue apron to her eyes and wept aloud and Lao Er made haste to comfort her.

"Now, my mother," he said "why will you always reach the end before there is the beginning? Have I said I am taking your grandsons away from you?"

"No," Ling Sao sobbed, "but if Jade wants to go, you will."

"How can we take three small children out secretly?" Lao Er urged. "It is only a dream of hers. We will not leave you."

But Ling Sao would not be comforted, "If Jade is dreaming, then I am afraid," she said, and though Lao Ta's wife brought hot tea to soothe her, she would not drink it, and so at last they parted and went to bed, and still none was eased.

Now in bed Ling Sao lay and thought how great a sorrow it would be if there were no children in the house and it would be worse even than if she heard her third son were lost, and then she felt herself wicked to think thus of her own son and she began to yearn for Lao San and soon she fell to weeping softly.

Now Ling Tan heard her weeping and he spoke sharply from his pillow. "Give over weeping, woman, your tears should be dry by now with so much trouble as we have had," he said.

"Am I to have my life end childless?" she cried out.

"You still think of yourself," he said heavily. "But you and I, old woman, we are as good as dead. Can we let the little ones grow up as slaves? Jade is right."

At this Ling Sao wailed afresh and he being very weary in his old age could not be patient with her for once and he reached out his hand and slapped her cheek. "Give over—give over—" he shouted, "lest you make me weak, too."

At these words, she paused, and, not minding his fierceness, she put her hand and touched his cheek and found it wet. Now she was quiet.

"You, too?" she whispered.

"Be still," he muttered, but his voice broke her heart.

171

"My dear old man," she said and yielded up her will. Let come what must—let come what must.

. . . And in the hot night Sheng sat frowning and remembering and Pansiao, beside him, remembered, too, and Mayli let them be alone, as though she were not there.

Pansiao put out her hand and Sheng took it and held it.

"Ai, my little sister," he said sadly, "why are you here? It is worse for you than for me. What can be your end?"

"But it is very lucky for me to have found Mayli and now you," Pansiao said cheerfully. "It might have been that I was here all alone," and so she told him how it happened that she had come here by one chance and then another.

"You have been like a leaf on a river," he said, "borne along without knowing how or why."

"But now I am quite safe," she said cosily, "now I am with both of you."

Over her head those two, Sheng and Mayli, looked at each other, and well they knew what each was thinking. Though they longed to be alone, how could they tell this young and trusting creature to leave them even for a little while? They had not the heart to be so cruel, and so they sat listening while she prattled, and looking at each other over her head.

And what she prattled of was always home and again home. "Do you remember how Jade used to try to teach me to read, Third Brother?" she asked. "I wish I could show her now how many letters I know and read to her out of my little book. I have the book still in my pack."

"Yes, she does," Mayli said. "I have seen her reading it sometimes."

"I learned to read it in the white woman's school," Pansiao said, "where I first saw you, Elder Sister," she said to Mayli. "And the moment I saw you I knew that you—"

She turned to look at her brother with sudden thoughtfulness. "The moment I saw this elder sister I said she would be a good wife for you," she said.

Sheng laughed aloud. "So have I always said the same thing," he

172

told Pansiao, "and so I still do say. But can you get her to agree with us?"

Now Pansiao was all eagerness. She took Mayli's hand and brought it to Sheng's upon her knees and she put them together under her two little rough hands and held them there.

"Now you t-two," she said, stammering, "you two—ought you not to agree?"

And as though to humor her Mayli let her hand lie under Sheng's, and Sheng closed his right hand strongly over her narrow one and held it and above these two clasped hands Pansiao's hands pressed down, quivering and hot. "Will you not agree with us?" she said pleadingly to Mayli.

"Child, Mayli said, "is this the time or the hour for such talk? Who can tell what tomorrow will bring to any of us?"

"But that is why we should agree together," Pansiao said anxiously. "If we were sure of tomorrow—there would be no haste. But when there may be no tomorrow, should we not agree tonight?"

"She is right," Sheng said in his deep voice.

Then Mayli felt her heart drawn out of her body. Would it not be strength to make her promise to Sheng and so be secure at least in that?

Then as though Heaven would not give her even so much, before she could speak they heard the sound of running footsteps and there was An-lan, pale in the moonlight, gasping with running, and her eyes were staring black in her pale face. She ran to Mayli as though the other two were not there and she shouted as she ran,

"Oh, you are here— Oh, I have searched for you everywhere! Chi-ling—Chi-ling has hung herself upon a tree! She—she is there!" And An-lan pointed to the further side of the encampment.

Mayli leaped to her feet and ran toward the place she pointed and Sheng came behind her. Behind him Pansiao stood still but none thought now of her. They ran to the further edge of the jungle, beyond where the men lay behind the barricade of their vehicles, and there upon a gnarled low tree whose small fan-shaped leaves quivered even in the silent air, they saw Chi-ling, a slender shape hanging loosely from a branch.

Sheng took out his knife and cut the cloth that held her and caught her as she fell and laid her on the ground. It was Chi-ling indeed, and she had torn her girdle in half and made a noose and by it had taken her own life.

But was her life quite gone? Mayli stooped and felt the flesh still warm. "Run," she bade An-lan. "Run—find Chung!" And she began to chafe Chi-ling's limp hands and to move her thin arms. In very little time Chung was there, girding himself as he came, for in the heat he had been sleeping nearly naked, and he stooped and felt Chi-ling's heart. He shook his head—the heart was still and she was dead. They rose and An-lan stood gazing down at her with no tears in her staring eyes, and only grimness on her mouth.

"Did she say nothing to you, An-lan?" Mayli asked gently. "You two were such friends."

"Nothing," An-lan said. "We ate our meal together tonight as we always do, she and I, a little apart from the others for the sake of quiet. Then afterwards she did what you told us was to be done for the wounded. She did for hers, and I for mine."

"I saw her," Chung said slowly, "not above an hour ago. She came in to tell me that one of the Australians had died. But I had feared he would. There was gangrene in his wound and my sulfa drugs are gone. But she knew that he might not live—besides, he was a stranger to her."

"She always took every death too hard," An-lan muttered. "I told her—I said, we shall see many die, and what are we to do if you behave so each time?"

"What did she say?" Mayli asked.

"You know how she never answered anyone," An-lan said. "She did not answer me. But I was speaking thus even as she went to the young dying man and it must be that when she saw him die, she came here to the jungle and died, too."

"Let us go and look at that dead man," Chung said. "It may be she left some sign on him."

"But we cannot leave her here," Mayli said quickly. "The jungle beasts would have her—the ants, the wild cats—they say there are tigers here, too."

Sheng stooped. "I will carry her," he said, and he lifted Chi-ling's

174

dead body over his shoulder, and so they went into the encampment. An English guard peered at them.

"Who goes there?" he asked.

"A nurse has killed herself," Chung said shortly.

"Oh, I say!" the guard murmured. He lowered his gun and put up the mosquito netting that hung from the brim of his hat and stared at Chi-ling. "Why, that girl," he said aghast, "she passed me not half an hour ago, and I said she had better not go out alone, but she pushed by me, and I let her go—it's hard to argue with them when they don't speak English."

"Put her down," Chung said to Sheng. "The guard will watch her until we come back."

So Sheng put Chi-ling down and Mayli stooped and straightened her body on the ground and there she lay peacefully, the white moonlight on her face.

"I'll watch," the guard murmured.

They went on silently then to the place where the young man had lain upon a pallet on the ground and there he still was, dead. But there was neither sign nor message there from Chi-ling. Only when they looked closely did they see how ordered was the young man's body, his hair smoothed, and over the foulness of the gangrene wound in his lower belly there lay a handful of fragrant leaves of some sort.

"She put those leaves there," An-lan said.

So they stood a moment and then Chung said, "Let us go back and bury her. In this heat it will not do to let her lie. The young man others will bury, but let us bury her for she is ours."

So they went back, and there beside the road in the edge of the jungle they dug a hole with sticks and a shovel that Sheng found and An-lan and Mayli put green leaves into the hole and they laid Chi-ling among them and then when the earth was covered over her Sheng and Chung together lifted the log of a fallen tree and laid it across the grave to keep the beasts away.

When all was done, Sheng and Mayli looked at each other and Sheng said in his old rough way, "Now I must get back to my men and you back to where your duty is."

They looked and Pansiao had come up and she was watching

them, but silently, her eyes strange and startled. They did not heed her, nor did they heed An-lan who sat on the end of the log, her head in her hands. Chung had gone already.

"Let us meet as often as we can at night," Sheng said. "Keep watch for me, and I will find you when I am free."

She nodded, and he went away and when she saw him gone, she went over to An-lan and put her hand on the girl's shoulder. "Come," she said.

And An-lan rose and now Pansiao came near and she was silent and afraid, and Mayli put out her hand and took Pansiao's, and so in silence the three went into the encampment to sleep, if sleep they could in the few hours until dawn would come again.

XVI

BUT not the next night nor the next nor for six nights after that did Sheng and Mayli meet. For at dawn the next day those whom the mosquitoes and the leeches had not waked, or the sandflies and all those many teasing insects and small creatures which dwell in wild lands, now were awakened by low-flying enemy planes which strewed fire even on the rear where Mayli and her women were. She had lain down for an hour or two and Pansiao beside her, after Sheng left, and she had commanded An-lan to stay within her sight, on the pretense that she might need her, but truly to watch the girl whose silence she did not trust.

When she lay down she would have said she could not sleep, for her thoughts were torn and troubled indeed, but she did sleep, being still so young and now very weary. From this sleep she too was awakened by the thundering of bombs very near and she leaped out of her sleep, dragging Pansiao with her, and they fled into the edge of the jungle. There in the half darkness they clung together. A flying rain had fallen a little while before, a rain which had not waked them in their shallow tent, but which had wet every leaf and bush, and now in spite of the heat and the stillness of the morning this rain made them feel chill. Nor was it safe even here, for all knew that the enemy crawled through the trees like monkeys, disguised in green, and so Mayli looked fearfully about her. But instead of that enemy, at this moment she saw near her a short thick serpent rearing its head from behind a rotting log.

"Do not move," she whispered to Pansiao. "There is an evil-faced snake watching us."

So, not daring to move, they clung together staring in horror at that snake, while above them the planes soared and dipped and soared again with loud whines of sound, and each time they dipped the thunder fell. The snake grew angry as it listened and now it began to weave itself back and forth lifting its squat head out of the nest of its own body and darting out a thin, split thread of scarlet tongue.

Pansiao watched it and her face grew pale. "I think that is no snake," she whispered. "I think it is a demon."

In this close wet heat, in the dripping wet, the two girls stood motionless, watching the creature. It dipped its head and then moved it slowly from right to left and back and forth, its two round black eyes fixed upon them, and though it was twenty feet and more away from them yet Mayli too began to be sure it had an evil intent toward them.

"We must not stay here," she whispered to Pansiao. "Let us move away so slowly that it does not know we move."

So they began to move slowly backward to the edge of the jungle again, forgetting in this terror the enemy above. But the instant they began to move thus in retreat, terror took them entirely and without thought and with nothing indeed except mad fear they ran into the middle of the road and not once did they look back at that serpent.

"Do you think perhaps it blames us for all this noise?" Pansiao asked anxiously, when they had stopped.

"Perhaps indeed it does," Mayli said. "That I had not imagined," she added, and in the midst of the danger and the explosions to the right and to the left of them she gave a second's wondering thought to the creatures in this jungle, used to silence since the world began and now crazed doubtless with what they could not understand.

She was to remember often in the next days the terror which had seized her and Pansiao together when they fled from the snake. For something of the same terror seemed to possess the armies in retreat in these days. The enemy made sorties over them five and six times a day as they moved toward the rear, and each time the dead were more than could be buried and the wounded more than could be cared for, and there was no sleep and little time for food and no appetite for the poor stuff that was given them to eat, for they had lost communication with the rest and must eat what could be found. In those few days Pansiao grew thin and white and Siu-chen's ruddiness was streaked with paleness. There was not strength now for tempers or quarreling. Those who lived did what had to be done for the dying.

And over them and under them and about them like blankets of wet wool was the eternal heat, which did not abate night or day. By day the sun was not to be borne, and they longed for the night. Then in the night the hotness of the dark was so hateful that they longed for the day again. This was the season of the mango showers, those light and fleeting rains which fall suddenly and soft out of seemingly sunny skies, the rains to which in better years than this the people had looked forward with thankfulness for the ripening of the fruit. Now while the showers gave a moment's respite from heat they sent a lasting chill through bodies weakened by battle. Indeed there was no good thing to be said of these days. They were an endless struggle and striving to retreat more quickly, until at last this retreat grew to terror in them all, a panic that spread from body to body, for it was flesh that feared and mind was dead.

Thus did six days pass and Mayli saw Sheng not once. She had not looked for him, it is true, for there had been no time in this retreat. But on the evening of the sixth day retreat was held because a heavy rain that afternoon had mired them and had clouded the skies too so that for a while the enemy did not come out. For the first time in all these days and nights Mayli took time to wash herself. The rain came down, steady and soft, and she took out from her pack the last piece of soap she had saved jealously since she left home. She called Pansiao a little apart and told her to hold up a piece of matting between her and the road, and behind that matting she washed herself clean in the rain.

178

It was while she did this that she saw Pansiao's face peeping over the matting, the rain streaming down her cheeks, and she said,

"Now what shall we do? I see that Third Brother of mine coming near."

"Does he come?" Mayli exclaimed. "Then I will dress myself quickly."

So she did and in a moment she was ready for she had only to put on her wet uniform and bind her wet hair and there she was.

So she came out from behind the matting and there was Sheng. The first thing she saw was that he looked ill and then she saw that his arm was tied into a rough sling with a short length of hempen rope.

"Oh, you are wounded!" she cried.

"I don't say it is enough to call a wound," he replied. "It is a nail hole that I had six days ago and I thought the wound clean, but now I think there was poison on the nail." And he told her how he had felt a sting and had found a nail buried in him to the head.

"Let me see it," she cried, and she drew him aside into the little tent, and made him unwrap the cloth he had torn from the tail of his shirt. There was indeed before her eyes a very ugly angry wound, for his arm had swelled and pus was coming out of the hole and small red veins ran up and down his arm and shoulder.

"Oh you stupid!" she cried, her fright making her angry, "how could you not tell me about this before now?"

"Who has had time to think of himself?" he said.

And what had she to reply to this? She turned to Pansiao who was looking at them with anxious eyes.

"Go and call the doctor," she said. "Tell him this time it is your brother." And away Pansiao went running to find Chung, and while she was gone Mayli washed the wound with medicines from her own kit.

Now shyness fell upon them, and yet it seemed good to them to be alone in spite of all their evil circumstances. It could be only a few minutes, they both knew, and each quickly set about to think what to say in those few minutes, and for some words that would last until they were alone again. And Sheng who was always outright spoke first and he said, "If ever we come out of this trap in

179

which we are I will not wait one day longer to know your true mind about me."

She had been making herself very busy at his wound, and now she looked up to smile but the smile stopped on her face for she saw that even the soft touch she put upon that arm had made him sick with pain.

"Oh," she cried, "this is very bad—you should have told me how bad. Sit down, Sheng—"

And she made him sit down on a box there which had once held bullets and which she had brought in for a seat. She went on washing his wound and she comforted him with humming. "Now, I must hurt you, poor fellow—I cannot help it. It makes my own flesh ache to hurt you like this, but the filth must be washed out and the poison. Then when Chung comes he can see it clean and he will know what next to do—"

And he sat still, not speaking because her words were sweet to him and the tone of her voice warm. How close—how close they were, and could anything part them, even death?

But that moment was only a moment long and it was gone before they could grasp it, and there was Chung at the flap of the tent.

"Now what?" he asked.

"This fellow," Mayli said. "A nail has poisoned him."

Chung's square face was like a death's head these days it was so thin, and the cords of his neck were like strings that moved his head, and the little belly he used to have in good times was gone now and in its place was a cavern around which he knotted his girdle twice. But he was not ill and he never spoke of weariness. He stared into the hole now cleaned and smelled its taint, and shook his head.

"This man should have the sulfa," he said, "but I have none. I used the last days ago."

"Would they have some—the English?" Mayli asked.

"How do I know?" Chung answered. "I have not seen an English doctor these ten days."

"We can't keep up with them," Sheng said wryly. "They are always ahead of us in retreat."

And now this was the first time that Mayli knew why they had gone back each day. "Is this why each midday we hasten so?" she asked.

"We get our orders each morning to hold," Sheng said hastily. "We hold at any cost. Then by midday the order comes to straighten out the lines. Then we spend the afternoon retreating to where the line is."

They looked at each other in deepest gloom.

"But where is the end of this?" Mayli asked.

"Who knows?" Sheng said. "Be sure the General is like a man gone mad. He who has never retreated in his life of war is now pulled back and pulled back, leaving his men dead. We who command under him—what can we do?"

"But the American?" Mayli breathed.

"What can the American do?" Sheng said shortly. "He is no god—he is like us—a foreigner, fighting on foreign soil. No, the battle is lost. We know it. The men smell defeat even in the rear and soldiers are deserting."

"Our men?" Mayli asked faintly.

"All men—" Sheng said. "Those who have the will to desert are deserting—white, yellow, black—"

All this while he had sat holding his arm stiff, and now the doctor recalled himself, and sighed.

"What to do with you I cannot tell," he said.

Then Pansiao spoke. She had stood silent while they talked of the war and she had paid no heed to their talk but only to her brother's arm.

"Do you remember, Third Brother," she now said, "that our mother used to make a poultice of baked yeast-bread wet and she put it on us when we had boils in the summer and it drew the boils and then they broke and went away? Sometimes she put in yellow rape seed too, but we have no such seed here. But I have a piece of bread in my pack that I have kept a long time against when I might be hungry and every day I have wiped the mold off and while a little is eaten I have saved the rest fearing there would always come another day when I would be more hungry than this one."

"It can do no harm," the doctor said, "though perhaps no good. Fetch the bread, child."

So Pansiao opened her little pack and took out a bundle wrapped in thin brown oiled paper, and this she unwrapped and another paper, and inside was the bread dried and molded in its pores, and she gave it to Chung and then he took the bread and made it into a poultice and wrapped it about Sheng's arm.

"Do not use your arm at all," he said.

"Luckily it is not my gun arm," Sheng said, "and so I can obey you."

Then he stood up. "I must not stay longer," he said. "The General has called us to him this midnight."

He did not put out his hand to touch Mayli, but he gave her a long deep look.

"Better for you if you come back tomorrow and let me look at your arm again," Chung said.

"If I can, I will," Sheng said, looking at Mayli still. "But if I do not come for some days, I cannot tell how many, do not think it is because I am ill of the wound. It will be because the General has put a command upon me. When I can come I will."

This he said to Mayli and she smiled and said with courage, "Be sure I shall not let myself fear anything for you."

And so they parted yet again.

. . . Now Sheng when he had left Mayli went his way among the disarray of the retreating army and then he turned to the left and toward a small tent which was the General's. He coughed at the door to signify his presence and he heard the General's voice calling him to come in and so he went in.

The others were already there, Yao Yung, his long face sad, sitting on a folding stool, and Pao Chen squatted on his heels. There too was Charlie Li, a ragged pair of trousers held about his waist and torn off at the knees.

"Sit where you can," the General said shortly. "This is no time to think who is what. I have called you here because Li brings evil news. The rear is already lost. That is, the men know the battle is lost. Supplies are stopped. Where there should be order there is none. If the rear is lost can the front be held? And yet in spite of this to-night I have orders from the American that we are to move quickly to relieve the white men who are in yet another trap. The enemy have beset them once again from the rear. Their armies have crept through the people, disguised and with the help of these people, until they hold the river where the white men must cross it. We are commanded to fight our way through and open up a space on the river enough for these white men to escape. There is a bridge which the enemy hold. We must force the enemy from the banks and hold them to the east of the bridge while the white men cross, then cross ourselves and destroy the bridge before the enemy can follow. It is a piece of work as delicate as an ivory maker's."

He said all this in a level cold voice, and when he had finished none spoke for a while, then Sheng asked,

"If it is true that the rear is lost, as Li Kuofan says it is, then what will become of these white men when they have crossed the river?"

"They will continue the retreat," the General said.

He lifted his haggard face and looked at their faces one by one.

"Let us not deceive ourselves by hope," he said. "The air support which we thought the white men would send, they cannot send. There will be no help of any kind."

"Do they leave their own men to die here?" Yao Yung cried out in horror. He was too tender for his task, indeed.

"Those above them count it less waste to let them fight their way out than to send more in to be lost, too," the General said.

"Then what do we fight for?" Sheng inquired.

"Let each man ask himself," the General said with gloom. "Meanwhile—here are the orders. Who volunteers?" Now the General remembered that the Chairman had said if there were a task too difficult for any other he should call upon Sheng, and he remembered that Sheng had said, "I will do it," but he was not willing to command any man to die, and so he waited.

Still there was the silence.

"Will one say he goes, or shall I choose which one must go?" the General asked when at last he saw that none would speak first.

Pao Chen spat into the dust and did not speak. Yao Yung thought of his young wife and little sons and did not speak. Chan Yu did not speak for he knew beforehand that the General would not let

183

him go, for it was his duty to support the General and be always near at hand.

Then Sheng looked around upon them all and he remembered his promise too. So he flung back his head. "Why, since all of you cannot speak," he cried, "and only I have my voice left, I will speak! I will go, sir, and I and my men will open the path for the white men. But let me know first why they are trapped so that I may feel the task a duty."

"I know nothing," the General said. "Nothing is told me. The orders are sent down. My choice is only whether or not I will obey. So far I have obeyed. If you go, I still obey. If you do not go—"

Then was Sheng secretly very torn indeed. It was true that nothing was told to them. What the white men did, or why, none knew. They fought to hold a line decided on by the white men, and without telling them the white men went back perhaps a day's march of thirty miles, or more or less. Now they were again entrapped and how it came about, who knew? His arm ached and pain shot into his shoulder and down his back as he stood and pondered all this.

"If it were not for the Chairman and his pride in us," the General said slowly, "then would I give the command for us all to turn our backs upon this lost battle—lost before we ever set foot upon the soil of this country. But how can I face the Chairman unless I have spent all he bade me spend?"

At these words Sheng sighed deeply and rested his sore shoulder against the wooden post that held the center of the tent.

"I will go," he said again. "I will be part of what must be spent— if so it must be spent."

"Stay here, after the others have gone," the General said, "and I will give you maps and tell you what the road is."

"I will ask only one price," Sheng replied. "I want this fellow to go with me," and he put his hand on Charlie's shoulder.

The General nodded, and so the others went and they three were left alone. There for two more hours they talked together, the General talking, and the other two listening, and Charlie now and again putting his finger upon the map to point out a shorter road or a path. For since they would travel by foot without machines, they could go by small footways and reach the river sooner.

"In a day and a half's hard march," the General said, "you should be there. Rest until the daylight ends. Then plan your attack by night as I have told you. Scatter your men widely as you march and do not seem to be together. But instruct your men well. You meet at the given place at the given hour, and let none delay."

"None will delay," Sheng said.

"When can you start?" The General asked.

Sheng did not answer for a moment. Under his uniform his shoulder throbbed with pain. But he had put the thought of it out of his mind and he would not heed it. No, he hesitated for another cause. Should he take a while to go back again to Mayli and tell her what he did? Suppose he told her, would she take it well or ill? Could he hide from her that his head swam with fever and that his eyes burned in their sockets, and that he felt his arm swelling inside its bandages? Then he knew he could not trust himself against the power of her will upon him. He had told her that it might be days before they met—let it be days, therefore.

"I will start within the hour," he told his General.

"Since you risk your life," the General said to Sheng, "I have no commands to lay upon you. Your own wits must tell you where your path is." And then he told Sheng the news which until now he had held back. "I have chosen the best men out of our three divisions for you to command."

Sheng heard these words which at any other time would have given him joy. But though his ear now heard, his brain could not comprehend. He tried to fix his eyes on his general's face, and he saw it double.

"You hear me?" the General asked.

"I will do my—very best," Sheng stammered and he forced his right arm to salute and he turned and went back to his tent.

185

XVII

A T DAWN of the next day Sheng had not slept for the pain in his swollen arm. In impatience with pain he now ripped the sleeve of his uniform and felt a little comfort, for the skin was so red and stretched that the weight even of the cloth on it was too much. Then he took off the bandage and poultice and, with this off, the yellow pus streamed out of the wound and he let it flow and now he was very much eased and enough so that he went out and met his men. When the bugle called them, they came together, and five young officers led them under Sheng's command.

Sheng stood before them, and the clear still air of the dawning day calmed his feverish mind. He saw his men with pride. They were good men, thin and sun-blacked but healthy enough. Their uniforms were faded and gray of a hue that it would be hard to say what they were when new, and they wore straw sandals on their bare feet and carried each an extra pair over his back. Each had a gun of some sort and his small pack on his back and a hat for sun or rain made of rice straw.

"Are you ready?" Sheng asked by way of greeting and the men shouted back in their various voices that they were ready, and so without more ado Sheng went at their head and they followed behind, swarming through the valley, and among them, although Sheng did not know it, was the Indian. Little Crab commanded the Indian to stay behind, but that one had waited until the march began, and then he had followed, to be near Sheng. Ahead of them somewhere had gone Charlie Li to gather together food and to spy out the enemy.

So they marched for some miles, and when it was full light, Sheng stopped and put his men at ease. Then he sent down his command thus:

"Now that it is day, we will scatter ourselves fanwise, but you are all to head for the Village of Three Waters, and that village is to the east of the river a hundred and two miles away from where we stand, and near it is a small lake of water which now is nearly dried. If each hundred of you part and walk a third of a mile and then walk due west, you will reach that lake. Then walk south if you now go north, and north if you now go south and cross the lake where you can, and in the middle on the other side is the village which you will know, for it has a lake on one side and a river too small for a map is on the other side and a narrow canal, which are the three waters. But do not keep together. Walk as though you were travelers or pilgrims or straying soldiers."

Then Sheng himself took with him a very young lad who had joined them at the borders and he chose this boy because he was silent. For now Sheng's arm was painful again and his head was hot and giddy and he wanted no talking. Throughout that day he walked in silence, saying not twenty words to that lad, who was afraid of him indeed and stayed behind him ten feet or so, and he did not speak at all except to say, "Yes, Elder Brother," whenever Sheng so much as turned his head.

Of half that day Sheng remembered afterward nothing at all except that he put one foot in front of the other. He did not stop for food or rest, but he did stop whenever he saw water and he drank whatever that water was. Villages they passed around, and it was easy to see them, for the large villages were fenced about with bamboo walls and the small ones were plain enough, since their houses were set high on wooden posts, and in a village there were seldom fewer than ten or twenty houses. But Sheng and the lad kept to the fields and where there were hills then behind hills. This was easy, for the paths were crooked and led it seemed wherever they willed. Sometimes where the rice was high they followed the paths between the fields, and sometimes they did not.

More than once a Burmese farmer stared at them and when Sheng saw this he pointed to his wounded arm, as though he were in search of a doctor somewhere, and the farmer nodded and some looked at him with pity and so they went on. Only once were they stopped and this time by an old man with energy in his look and in his bright black eyes, and when he saw Sheng's arm he shouted and pulled Sheng by his other hand and Sheng, not wishing to make a quarrel here, went with him into a village near by. There was but one street in that village and along it were open shops selling small things and a blacksmith shop or two and at the end of it a monastery. Through its gate the man led Sheng without delay and into a

187

room where an old man sat, a venerable good old man in a robe, and the man pointed to him and said loudly to Sheng, *"Pong yi—pong yi!"*

But how could Sheng understand this word? He could only look stupid and so the man spoke quickly to the older one, and that old one lifted the torn sleeve from Sheng's arm and stared into the wound and shook his head and sighed a few times as if to say it was very grave, and then he rose slowly and moved slowly away into another room and he came back with a little pot of white porcelain and in it was a smooth black ointment. This he dipped up with his long thin forefinger and he motioned to Sheng to hold out his arm and he smeared the ointment over the angry wound. At first Sheng thought he must cry out with pain for the ointment was like fire on the wound. But he held himself silent for decency's sake and soon the fire changed to coolness and then his arm felt numb and then in a little while more there was no pain at all. How grateful was he for this, and he took out his purse from his girdle to pay the old man, but no, the old man would take nothing nor would he who had brought him here. That one led him back to the entrance of the village and though Sheng pressed him yet again, still that man would take nothing. And so Sheng went on his way, wondering that even here in this enemy country there was one to be found who could be kind and for nothing.

Now that the pain was stopped for awhile he could go with ease and this he did, and he bethought himself that the boy behind him must be hungry and indeed so was he and he said,

"The next time we see food we will stop and buy rather than eat the little we have with us."

So they went on again awhile and now Sheng could look about him and see the country and indeed it was as rich and fertile a land as could be found anywhere, and he saw what he had never seen elsewhere, seed rice and rice harvest at the same time, for there was no winter and no summer here as in his own country, but the land was always green.

After while they met a man carrying a food stand and he sold fried rice balls, and they bought each four or five of these hot balls, and they sat down beside the road under a tree that had very fine leaves and flowers of a delicate purple so fragrant that all the air about its top was busy with insects and bees. Under this tree Sheng sat down and the lad at a little distance sat in respectful silence. Sheng thought to himself that he ought to ask the lad a question or two out of courtesy but indeed he could not. The fever in him made him drowsy and it was now the heat of afternoon and the sweetness of the flowering tree above him was heavy, and after he had eaten a little and yet less than he thought he was hungry for, he lay back and fell asleep.

He was wakened by the pain in his arm beginning to throb again and he stared about him, not knowing for a moment where he was, but his body was heavy as though his veins were full of hot lead. He struggled up and there the lad sat still.

"Have I slept long?" Sheng asked.

"Not very long," the lad said, "but I was beginning to wonder if it were my duty to wake you."

Sheng did not answer, but he pulled himself from the grass and rubbed his face and his head with his good arm and he took up the march again and the lad fell in behind him.

And of that day there is nothing more to be told except that at dark they came to the lake, now dried into a big pond, and they walked around the water upon its bottom of curling cakes of dried clay, and there on the other side they found their comrades waiting, not together so that men could see they were indeed an army, but a hundred here and a hundred there among the low trees. To his pleasure Sheng saw Charlie among them, and Charlie came forward and held out food to Sheng. Upon a green lotus leaf he had put hot rice and egg mixed with it and on the ground near by was a teapot full of hot tea and Sheng sank down with a great sigh that all so far was well. When he saw that teapot a mighty thirst fell upon him and he picked it up in his right hand and put the spout to his lips and drank as long as his breath held, and Charlie stood there watching him and waiting until he had drunk his fill.

When at last Sheng put the pot down Charlie said quietly: "Now I can tell you the news. You must make a forced march and it will not do to rest tonight. The white men will all be dead unless we

189

reach them by another day and night. This I know and can swear by. Let us eat and be on our way."

This Sheng heard but while he listened his arm began to throb again and he gave one grunt for answer.

But he sent word to his men that they were only to rest and not to sleep. When he had so sent his command he went alone to the side of the lake and he put his head into the muddy water to cool himself, and he dipped up water in his hands and over his garments for coolness. But so great was his fever that when in an hour it was time to march he was dried and hot again.

. . . All that night the division marched, stopping only to rest at the end of each two hours. Sheng had marched many times before this through day and night, and well he knew that the only way to keep the pace was to rest at given times, whether in day or night. They marched together through the darkness, but when dawn came they scattered again and chose the village where they must meet once more. There in the fields they would sleep for three hours before they made attack.

Now all went well enough, except that by noon the next day his wound began to ache beyond bearing. Whether the showers of rain which fell now and again had washed away the ointment or whether his constant sweat had washed it off, Sheng did not know, but the old throbbing agony came back and his head began to swim and he wished he could find another old man like that one who had given him the black ointment but how could he delay? There was nothing he could do except to go on and so he did.

And yet there was some good in that day, for the low hot jungles through which they traveled gave way at noon to great trees of teak forest and the leaves upon the ground made a carpet very comfortable for their tired feet. By now all had worn out their sandals and many were walking barefoot and so they were grateful for the new comfort. Yet there was this hardship in that great forest and it was that the paths were many and when Charlie had looked at the footprints on the worn earth he said, "These are the feet of elephants where they have been pulling out the trees and we must be careful for to be lost in one of these trails may mean days before we find its end."

So they watched their compasses closely and they came to the end of that wood.

But since the night was near Sheng commanded them that they would take their long sleep here. And so they lay down where they could, upon their blankets or two sharing a blanket, and only Charlie did not sleep.

"Do you never sleep?" Sheng asked.

"I sleep upon my feet," Charlie said with his grin as wide as ever. When all was quiet and he had eaten and drunk he said to Sheng, "Before you wake I will be back to tell you where the enemy is closing in and where the white men are."

And he went with his long silent step through the forest, taking with him only the silent lad.

. . . Sheng would have said he did not sleep, so vivid was the pain in his arm, and yet he did sleep for it was out of sleep that Charlie waked him at the end of three hours. Sheng felt Charlie's touch on his wounded arm lightly enough, but he leaped to his feet with a yell, and stood for an instant in the hot darkness shaking with agony.

"Elder Brother, what is the matter with you?" Charlie whispered in amazement.

Now Sheng was awake indeed and he licked his dry lips. His whole body was as dry as bone, and his skin was tight and burning.

"Nothing," he said shortly. "I was dreaming of an evil thing."

"Well, then, put it aside," Charlie said. "For I have found the white men. They are caught in a trap indeed. The devils are between them and the river, and between them everywhere. But they are too strong to the south and the east and the only hope is toward the west and the bridge. There you must attack. The enemy are stretched thin there in a line not more than a half a mile along the river. I say that if you press through that half mile you can relieve the white men, and they will push to the bridge. But it must be suddenly, so that the devils do not destroy the bridge, for then shall

191

we all be trapped. The river is swelling with the new rains, and there are no boats."

"No boats?" Sheng asked. "It is very strange to see a river with no boats."

Charlie wiped his sweating face with the tail of his coat.

"The white men are leaking away from their leaders," he said. "But they are not all white—some are men of India. Yet they all know that they are caught, and who can blame them? Every time one bribes a Burmese with his gun for a boat, why, the boat is soon gone, and it drifts down the river on the current when the men leap out on the other shore."

"Do they give their good guns to these Burmese traitors?" Sheng cried. For a moment his head cleared with rage.

"What have they else to offer as a bribe?" Charlie said. "They are human, as other men are, white men and brown."

"But a good gun!" Sheng groaned, "when we have no good guns!"

His throbbing head caught these words and his hot brain spun them into a twist—"a good gun—" he muttered, "a good gun—a good gun—"

"Are you drunk?" Charlie shouted.

Sheng's brain cleared again for a moment. "No," he said.

But he thought to himself that he was drunk with pain, but could he heed pain now? He laughed out loud. "I am only drunk with what lies ahead of me this day," he shouted to Charlie, and he went back to his men and roared at them and he bellowed that they were to delay for nothing but they must follow him.

He did not stop for food and they followed him without food, frightened at the sound of his voice. He ran ahead of them and they ran, and he felt his whole body filled with strength and fire, and his brain whirled, and his eyes burned, and he ran on, and there was strength in him beyond anything he had ever known.

Behind him he heard men gasping and muttering, but he paid no heed, but he kept them to the utmost speed of forced marching. Before the dawn broke, he saw ahead the low tents of the encamped enemy. But still he would not rest, and he bellowed like a bull when he saw them, and he shrieked to his men to bellow with him and roaring together they fell upon the enemy while they were still half asleep and expecting no attack.

Now those who followed Sheng followed him as though he were a god, and when they saw his madness and rage, they became mad, too, and they plunged their bayonets into the enemy wherever they found them. First they fired, but the weapons of many were old and could not fire more than once without delay for reloading, and rather than delay, they stabbed and cut and tore the enemy, and they choked men with their bare hands and gouged out their eyes with two thumbs digging into their eyeballs, and they jerked off men's ears and ground their heels into their bellies and mauled them and threw them dying into the river. And ahead of them all was Sheng like a demon, his eyes red and burning and his square mouth open and yelling without stop. All who saw him were filled with fright, and his own men swore to each other that never had they seen any man so fierce as Sheng was in that battle. He used his wounded arm as though it were whole, for now his entire body was filled with pain as a vessel is filled with dark wine, and he was drunk.

Thus led, his men swept aside the enemy, and into the breach the weary white men poured, and the Indians with them, and they escaped from the trap in which they had been held. Those of Sheng's men who were in the rear, holding fast, saw white men stream by on foot, wounded, some in broken machines, some in whole machines. A few waved their arms and shouted to their deliverers, but they were few. The many went on without heed to any except themselves and to save their lives. Six and seven times, pushing and pressing each other, some fell into the swirling muddy water of the river, but none stayed to help whose who fell.

Now at the head of his men Sheng had pushed on after there was need, and in his feverish strength and confusion he had forgotten why he was here, except that he was sent to defeat the enemy. He led on and behind him pressed the ones who followed, and they fought until suddenly Sheng felt himself laid hold on by a hand, strong in his girdle.

"You fool!" he heard Charlie shout. "Do you plan to fight straight through to India this day? Turn—turn—your men are being murdered at your rear! The enemy is counter attacking from the south, you son of a dog!"

Then Sheng turned, staggering and panting, "Have we—have we passed the bridge?" he gasped.

"The bridge is a mile-and-a-half behind you!" Charlie shouted. He gave Sheng a great push as he spoke, and Sheng began to run back and with him his men whom he had led too far, and they ran like hounds that mile-and-a-half along the river bank to the place where the bridge had been. There they stood, and they stared across the river.

The span of the bridge was broken at the other end and the river rushed between. The current caught the hanging farther end and twisted it hard, and before their eyes yet another piece of the bridge was wrenched off and carried it in triumph away.

"The bridge—" Sheng stammered, "the bridge—" But his giddy brain could not finish. It was the silent lad who finished for him. His young voice rose in a clear and piercing scream. "Oh my mother, my mother!" he wailed. "The white men have cut the bridge!"

At these words Sheng's blood rushed upward and filled his head. He laughed in a great howl of laughter, "Our allies," he howled—"our allies—"

He felt his head burst and split in two, as though an ax had cleaved it and he knew no more.

XVIII

HE woke, how many days later he did not know or where. He was enveloped in a soft green light which he could not understand, for it was neither the light of day nor of night. For a moment he thought he was under water. His body felt clean and cool and thin. He lay on his back and above him and about him there was nothing but the green. Then he heard a sharp clear whistle made from some one's lips, and a voice began to speak in English. But he could not understand English and these strange harsh sounds made the place more strange to him. Where had he waked out of death? He could not lift his head to see, and he opened and closed his weak eyelids.

Again he heard the sharp harsh sounds. Now some one answered, and this voice he knew. It was Charlie's voice. Still he could not make a sound. He forced his eyes open and lay staring up into the green. Then a face came between him and the green and it was the dark face of the Indian. This fellow shouted with joy and now his face changed and it was Charlie's face, looking down at him from very far up above him and he heard Charlie's voice, speaking now words which he understood.

"Sheng, you are awake?"

Sheng could not make his voice come. He opened his lips but only breath passed through them. Charlie's face came nearer. He had dropped to his knees.

"Sheng, can you hear me?"

Sheng made a mighty effort and his voice came small like a boy's voice.

"Yes."

"Do you know me?" Charlie asked.

"Yes," Sheng said again.

"Now I know you will live," Charlie said gently.

He took out of his bosom an egg and cracked it carefully so that the meat inside ran out of a hole. This he put to Sheng's open lips. "Drink," he said, "I have been saving this hen's egg for you."

Sheng felt the soft smooth flow of the egg slip down his throat. He swallowed twice and thrice and drifted off again into the green and floating light.

Charlie Li sat on his heels for a moment watching him, holding the empty egg shell in his hand. Sheng's face was still a pale yellow, but the yellow was clear.

"He will get well," he said to the Englishman.

"Thanks to you," the Englishman said.

"It was you who gave him the sulfa," Charlie replied gently.

The Englishman smiled slightly. "I wish I had a cigarette," he remarked.

"If there were a Jap around I would kill him and take his cigarettes for you," Charlie said.

195

"Why do all Japs have cigarettes?" the Englishman asked lazily.

"Because they all have guns also," Charlie answered. He stared down into the empty egg with one eye, broke the hole somewhat larger and then, putting the egg to his lips, he thrust his tongue into the hole and licked the inside clean.

"I have not tasted an egg for months," he said. "But this morning God was with me. I stumbled upon a black hen in her nest in the edge of a rice field. She had not laid the egg yet, but I persuaded her."

"Midwife, eh?" The Englishman grinned. "What fellows you are, you Chinks!"

Charlie glanced up sharply at the word "Chink." No, the Englishman's haggard young face was kind. He had used the word without thought. Charlie rose from his heels and crushed the egg shell in his hand.

"Here is the trouble with you damned English," he said in his pleasant voice, "you do not even know when you insult us."

"Insult you?" the white man asked amazed.

"You insult us as naturally as you draw breath," Charlie said. His face was quite calm but his eyes were cold.

"But how?" the white man asked still amazed.

"I don't even know your name," Charlie said.

The Englishman sprang to his feet from the bank on which he had been lounging. His blue eyes were honest, though a little stupid. "Sorry," he said, "I'm Dougall."

"I am Li," Charlie said quietly. Neither put out his hand. They stood looking at each other, Charlie at ease, the Englishman embarrassed.

"We have been together two days and a half," Charlie went on, "but you have not asked my name. Because you did not ask mine, I did not ask yours. You see I am not a real 'Chink'—as you call me. A real one would have been polite to you whether you were polite or not. But I'm a new kind of 'Chink'—I'm not polite to a man just because he is a white man. You can call me a communist."

"I say," Dougall murmured. His good-looking face blushed under the blond unshaven beard.

"I know you don't mean anything," Charlie said. "It is that of which I complain."

196

"I'm afraid I don't understand," Dougall said stiffly. His flush was receding and his blue eyes began to blaze mildly.

"I know you don't," Charlie said. His voice had not changed or lifted. The pleasant level was like quiet green fields. "And I am sure you don't think it is your fault that you cannot understand anything."

"Really—"

The young Englishman was biting his lips. They were cracked with heat and his fair skin was dirty. "You are so honest," Charlie said. "You are so wonderfully honest, all of you!" He laughed suddenly and rubbed his hands over his stubbled black hair. "Oh God, deliver us Asiatics from the honest white men!" he prayed as suddenly as he had laughed, and feeling something breaking inside him, he turned and tramped off into the green jungle.

When he was quite hidden by the great ferns and low brush, he cleared a small space about a fallen log, watching sharply for snakes, and picking off two leeches, and then he sat down. Where were the rest of the men? When he saw Sheng fall he had seized him under the arms and even as he ran a lithe dark figure had sprung out of the bush and had shared the burden of Sheng's body. It was the Indian. But how could he ask the man how he had come there? They had plunged away from the river bank into the forests beyond. They had not stayed a moment for two hours. Sheng's inert body had hung between them. He wondered if Sheng were dead but he had not dared to stop and find out. The Indian was tireless and silent and easily forgotten. Behind them he knew very well what was happening. Caught between the river and the enemy, Sheng's poorly armed men were simply cut to pieces and thrown into the river. If any had escaped it would be only by the chance he himself had taken. They had put Sheng down at last, and Charlie knew the moment he looked at him that he would die unless there was aid. But where could there be aid in this foreign country? Nevertheless, bidding the Indian to keep watch and not let the flies consume Sheng, he had crept to the edge of the jungle, which was now half a day away, and he had stared out into a burning countryside. Fires blazed on the horizon like volcanoes, and he knew what they were. The Burmese, in madness, were firing their own towns and villages.

197

Why he could not imagine, but so he had seen them do, as though they were delirious with the chaos around them. He had stared awhile and then he turned and made his way back again.

But while he was on his way back he had come upon the Englishman hiding in the jungle, too. He had almost stepped on the fellow, and for a second he saw nothing but the muzzle of a gun. In that second he had leaped on it and saved his life, for Dougall had taken him for a Jap, and had thrown his long arms about him and borne him down. They fell together, and there face to face, the white face not six inches from his own Charlie Li, had cursed and sworn and gasped out that he was Chinese. Dougall had released him instantly.

"Good God!" he said. "I nearly killed you. I thought you were a Jap."

They had gone on together then, and with few words, until, finding Sheng still alive, Dougall had reached silently into his pocket and brought out a small sealed packet which he unwrapped. Inside were a few drugs and from these he chose some flat white pellets.

"He'd better take these," he remarked. The Indian had found a wet hollow while they were gone and had scraped it out and water had seeped into it, dark jungle water. This Charlie scooped with his hands and poured into Sheng's open mouth, and Sheng had swallowed the medicine with it.

That had been yesterday morning. Dougall had been kind again and again. He had made a better bed for Sheng to lie upon, breaking ferns and laying them into a mattress. He had washed his handkerchief clean and filtered clear water for Sheng to drink, and he had sat holding Sheng's wounded arm to the sunshine that fell in stray slanting beams through the green arch of the teak far above them and watchful against a midge or a fly. "The sun will heal this sort of thing," he remarked. "We learned that, over and over again."

Of the retreat neither had said a word.

Charlie rose, sighing. He hated these forests. In the stillness small noises were beginning to stir about him. The beasts were stealing out to see him. A lizard crept from under the log at his feet, glanced up and, seeing him, darted across the crushed grass in a panic, its sky-blue tail like a comet behind him. Midges twirled about his head. There was no peace for man in the jungle and no safety. What now?

198

They must get out of it somehow and move west again until they found the General. At least what they had been sent to do was done. They had delivered the English.

He followed the path by which he had come, through already it was nearly lost. The twigs he had bent were straightening themselves and the crushed grasses rising. In another hour it would look as though no human foot had ever walked that way. But in less than that hour he came into the small clearing they had made for their hiding place. He found Sheng awake, his eyes sensible and clear. The Englishman had propped him up against a pile of small branches, and he was standing there, his hands on his hips, looking down on Sheng.

"I was just hoping you'd be back soon," he remarked to Charlie with great cheerfulness. "This beggar came to when you'd only just gone. I expect it was the egg. But he doesn't know a word of English, does he?"

"Not a word," Charlie said.

And then as though the Englishman were not there Sheng began to talk in his own voice, weak enough but resolute again.

"Where are my men?" he asked.

For a moment Charlie thought to himself that he must shield Sheng a little longer from the truth. But he decided quickly that the truth must be told. Let Sheng bear it as he could, and get his strength together for the return.

"Those men are destroyed," he said.

"Destroyed?" Sheng repeated.

"The white men cut the bridge after they had crossed," Charlie said. "You remember that?"

Sheng nodded, his black eyes fixed on Charlie's face. "The enemy came out from the village at the same instant and with them were yellow-robed priests," Charlie went on. "I saw them plunging at us and at that moment you fell, and I caught you. Suddenly the Indian was there—he had followed us. And he helped me and we escaped here but how do I know where the others are beyond that? I saw the enemy fall upon them, their guns blazing and their bayonets shining and plunging. But I and the Indian were bearing you away into the forest. We did not stop even to rest for half a day."

199

Sheng lifted his eyes upon the Englishman and let them move up and down that tall thin young man, who had not understood one word of what was being said. Now he stood there grinning like a boy, full of good nature.

"Who is this long white radish?" Sheng asked Charlie.

"I stumbled upon him in the forest, and he nearly choked me, mistaking me for a devil, and then he came with me when I persuaded him otherwise," Charlie said.

The two Chinese and the Indian stared at Dougall and he stood patiently, still good-natured, under their stares.

"Does he say why they left us without a way of escape after we had rescued them?" Sheng asked.

"I have not asked him," Charlie replied.

"Ask him now," Sheng commanded.

So without ado Charlie changed his tongue and he asked the Englishman, "Why did you fellows destroy the bridge after you had gone over and so left us with no retreat, when we came to save you?"

Dougall opened his blue eyes wide. "I'm sure we couldn't have done that," he said.

This Charlie told to Sheng, changing his tongue again.

"Does he not know what happened?" Sheng asked.

"He knows nothing," Charlie replied.

"This fellow," Sheng declared after a moment, "is a deserter. Ask him why."

"Why have you left your army?" Charlie asked Dougall.

The young face of this Englishman burned red again under the thin white skin. "I was fed up," he said. "Any one could tell we were licked," he said again after a moment. He examined his long pale hand. It was covered with red scratches and the nails were broken and black. "It was simply too silly," he said at last. "The commanders themselves didn't know what they were doing they were retreating so fast. It was every man for himself." He smiled, shamefaced. "After all," he said in his bright confident way. "What's the use, you know? If we win the war, this'll all come back to us. If we lose—well—" he shrugged: "Then what would be the use of fighting for this bloody bit of heathen ground?"

200

This Charlie translated to Sheng and Sheng groaned in his weakness. "Ask him what he will do now," he commanded again.

"What will you do now?" Charlie asked.

"I?" Dougall lifted his head and looked at one face and another. "Why, I'll simply come along with you, if you fellows don't mind. It was most awfully lucky my finding you—I mean, because you can speak English, you know."

"He says he will come with us," Charlie told Sheng.

Sheng closed his eyes.

"He did give you some white pills he had," Charlie said, "and it is also true that he has made your bed of those ferns and he has held your arm in the sunshine to heal it. Can a man help it that his mother gave birth to a fool?"

Sheng smiled bitterly without opening his eyes. "Since he is our ally," he said, "let him come."

Two days later they set out for the west again. Sheng was on his feet, weak but ready to live.

XIX

THE General looked at the American. He made his face blank to hide the repulsion and the refusal which tingled inside him to his very fingertips. He wanted to say what he felt, that nothing this American could do would save any of them. He wanted to say what they all knew, that the battle here had been lost before any of them ever trod upon the soil.

"I have sacrificed one division," he said. "Not one of the Fifty-Fifth has returned. Where are they?"

"Heaven knows," the American replied. "I have never heard of such a thing as a division disappearing, but so it is."

The General determined to be patient. "It is impossible for one army alone to fight, you understand," he said. He made his language simple and plain for this foreigner. The foreigner was proud of his

Chinese but he did not know that he spoke as a foreigner does, having learned from simple men. "You understand? I am given orders to hold a sector of the line. I hold. My men fight without regard to life. Then we are given the order to retreat so that the line can be straightened. What do we find? While we have been fighting our allies have been retreating without notice to us. We have to give up what we have been holding at the cost of our lives. Is this the way to fight a winning war?"

The American's thin cheeks flushed. He did not answer.

"You white men," the General said distinctly. "You are determined to save each other's faces."

He slapped his knee and rose, saluted with sharpness, wheeled and went away. He nodded at a guard curtly, his own guard waiting at the door fell in behind him and he marched to his own quarters, holding his slight body very straight. He had now made up his mind that he would never see his wife or his sons again. The conviction made him cold inside as he had once felt when he had eaten a foreign frozen dish—ice cream, they called it. The pit of his stomach felt like that now. He suddenly wished that he had a woman to talk to as he might talk to his wife. His wife, though younger than he by six or seven years, was sensible and quick to think of a way out of trouble. But she was thousands of miles away. He entered his own gate and passed the guards without seeing them. In his tent he sat down and closed his eyes and rubbed both hands slowly around and around his head. He was really desperate. Sheng had never returned. Meantime the rate of advance of the enemy was tripling itself. At first the advance had been at not more than ten miles a day. Then it was twenty and now it was thirty and forty miles a day.

He sat still, thinking, his hands outspread on his knees. He would echelon his men along the line of the Lashio road. At least he would protect that road, "since they never think of us," he muttered, "let us think of ourselves."

He suddenly felt the impulse to weep and was surprised at himself. "It is this eternal retreat," he told himself. "I must get into action. Well, I will act for myself."

He unbuttoned the collar of his uniform. It was very hot, day and night hot, and while he did not mind heat, for his own town at home was at the bottom of a valley between two mountain ranges, still it was not like this. The snakes alone were an enemy and the mosquitoes another. Two nights ago he had been bitten by a scorpion on his ankle and it was still swollen. Only the quickness of one of his men who had pulled out the sting with his thumb nails had kept it from being dangerous. He sighed and thought of his lost men. Sheng was lost, that great brave fellow from the Nanking hills! He thought of Sheng and then it occurred to him that he should tell that pretty girl about him—warn her, at least. If he was never to see his wife again, she need not be jealous. He shouted and an aide ran in.

"Send Wei Mayli to me," he said shortly. And then for an excuse he said, "Tell her I wish her to go as a messenger for me to the American. Her English is good enough—I cannot understand his Chinese."

He thought with a sparkle of pleasure that he would send Mayli and shame the American by saying that he could not understand his Chinese of which he was so proud. He smiled, and a little of his old quiet arrogance came back to him.

. . . "Yes, of course I will come," Mayli said. She wiped her hands on her apron as she spoke. "I will only change my coat—it is blood-spattered."

The messenger nodded, and she hastened toward the operating room where a moment before she had been helping Chung deliver a Burmese woman of a large fat boy. The woman's husband was a Chinese merchant. He was waiting now at the door and stopped her as she passed.

"Tell me," he urged, "has the child a mole on his left ear lobe?"

"Now have I time to look for that?" she said and laughed.

But the man was grave. "You do not know these Burmese women," he said solemnly in his old-fashioned Chinese. He had not been home for many years and he still spoke as he had when he was a boy before he set out to find his fortune. "How shall I know this is my son if there is not my mark on him?" he asked.

He turned his head and there on his left ear lobe was a round black mole with hair growing out of it.

"But not every child you have will bear your mark," she cried. "What—will you test your wife's virtue by a mole?"

She laughed again but still the man would not laugh. "Look for it, for I do not want to waste any red eggs on another man's son. She is pretty and young and I cannot always be at home."

She pulled away from him, promising, and in the room she found Chung carefully washing and polishing his instruments before he put them in the closed can which was his sterilizer.

"Chung, the General has sent for me," she said. She began to scrub her hands in the bucket of hot water which stood on a bench. "Oh, Chung, is it Sheng, do you think? Why else should the General send for me? I have not seen him for weeks."

"Sheng should be back by now, certainly," Chung said. It had been strange to see so many men march away and not one return, no wounded, none living. This had been a strange pause, indeed—no orders to move, only waiting here now for nearly eight days.

The women came in and lifted the stretcher on which his patient lay and took her away. He had been undecided whether or not to waste anaesthetic on her. Then he had done so. After all, it was a boy.

Mayli reached for a clean uniform and he turned his back modestly. He was never sure whether or not she was immodest or only unthinking, but there was no need for him to find out. In a moment she was clean and at the door again, when suddenly the child wailed. He had been forgotten and was lying wrapped in a towel on some straw in a corner.

Chung hurried toward the child and picked him up. "After all this trouble you are forgotten," he remarked. Mayli paused, and ran back again. "Give him to me," she said. "I will tell Pansiao to look after him until I come back." She seized the plump little bundle and hurried toward the door once more. There outside was the patient father and seeing him she remembered what he had wanted. "Here," she said, "see for yourself."

What small chance there was that the child had inherited a birthmark she knew, but she moved the end of the towel from the black head and there was the little left ear, perfect except for a tiny dot of black.

"It is here," Mayli cried with joy, "so small that it can hardly be seen, but then he is so small."

The Chinese merchant rose, felt in his bosom for his spectacles which he put on and then he examined the tiny lobe.

"He is my son," he said, solemnly. A smile came over his face. "My first," he said. He put out his arms. "I will take him."

"But I was about to wash him and put on his clothes," Mayli protested.

"I will take him," he repeated firmly. "I can wash him and put on his clothes."

She gave him the child and watched for a moment while he strode away, his robes swinging, the child laid across his two arms like tribute being borne to an emperor. He disappeared down the street and she came to herself. How foolish was life, she thought, that in the midst of war and death and evil news of every kind, one could forget for a moment all except that a son had been born to a man again!

She hastened on, smiling and sad.

. . . "Of Sheng I have heard not one word," the General said. Mayli clasped her hands a little more tightly on her lap. He was not looking at her. "What there is between you two I do not know," he went on, "but I ought to tell you that not one man of his command has come back. They went across the river of course with the allies, but by now I ought to have had Charlie Li here at least to tell me that they were rejoining us. It is in my mind to put my armies along the Lashio road, but how can I do this unless they return? The line will be too thin. Nevertheless I will do it."

"Does that mean we move?" she asked.

"It means we move at once," he replied. "And I want you to go for me, as my private messenger, you understand, and speak to the American in his own language so that I can be sure he understands and tell him that I move, regardless of all others. I am wearied of this constant retreat. I will retreat no more. I will take my own stand and guard the borders to our own country and let the white men do what they like."

He was very tired, she could see that. His bony face, always thin,

205

was now a series of hollows and cups, the temples hollow, the cheeks hollow, hollows under the jawbones and under the ears. But the retreat had been swift. She had been troubled enough at it herself, moving every few hours as the orders came down. How could Sheng find her? She was a hundred miles from where he had left her.

"Shall I go to the American now?" she asked.

"Now," he answered, "for tomorrow we march."

She rose, and he lifted his haggard eyes to regard her. "I think I shall never see my wife and children again," he said abruptly.

"Do not give up hope," she said quickly.

"I have not given up hope," he replied, "but hope has been torn away from me." He hesitated and then went on. "And I am afraid," he said, "that this young man—this Sheng—whom you—"

"Oh no," she said. "Don't speak of him—I do not give up hope. You have no idea how strong he is—he cannot be killed."

"Yes," he said. "He is strong. But then—so am I."

"Shall I go?" she urged. She was uncomfortable. This man was deeply moved and desperate. She was not afraid of him, but he was clutching at anything, at anybody. "I will go and come back quickly," she said, and went away.

She knew of course where the American was. They all knew that he lived in a little tent like any common soldier's tent. It was under a banyan tree for coolness, and through the arches of this great tree with its hundred trunks she now walked. She was not afraid of the American, although she had never spoken to him. Gossip had made him known, the talk of men and the talk of women. She knew that he made friends easily with the common soldiers and not so well with the officers. "The old dislike of equality," she thought with scorn. "The white men want us all to be common folk so that they can continue to be our lords."

When she came to the white guard at the entrance of the tent she said curtly in English, "I come as a messenger from the Chinese General."

"Righto," the guard replied, without saluting, and went inside. In a moment he came back. "The boss says to come in," he said. She went in and there she found the American sitting on a folding stool, eating a green-skinned melon. Inside the melon the meat was a clear golden yellow. He looked up, smiled and rose, the half-melon in his hands.

"I can't shake hands," he said in his slow pleasant voice, "but I'll give you a piece of this."

"No, thank you," she said. She sat down on a second stool.

"It's rather good," he remarked, sitting down again.

"It looks so," she agreed, "but I have only a message to give you from our General. He wishes me to say that he will march tomorrow and move to the Lashio Road."

The American swallowed a mouthful of the golden juice. "I'll be sorry if he's made up his mind," he drawled, "because if he does what he told me he wanted to do, he's planning too narrow a front and he is putting his units at a disadvantage. Try to persuade him, young lady—I can't. He doesn't take my orders."

"He is discouraged," she said warmly. "We are all discouraged."

He put the melon down on a small folding table and wiped his hands on a surprisingly white handkerchief.

"I know," he said gently—"I know."

She waited but he said no more. She could feel little separate withdrawals of his whole being, the eyes retreating first, the lips next, pressed firmly to silence, the shoulders stiffening, the hands busying themselves with folding the handkerchief.

"You all defend each other, you and the British," she said suddenly.

He gave her a swift look from under his lids. "We're strangers in a strange country," he said.

"Are not we?" she replied.

"You are not so strange as we are," he said.

She was suddenly ablaze with anger. "You white people," she cried. "You sacrifice all other human beings on your own altars for yourselves."

"I was twenty years in your country," he reminded her.

"Always being a white man," she retorted.

"For so I was born," he replied.

She turned away her head, and rose, having fulfilled her mission. But he delayed her a moment more. "In spite of all that you are thinking," he said, "I have never seen braver men than these British.

207

They have known that they would have no reinforcements—that planes were not being sent, nor ships, nor additional troops—nothing. They have been fighting what is called a delaying action. Their lives are the scraps thrown to the advancing wolves that others might be saved."

"You always make heroes out of yourselves," she said harshly. "You forget that we should have had allies here in Burma instead of enemies, had white men been human beings all through these decades of your possession instead of always white heroes among dark savages."

"Do not forget I am American," he reminded her.

"I can only remember that you are white," she retorted, and she bent her head away from him and went away.

She hastened, winged by fury, and was almost back to her own quarters before she remembered that she must return to the General. But when she reached his quarters he was busy with his commanders, and she was not taken inside. Instead he came out to her and she told him, standing in the presence of soldiers and guards, "I have delivered your message and he advises against it."

"I will not heed his advice," the General replied.

"Then tomorrow?" she inquired.

"At dawn," he replied.

She nodded and made haste indeed now. For the severely wounded must be left behind, scattered as safely as could be in the homes of Chinese wherever they could be found, and those who were a little wounded must be made ready to be moved. Chung must be told first and then her women. All the hundred small things must be done when they marched again.

She frowned and the careworn look that was now natural to her came over her face. This time at least it would not be retreat. She was eager to be gone—yes, the General had decided wisely. They would form their own lines. How she had talked to the American! When she and Sheng met she would tell him, and he would say he was glad. But whether she had been right or wrong she did not know. The American was an honest man. But when honesty was blind, was it still honesty? She saw the honesty and Sheng saw the blindness. Sheng was right, Sheng was wiser than she.

"Oh, will they never *see?*" she muttered between her teeth. No, she knew they never would. These white men, retreating before the Japanese, would still not see. They would be planning even while they retreated, that they would come back again and be as they had always been, White Heroes.

She ground her even teeth together and pressed her red lips and felt her eyes grow hot. Upon the wings of her scorn she sped to do what must be done, and she bustled and hastened as she went, driving Chung at last to rebuke her thus, "You are as bad as a foreigner sometimes."

She paused at this and after a moment she said, "Well, perhaps you are right." And as though he had given her a medicine, she grew quieter, her step moved as swiftly but the haste was gone. Her voice lost its sharpness and was calm again. Now Pansiao, who had stayed out of her sight, came near her.

"Are we moving?" she asked in her soft voice.

"Yes, but this time nearer home," Mayli replied. She thought as she spoke that the girl would be comforted, but instead a look of dismay came over Pansiao's face.

"Doesn't that please you?" Mayli asked. She was folding uniforms into a wicker basket.

"Yes, but—" Pansiao began and stopped.

"But what?" Mayli asked.

"Sheng," Pansiao faltered, "how will he find us?"

Mayli paused for one instant. "I have been thinking of that," she said. "See, we will leave a letter here with the woman who had the baby today. We are sending her home tonight and her husband is coming for her. I will give a letter to him and tell him he is to look for anyone Chinese coming here. It is natural that when Sheng finds us gone he will go to the Chinese."

Still Pansiao was not satisfied. She hung her head and twisted her fingers and looked sidewise at Mayli now and then as she worked.

Mayli watched this for a while and then she said, "Speak what is behind your eyelids, for I can see something is there."

"There is nothing behind my eyelids," Pansiao said warmly. "Nothing, that is, but something that doesn't matter. That is, it matters nothing to me. But if we leave a letter for Sheng—"

209

A guess darted into Mayli's mind. "We ought to leave one for Charlie Li," she said laughing.

She sharpened her two forefingers at Pansiao as though they were knives in the old childish gesture of derision by which girls tease each other, and Pansiao threw the end of her jacket over her face and ran away.

And Mayli, left behind, ceased laughing suddenly and sighed, and stood motionless for a long moment, her busy hands resting on the edge of the basket. It was possible that she and Sheng would never meet again.

XX

THAT last night Mayli wrote a letter to Sheng. She made it short and plain, for she did not know whose eyes would fall upon it, and what she said was this:

"Sheng:

"We leave tomorrow morning at dawn, under orders. The American will tell you where we go, if you cannot find out otherwise. If you can follow, I shall be watching for you day and night and so will your sister. I believe you live. Would I not know it if you were dead?"

When this short letter was written, she sat for a while thinking whether she ought to write to any other. Well she knew that from this campaign which the General planned she might never return. She knew that the General must be obeyed and yet she could not forget the American's warning, that what the General planned to do was folly, since he had not enough men left to do it. If she were to die in this campaign, for the enemy spared no woman or man, then to whom should she now write?

She thought of her father in America. Surely to him she should write? And yet she could not. He seemed far away, he was ignorant of her life and its necessity, and how could she begin now and explain to him where she was and why? She had been silent so long that now silence could not be broken.

Was there no one to whom she cared to say that this was the last night before a great campaign? And as her mind wandered, she thought of Sheng's family in the village near Nanking, and she knew that to them she could write. They would know what battle meant and what the enemy was and what the danger would be tomorrow.

So in quick clear characters she wrote one of her letters to Jade and she told that one exactly what was the truth—that Sheng had not returned but she would not think of him as dead and that she went with the others tomorrow to a new camp and battle front. When she had written this she sat pondering if there were anything else she ought to tell. The night around her was very dark, the air thick with heat. She was in her small tent, and the light she wrote by was a paper lantern. Around it a cloud of moths and beetles circled and swarmed and fell bruised upon the paper. She brushed them away with her hand, and then she wrote, "I ought to tell you —our allies have not upheld us here. Do not have great hopes, for we are in retreat. I tell you this—those whom we came to deliver have betrayed us. Tonight is dark—who can see tomorrow? But I send good wishes to you all. If we live, Sheng and I will come home again some day."

Now this was as near as Mayli had ever come to saying to that family that she and Sheng would one day be wed, and as she wrote the words a deep heat came up out of her heart and made her warm and she said to herself that she would never believe Sheng was dead until she saw his body or his bones. And so she sealed the letters and she mailed the one to Jade, but the one to Sheng she gave to the Burmese woman to give to her husband and she said,

"Tell your husband to look for a tall fellow with frowning eyes and a wounded arm, and give him this letter."

The Burmese woman, pleased with her child, promised that she would do what Mayli asked in thanks for the healthy son she had. All this was on the last night before the new march began.

. . . Now that letter which Mayli sent to Jade went by carrier and by plane and by carrier again, and then over the enemy country by the hands of hill men and then by carrier again, until by devious means it came to Ling Tan's village and was brought to Ling Tan's house. No one in the village could read outside of Ling Tan's house, since the old scholar was dead, and so every letter was brought to that house and to Jade. And Jade because of her learning had come to be looked upon as a woman of great wisdom and skill, so that women came to her from a distance and asked her to cure their troubles. Some would ask her how to bear a son and some would ask her why their hens did not lay and some asked how to put down a wen or heal a flux or how to mend a child's crossed eyes and many other like troubles they brought to her. Such answers as she could get from books she read to them, and then out of her own increasing wisdom she began to devise cures and answers which were so often good that all over the countryside quietly this woman Jade began to be known for her good works.

Even Heaven thought well of her, for Lao Er never looked at any other woman. His whole heart was upon her and her children grew without illness, and when she weaned her twin boys they did not grow thin or fretful and even Ling Sao had to give over her complaints against Jade. More and more she leaned on Jade for the direction of the household, and Jade without worry or talk took upon herself the duties of Ling Tan's house, and always so gently that no one felt the weight of her tongue or hand. Even Lao Ta's wife, though she was the elder, allowed the younger to be her guide, and it was now Jade who kept peace between this woman and Ling Sao and it was she who soothed the tempers which Ling Sao let out more easily as she grew older, and she who comforted the other woman's tearfulness. All Jade did was done so delicately that Lao Ta felt himself always the older brother and Ling Sao had always the place of honor among the women, and as for Ling Tan, he shouted for Jade whenever a fly buzzed near him when he wanted to sleep, or when he wanted hot water to bring the wind of old age up out of his belly, and he thought Jade had nothing to do but serve him.

So this household went on even in such evil times, and Ling Tan and Lao Er spent their time in devising cunning ways to deceive

212

the enemy as to their crops and the number of their fowls and fish, and secretly they ate well enough and outwardly they looked as though they had nothing. That cave under the kitchen they kept as a hiding place for salted fish and dried fowl and ham and salt pork and cabbage and turnips and bins of rice. Thus fed, the children grew so well that Lao Er taught his sons to hide if an enemy came by, lest they look too fat for people who are conquered.

In these years there had been only one real trouble in the house and it was that Lao Ta's wife for two years had no children. She could never forget that she was older by nearly ten years than Lao Ta, and in her impatience this woman once and twice and three times thought that she was with child and she told it too soon, and then must confess that she was wrong. When this had happened the third time, Ling Sao grew angry and she said,

"Do not tell me that you have a child in you until your belly is big and I can see it for myself."

At this Lao Ta's wife began her ready weeping and Ling Sao seeing it went on morosely, "Even then it may be nothing but I have known women who were so full of wind that they deceived all and came to childbirth and they brought out nothing but a bag of wind."

When at last the woman was truly with child Ling Sao would not believe her until the child was born. Alas that this child was a small and wizened girl, and Ling Sao disliked her at sight, and so here was another trouble in the house. But Jade took that little girl's part secretly and made such amends as she could for Ling Sao's hatred of her. The truth was that Ling Sao had always been so full of hearty health and her children so good, that she was ashamed that something of hers should be so small and yellow as this child.

"Eat!" she would cry at her. "Eat!" and when the child cried in fright at her fierceness and could not eat Ling Sao's heart smote her and still she was more angry, and so this was a trouble in the house. But Jade took the child away into her own room as she grew older and she coaxed her with an egg or a dish of noodles cooked with bean oil or some such dainty and because she smiled and was gentle sometimes the child ate.

And all this time under her calm face and behind her kind eyes Jade kept her own thoughts, sometimes even from Lao Er, her husband. And these thoughts hovered continually about Mayli and Lao San, or Sheng, as she knew he was now called. So she had done since the day now many days ago when Lao Er had told her she must dream no more of leaving this home again and going to free country.

"It is our duty to stay here with our father and hold the land," he had told her, "and we must wait for the day of freedom to come here."

To Mayli and Sheng, therefore she looked with constant unchanging hope that some day they and others like them would free the people from the hold of the enemy. If these did not free them, then indeed there was no hope except that her fine sons would grow up slaves and conquered. She could feed them hidden food now and do all to make them strong and straight, but of what use were straight strong men if they were still to be slaves? Again and again this thinking woman would lift her eyes to starlit night skies, or gaze out over the green fields, and her heart would swell and ache with the longing to be free. Then she would cry inside her heart where none but she could hear, "If we are not to be freed, I had rather my sons died now in their childhood."

To Jade, then, did Mayli's letter come saying that Sheng was gone to rescue the white men and that he had not come back and none knew where he was and she read what Mayli had written last. "We are in retreat," she read, and again she read. "Those whom we came to deliver have betrayed us."

Now when Jade read this it was lucky that she was alone. The summer was beginning to be hot and the others lay sleeping after the noon meal. But she was always sleepless because of the longing in her heart after freedom. So it was her custom while the others slept to sit in the shade of the bamboos in the court and sew on a shoe sole. There the letter had been delivered her this day by a passing farmer who had taken it from the secret postman. When she had read the letter this woman who never wept allowed her tears to rise to her eyes and flow quietly down her cheeks. If the ones to whom she trusted for freedom were now defeated and betrayed, what hope was there for her sons?

She pondered for awhile, the tears still wet on her cheeks, whether

214

or not she would read the letter to the others and so destroy their hope, and she thought to herself, "It would be easier for me to hide this letter and keep the evil news in myself, rather than to hear the wails of my husband's mother and to bear the the curses of my husband's father."

And yet she did not wholly dare to keep from these two the news of their own son, and so at last she rose and went into her room where Lao Er lay sleeping. He lay stretched out on the mat on the bed, naked except for the blue short trousers he wore, and she looked at him sadly as he slept, loving him and grieving for him. His life was spent in deceiving the enemy, and he was often in danger lest he be discovered. Yet they had ceased to speak of danger since one day when she had cried out her anxiety and he had said, "What I do I must do, and I do it more easily if you do not speak of it."

So now she only sighed and she laid her hand gently on his bare shoulder. But however gently she laid it he woke with a great cry, and this showed the constant fearfulness of his inner being. When he saw it was only she he was ashamed and he wiped the sudden sweat from his face and said, "I am a fool."

She did not answer this, knowing very well why he had cried out, and she said, "I have a letter from Mayli and it has bad news. You must tell me whether we will keep the news to ourselves or tell the others." So she read him the letter and he listened and cursed under his breath and frowned, and slapped his knees as he sat on the edge of the bed.

Then he thought awhile and she waited and at last he said, "Of what use will it be to tell the old ones? They know they will die before they are free, but they have the hope that we who are their children can be freed. You know how my old father still trusts that promise the white man made. What will he think if he hears the white men have betrayed us? Can he live? And if we tell my elder brother he can never keep it from his wife and she can hide nothing from my mother. No, let us keep all to ourselves, at least until we know whether my third brother is dead or not."

"I am glad you say this," Jade replied, "for it is what I wanted to do and feared."

She rose as she spoke and she took that letter and put it down

215

into the bottom of a box of winter clothes. When she had done this she looked at Lao Er and he looked at her and each read the other's thoughts and she came to him and they clung their hands together for a moment as they thought of their sons. Then Lao Er cleared his throat and he said, "I must get back to the field."

And she wiped her eyes and said, "It is time for them all to wake and I must see to your mother and father."

And so these two carried in them secretly from that day on their own despair.

. . . Now the Burmese woman had put Mayli's letter to Sheng in her inner pocket and she forgot it for six days together after she went home. First her house was dirty and needed cleaning and then her husband, who had been joyful at her coming, grew moody when he had looked awhile at the child, and he imagined that he saw something in that small face that was not like his own in spite of the mole on the child's ear, and so she had to coax and please him, and what with these matters she forgot the letter. It was only when she came to wash her garment one morning at the pool that she put her hand into her pocket to see what was left there before she wet the cloth and found the letter still there. But she thought it no great wrong, since at least the letter was not lost, and she put it into the pocket of the garment she wore and forgot it still another two days, and only then did she remember and bring the letter out and give it to her husband.

Now it so happened that this man had that very day heard in a meeting place of the Chinese merchants of the town, that one division of their army had been totally lost except for two or three men who had strayed back dazed and lost and looking for their comrades who were not here. So he seized the letter and when she told him how Mayli said he was to give it to a tall soldier he slapped his wife for having been forgetful, and he hastened with the letter to the meeting place, and there he found some other merchants and they talked together of the lost men. But how could merchants know what armies do?

"Let us go to the American," one said at last. "He is still here."

All agreed that this was well, and so these merchants went to the camp near by and asked for the American and he received them kindly enough.

"Can you tell us what road the lost men might take to find the Chinese armies?" they asked.

"Northeast," the American said, "and more than that I should not tell."

But this was enough and so the merchants bowed and went away and they hired small asses and mounted them and went on the main road to the northeast for half a day, and they watched the roads and searched the villages as they went until they came upon not three but four men walking ahead of them. Then they hastened their beasts, and coming to them they found two Chinese and one Englishman and an Indian, all ragged and filthy and weary. But one of these Chinese was so tall that the merchant put his hand in his pocket and brought out the letter and gave it to the tall one, saying, "Are you this one?"

And Sheng looked down and saw his own name. "I am," he said.

"Then my duty is finished," the merchant said, and he put some money into Sheng's hand for a gift and bade him farewell and they all turned their asses homeward again.

Now Sheng was full of wonder at this letter, but who can understand how strange things come? He could not know that he had this letter because Mayli had delivered a Burmese woman of a son to a Chinese merchant who until now had no son. He only marveled that a letter from Mayli was put into his hand and he thanked Heaven secretly that he knew enough to read what she had written. It was true she had written the characters large and clear, knowing that it was still not as easy for him to read as to breathe. He read her letter three times, and he sat down under a banyan tree to read it, and the men with him sat on its arm-like roots and waited. Then he said,

"We must turn back to see the American and ask him where the armies have gone."

He rose as he spoke and put the letter into his girdle and the others rose with him except the Englishman, who continued to sit. When Charlie told him that they must turn back to the American to inquire where their armies were, the Englishman looked abashed.

"I will not turn back," he said. "You go and ask whatever you like, but I shall sit here and wait for you."

At this Charlie Li laughed and he said to the others in their own language which the Englishman could not understand, "Since this man is a deserter, it is only natural that he does not wish to see a white officer."

So they left the Englishman sitting there looking after them and they turned and walked for half a day and came to the encampment where the American was and such troops as he still had left, a motley handful of Chinese and Indians and whatever he could save from the retreats and losses which he had had.

They found him sitting outside his small tent in his shirt and trousers like any common soldier, and his gray hair was streaked with sweat, for the heat never changed night or day in this place, and Charlie went up to him and asked him where the Chinese armies were.

That American was staring at a map and writing on it with a pencil and when he saw the ragged handful of men before him in the uniform of the lost division, he began to swear in his mother tongue in mingled wonder and anger. When he came to what he wanted to ask it was simply this, "Where have you been, you fellows?"

At this Charlie told him straightly and simply how Sheng had led his men to rescue the white men and how the bridge had been cut and there was no retreat and so they had been hewed to pieces except for a few who could escape, but who had escaped except themselves none knew.

The American listened with his blue eyes hard and his head lifted and he said not one word.

So when Charlie saw that nothing was to be said, he asked, "Where are our men?"

"They have gone toward Lashio," the American said in English, "and I have told your General that it is a fool's decision to do what he is about to do. He is stringing out his men to an absurd depth on a narrow front. The Japs will get him sure, but he won't listen to me."

Now Charlie put this into Chinese for Sheng. The Indian who

218

was with him could only stare, for he knew nothing, but Sheng instantly perceived what the American meant and he knew he was right. Unwillingly he said, "Tell the American I fear he is right, and let us hasten ourselves and tell our General so. It may be it is not yet too late."

"I can understand you," the American said.

He cast a hard blue look at Sheng and Sheng caught the look with his own black gaze, and these two liked each other.

"I have seen you before," the American said.

"Once," Sheng agreed.

"You're the Nanking hill man," the American said next in his rough simple Chinese. "I wish you were the General instead of that other fellow," he went on. "You have more sense than he has."

This Sheng would not answer, for he could not allow it that his own officer was less than he was. He only said quietly to Charlie, "Let us go quickly."

So with their thanks, which the American received without politeness, they hurried on their way.

When they came back to the Englishman they found him lying in a curve of the root of that great banyan tree, sleeping. When he heard what they planned to do, he was very reluctant.

"We ought to get on to India," he grumbled to Charlie. "That's the only hope of saving ourselves."

"India!" Charlie cried aghast, "why, man, do you know that mountains lie between us and India?"

But the Englishman would not change his mind. "If I could get to India, I'd be all right," he said. "I know people there."

Nevertheless, since he was helpless in the enemy country, for the Burmese shot an Englishman whenever they saw one, he could do nothing but come with them, since he was afraid to be alone. So he went with them and they went by small paths and avoided villages and towns and when along the country roads they saw someone coming in the distance they went into the fields or into the low jungles that lined the roadways where there were no fields.

Now when they had been traveling thus for some days, they perceived by many signs that they were behind an enemy army of some sort, large or small who could tell, but there were increasing signs that the enemy was ahead of them. Villages were half burned, or where they were whole they flew an enemy flag and the people were excited and triumphant at the defeat of the white men who had ruled them.

When Sheng perceived this he said to Charlie, "If we do not creep around the enemy somehow, the battle will be over by the time we reach our General, and if the American is right we shall be too late."

XXI

THE General had placed his units according to his plan. He was silent and stubborn day and night, for he could not forget what the American had said and yet he would not acknowledge that he himself was wrong. With great care he set his men out along the narrow front which he had chosen, and when in the night he grew uneasy, he fortified himself by saying that the American had no right to advise since he had not himself won a single battle. "That American clings to the English, so how can we trust him?" he thought bitterly. "The white men are leagued together against us and they have let us come into this enemy country and they have not taken us as equals. Let them cling together and we will act for ourselves since we are not to be treated as allies."

Day and night he had such thoughts as this and he strengthened himself with his anger, and he told himself that he and his men could vanquish any attack from the enemy, for had he not fought this same enemy at home and now?

Among the women none knew anything except to do each day's work as it came, and there was much to do, for the men's sandals were gone and many marched barefoot and their garments were in rags and they were stung by insects and bitten by scorpions and spiders and by snakes which were everywhere and some were ill of stomach poisonings from bad wells and stagnant jungle water which they drank because they could find nothing else.

But Chung as he worked to heal them was uneasy, for he heard rumors among the men more quickly than the women did. One evening he went to Mayli as she sat sewing a ragged coat of her own, and she still had by her the small sewing bag that Liu Ma had made for her. He sat down near her on the ground and he said in a low voice,

"Should we be attacked, should we be defeated, what plan have you to save yourself and your women?"

Now Mayli had often thought what she would do in such a case for she knew that her women would look to her, and she now said, "We will stay by the armies if we can, but if we cannot we will strike out into the jungle and hide—what else can we do?"

"I want to give you a small gift," Chung said, and he put his hand into his pocket and took out a little compass. "Take this, so that you will know how to walk west away from the enemy."

She put out her hand and took it and put it in her pocket. "I thank you for it," she said, and went on sewing. And he looking at her face thought to himself how changed she was from the beautiful careless impetuous girl she had been when he first saw her. She was lean and hard now as a peasant and her black hair was burned in brown streaks, and her face and arms were brown and her lips were less full and very set and firm and her brows were thoughtful. Her hands were gnarled and the nails broken, for there was nothing she did not do of the hardest sort of labor. Her ways had changed, too. There was no time in these days for coquetry and smiles, and indeed she seldom smiled.

She felt his gaze and looked up, and he caught that straight gaze. But she did not speak nor did he, for what was there to say about today or tomorrow which it would be well to say? He rose and nodded and went away, not knowing that never again would he see this woman whom he had learned to lean upon as he might upon a comrade and a man.

. . . At dawn the next day, out of the seemingly peaceful countryside, the enemy came down upon them. The first men to rise saw a cloud on the horizon toward the south, but what is a cloud? Here the mornings were often cloudy until the sun rose full, and if a

221

cloud was more yellow than others, in this foreign country nothing was strange.

But that cloud came from the dust of trucks and vehicles which carried the enemy army, and above them and beyond them were airplanes, and these airplanes suddenly roared down out of the sky.

"Evil—evil!" they cried, and they hurried hither and there and everywhere to get themselves ready for escape.

The General had not slept, and when he heard the commotion he leaped from his pallet and ran out of his tent. And at that moment a small enemy plane swept downward and let fire out of its little twin guns and this fire caught the General in the shoulders and he fell. He had no time to think of fear for in that one second his life was over.

Few saw him fall, for now the enemy was everywhere on sky and earth, pushing and attacking and scattering and felling all as they ran. Under such fire who could think of another? Chung flung up his arms and stood still. "I am caught," he muttered, and he turned his face to the sky, and the enemy dropped down on him and he fell.

The enemy pushed between the General's men, between regiments and battalions, and they circled the men who were in the rear, and separated and honeycombed them, and then they fell upon them in these small pieces and destroyed them, and this division disappeared as though it never was.

Wounded men and whole, all were alike, and what the enemy in the sky did not do, the enemy pressing furiously from the earth finished. In so little time that the sun had scarcely crept above the clouds, the battle was over, and the enemy vehicles and the marching men and the airplanes were sweeping furiously northward, a typhoon of men and metal. And what lay behind lay unburied by the road that ran through the jungle.

. . . Now some escaped by the jungle, and of these were Mayli and Pansiao and the three women, Siu-chen, An-lan and Hsieh-ying. For after the doctor Chung had left Mayli last night, she grew very troubled and she did not sleep. "He would not have come to me unless he had been fearful," she told herself, and the more she

222

thought of the enemy and of their evil ways with women the more uneasy she grew. At last she gave up sleep and she got out of her bed and she went to Pansiao and to the other three and she woke them and whispered,

"I feel uneasy somehow. Get up, all of you, and listen to me."

She stood hesitating, under the small hand light which she let fall upon them, looking at the other sleeping women. They slept huddled together, weary and muddy as they were and her heart pitied them. "Shall I wake them all or not?" she asked herself. She gazed into the blackness of the sky and then passed the cone of her light over them again. None stirred. The night was so still that she began to be sorry that she had yielded to her fear and she did not wake the others, and she went back to the few she had waked, and she bade them sleep again. "I ought not to have waked you because of my own fears," she told them, "what have I to judge by except this uneasiness inside myself?"

So they lay down again, and she downed her fears except enough to say, "Still, should my fears have a reason, then you are all to go straight west into the jungle. Choose a spot a mile or so inside, and wait for me."

They heard this, awestruck, and Pansiao cried out softly, "You do make me afraid, Elder Sister."

"You need not fear," Mayli answered quickly. "Go back to sleep," and she went away then to her own bed.

Privately she blamed herself because she knew much of her sleeplessness and restlessness now was because of Sheng and because she did not know whether he were living or dead, or if he were alive whether she would ever see him again, for he might be a prisoner. Nothing was good to her in this uncertainty. She had not slept and her food was dust in her mouth.

So she was still sleepless and when the first distant roar began in the sky she heard it and she leaped up and searched the skies. Be sure she saw that yellow cloud, and she saw it was no common cloud, and she screamed to her women to wake, and she ran to where the sick and wounded were. "Run—run for yourselves, those who can!" she screamed, "and those who cannot—lie upon your faces!"

223

Even as she spoke the enemy came down from the sky and she threw herself on the ground, but seeing before she did that Chung had fallen.

Who can tell why one is spared and another killed? She lay motionless, her face upon her arms and nothing between her and the enemy and she felt the heat of fire upon her and around her and she heard the roar and whine and throb of guns and nothing touched her. She did not lift her head as she lay there.

"I am dead," she thought. "This is death. I shall never stand upon my feet again, never speak a word. This thinking I now do is my last."

She felt her brain alive and masterful, ready to live forever at this instant of its death. "A good brain," she thought, "it's been a good brain."

Her body, too, was quivering and alive and she felt her blood running smoothly in her veins and her supple muscles and her strong bones. She had never been so living as she lay waiting for the quick death which would end her and forever. "I wish I had married Sheng," she thought passionately. "I wish I had even once slept with him—what waste to have lived lonely all these months!"

These were her thoughts, and she thought of nothing else, for she was sure she was about to die. "Sheng, Sheng!" she thought. "This body of mine dies without having lived." And this was what she sorrowed for most, awaiting death.

But death did not come. The enemy went on and she lay there still alive in a field of dead. The noise grew less and the planes went echoing over the sky and she heard them no more. The battle here was over and the sun rose as it ever did. She lifted her head and saw that the dead were all about her, but she—she was alive. She rose and stood, lost and small, because she was alive and all these others dead. She stood one moment staring about her at the twisted shapes, the torn, the bleeding, the wounded and the dying. These were her other women, killed while they slept. "I ought to have waked them, too!" she cried. Then she turned blind and sick and ran, stumbling and moaning, toward the jungle.

. . . Try as they could, Sheng and his companions could not circle

224

the enemy, for the enemy went in vehicles faster than human feet could walk.

When at last they did come up to where the enemy had been, there were only heaped dead, rotting in the sunlight and in the sudden hot rains that fell every hour or two. Eye would have taken it that not one escaped. The General they found dead. He lay before his tent, on his face, as he had fallen. The enemy had stayed to seize his weapons and his insignia. Sheng lifted him and turned him over and there he was.

Yet how could he mourn even for this one? "Where are the women?" he muttered to Charlie. "There was one among them whom I knew—"

"Was there?" Charlie asked. "There was one among them whom I knew, too."

The two men stared at each other in this field of death. The enemy was gone, sweeping northward toward Lashio to cut off the Big Road into China. They were safe from the enemy, but who could save them now from sorrow? It seemed to Sheng that he must speak Mayli's name only to ease himself of fear, and he said to Charlie, "I mean that tall one—surnamed Wei and named Mayli."

"That one?" Charlie exclaimed and for one evil instant Sheng feared that he and Charlie loved the same woman. But Charlie went on quickly, "And the one I know is a little thing, like a child, who follows Mayli all the time as though she were a small dog."

"Why, that is my sister!" Sheng cried. "That is Pansiao."

"Is Pansiao your sister?" Charlie shouted.

And these two young men in the midst of the death around them seized each other's hands, and they let the tears come into their eyes. Each would have spoken to the other but the Englishman spoke first.

"What do you chaps plan to do? I say, what next? I hope you know now I was right—we should have gone straight to India."

. . . What was there for Sheng and his companions to do indeed but to move toward the jungle where they would be out of the stench of the dead, so that they might plan what step lay ahead? Yet neither Sheng nor Charlie could leave the dead until they had walked everywhere among them to see whether or not Mayli and Pansiao were there. There were many others whom they knew, but what hope had so few of burying all these? They moved those whom they knew best so that they lay decently and they found a torn piece of tent cloth and covered the dead General against the flies. They searched everywhere for the two women, and when at last they could not find them, the heat being now very intense and the flies fearful in number, they went into the jungle for shade and to find water and to eat the little food they had in their pockets, which they had bought with the money the merchant had given Sheng.

Now the jungle was as all are, and it was difficult to find a path into it, and now it was the Indian who led them. He searched out the only slight path he saw and thus they went by the very way where Mayli and the women had gone that morning, some four hours or five before this. By this same path Mayli had found the women easily when she went stumbling into the jungle, and she found them there clinging together in fearful silence. A rain had begun to fall, as rains did fall out of these low skies and all around them the sound of the rain drummed down and they looked here and there for the enemy, lest they could not hear a footfall because of the rain. So indeed they did not hear Mayli, and she came upon them before they knew and they put out their hands and drew her into their midst, tears streaming down their faces with the rain. And she put back her wet hair from her face and asked herself what now could be done. Where would they go in this enemy country and how could a handful of women escape and where would they find their own again? The trees about them were vivid green in the rain and small monkeys stared down at them, parting the leaves like humans to peer at them, and Mayli shivered to see those little dark faces, for so the enemy hid, too, in the trees like monkeys, and who knew whether monkeys and men were not hidden there together? So they all felt the presence of the enemy, and this terror passed from one to the other like cold flame, until seizing each other's hands they ran in blindness toward the road.

Mayli came first to herself and she pulled back and shouted at them, "Stop—stop—we are all fools—where are we going?"

226

At the sound of her voice they stopped and they all looked at her, and Pansiao began to cry because she was so hot and weary and frightened. Then looking at these faces Mayli knew that indeed she must think for all of them, and she tried to quiet her own panting while she thought what indeed they could do.

The rain had stopped again and around them the wet green light shone deep and soft. If they had been able to see beauty, they could have seen this beautiful, but to them the light seemed only strange and dangerous and the dripping leaves and trees only drenching and shelterless and they were hungry and even thirsty for the rain had sunk through moss and loam and there was no stream near.

At this moment they heard men's feet crashing through the jungle near by and men's voices. They shrank together at the sounds, fearing enemy men more than all else. Suddenly they were women, these who had been so strong and ready to suffer, who had shared the hardships of battle and had walked stride for stride beside the men in their army. But when they now heard these voices of men they forgot everything except that they were female and therefore at the mercy of the male. Clinging to each other and motionless and silent they stood close together, staring in the direction of the men.

The path ran near to where they stood, and there was no time to run back, nor did they dare lest they be heard. The voices came nearer and they listened, and what Mayli heard was a complaining English voice, speaking English words.

"I say, you chaps," the voice said. "I shan't have any boots left on my feet for tomorrow if we keep this up."

She put her finger to her lips, and she loosened herself from the others and crept forward, and parting the green branches a little she looked through them and saw sitting on the edge of the path three young white men. They were ragged and empty-handed except for the rifles which each clutched. One of them had taken off his boot and was looking at it sorrowfully.

She crept nearer. Should she speak or not? They were pale, weary, lost-looking men, very young, she saw, little more than boys. Yes, she would speak.

"Hello!" she said softly, "hello!"

They leaped to their feet, their eyes staring, their guns ready.

227

"You there!" the one without the boot said sternly, "are you friend or foe?"

She stepped out from the bushes which hid her. "Since I am Chinese," she said, "I must be friend."

XXII

THE three young Englishmen looked at Mayli. She saw in these three pairs of pale eyes the white man's old doubt. Chinese! Friend or foe?

"You need not be afraid of me," she said quietly. "Even if I am not English, still I am only a woman."

"Are you alone?" the first young Englishman asked. He had lowered his gun, but he still grasped it so hard that she saw his thin dirty hands were white at the knuckles.

"No, I am with four others," she replied. "We escaped from the battlefield today."

"What battlefield?" he asked.

"Did you not come from the road?" she asked.

He shook his head. "Quite the opposite," he said. "We've been wandering through the jungle for days without seeing a road. We don't know where we are. We had an idea we were going toward India, you know, but not seeing the sun rise or set in this beastly green darkness we may be entirely wrong."

She took from her pocket the little compass Chung had given her. "You are going southeast," she said.

"Good God!" he said in a low voice.

The Englishmen forgot their fear in their dismay and they lowered their guns. One of them, a short square fellow who had been thickset and was now so thin that his flesh hung on him, took off his ragged sun helmet and scratched his head that was bald from heat and filth. The third, the youngest, turned very pale under the grime streaked on his unshaven cheeks. "Do you mean all this time we've been walking in the wrong direction, Hal?" he asked of the first one.

"Looks like it," that one replied.

He buttoned the ragged coat that was open over his naked body. "Are the Japs south of us or where?" he asked Mayli.

"They passed through here this morning," she said, "going north and east. How far from here they are now I cannot tell."

"If they were here only this morning," he said, "then we ought to move quickly. But where? We've been running from them for days. They were behind us up there—" he nodded northward. "We thought that we were getting away from them."

"We must get out of this jungle," she said. "We cannot see anything until we are out of it. I will call my friends."

She lifted her voice and called. "An-lan—Pansiao—Siu-chen— Hsieh-ying!"

At the sound of her voice the women, who had until now been hiding behind the bushes came timidly out, Pansiao clinging to Hsieh-ying's hand. They looked at each other, English and Chinese. The men, Mayli could see, were not too pleased. Women, they were doubtless thinking—women would be a burden.

"We can walk as swiftly as you," she said, "we are used to walking with the armies."

"Think of comin' this far to find a lot of women!" the short one remarked.

"Shut up, Rick," the first Englishman replied. There was a long moment of shy silence, then he shouldered his gun. "Well, come along, everybody," he said, "we'd better be on the march again." He tramped off in the direction in which they had come, the men taking the lead and the women falling in behind, single file.

Now these two kinds of people, men and women, light and dark, walked hour after hour in the sultry dusk of the jungle, each kind dubious of the other, and therefore continuing in silence. Once and again they muttered together concerning each other. Thus the Englishmen, glancing backward at the women, spoke in low voices:

"The little one doesn't look more than seventeen," one said.

And another one said, "They'd be pretty if you didn't remember your own girls."

"They're too yellow, too thin, and I don't like their eyes," the third one said.

"Still they're girls," the first one said.

"I suppose you'd call them that," another answered.

The women spoke freely, knowing the men could not understand them in their own language. "Are all Ying men tall and thin and bony like these?" Hsieh-ying asked Mayli.

Mayli could still smile, hot and tired though she was. "Ying men come fat and thin as any other men do," she said.

"They scare me," Pansiao said plaintively. "Their eyes are cruel blue, and their noses are like plowshares. Why need they have such noses? Do they smell as dogs do?"

"They come from their mother's wombs with those noses," Mayli replied.

"They looked like peeled fruit," Siu-chen said. "Why should their skin be red?"

"The sun burns them red instead of brown," Mayli said.

And then being women they fell into yet more intimate talk. "Are these men as other men are?" Hsieh-ying asked, for she was one who had a warmth toward men and this she could not help, although for shame's sake she hid it as much as she could.

"Certainly they are," Mayli said with coolness.

"My flesh pimples to think of sleeping with such gawks," Hsieh-ying said.

Mayli smiled drily. "I am glad to hear that," she said and the women laughed.

Yes, they could laugh, looking at these Englishmen and seeing their knobby bare legs and tall lean bodies and lank necks burned crimson, so young were these women even after the sorrows of the battle and the plight they were now in.

"It is their hairiness which I cannot bear," An-lan now said. "I never did like hairy things such as cats and dogs and monkeys, and these Ying men are covered with hair. Look at their beards!"

"They could not shave for all these days," Mayli said.

But Anlan said, "How can they shave themselves all over? Look at their arms and their legs, as hairy as their chins, and did you see their bare bosoms? The hair was as thick on them as the hair on a

230

dog's breast. Have they hair all over their bodies under their garments?"

"I have never seen a Ying man without his clothes," Mayli said shortly. "Nor any other man. But I think white men are not as hairy as dogs."

With such talk they lightened some miles of walking, but it could not go on forever. They must think of food and shelter and as night came on of sleep. So when afternoon wore on to evening Mayli called to the Englishmen and she said,

"Had we not better talk together and decide what we should do about food and shelter? There is no end to the jungle yet, and somehow we must eat and sleep."

The men stopped at that, and waited for the women to come up.

They sat down on fallen trees and they wiped their faces with their sleeves and plucked broad leaves and fanned themselves. The gnats and midges were thick about their heads and they needed to keep the leaves moving against them.

In a moment the short Englishman leaped up, "God, I can't stand this," he shouted. He slapped his bare legs and knees. In the orange red hair that grew on him there were entangled dozens of small insects. Now Hsieh-ying had been staring at him with large eyes, and she had smelled the leaf she held and it was very pungent, and she perceived when she crushed it that it gave out a yet stronger, hotter odor. So she went over to the man and motioned to him to rub the leaf up and down his legs, which he did, and the insects disliked the rank smell of the leaf and so he had a little peace from them.

"You're a good girl," he told Hsieh-ying and Mayli translated it and it made Hsieh-ying laugh behind her hand.

Yet so poisonous was that leaf that he had scarcely said this when his legs began to itch, and he began to scratch and yelled, "Damn, I believe that leaf was poison!" and they all looked at his leg and Hsieh-ying stopped laughing, and what between this and the insects, they all decided against staying and so they took up the march again. But now Mayli and the tallest Englishman walked side by side to talk, since they were the leaders and the others walked behind, together, too, and no longer separate.

231

The more the Englishman looked at Mayli the more he liked her. "It's luck that we should fall in with someone who can speak English," he said. "Perhaps we can help each other."

"It is not easy for women to travel alone in this inhospitable land," she replied.

"Shall we make a sort of plan?" he asked her next.

"I have been thinking what we could do," she said. "If we could strike the great road which leads into India, it might be best for us all to go in that direction for I know there are no main roads into China. But I have often heard that there is a great road leading into India."

He pressed his swollen lips together. "You are wrong," he said brusquely. "There is none."

"No road to India?" she exclaimed.

He shook his head. "That is why the retreat is so hard—" he said slowly, "the roads are narrow, old winding roads and they are clogged with people. Besides, nothing leads directly into India."

For a moment she could not answer, so astonished she was. She had heard many times of the fabulous road into India, a hundred feet wide, hard as a floor, fit for great armies to march upon. "What incredible folly of your generals," she cried, "to bring into this country armies too few for victory, and knowing that there was no way for retreat!"

"You don't say anything that I do not myself say," he told her. "I've said it over and over. But that's the way it is. Dunkirk was easy compared to this. I was at Dunkirk, mind you. It was only a few miles of water we had to cross and all England turned out to help. We knew England was there, you see. But here—hundreds of miles of this horrible jungle—and England thousands of miles away. Even India—" he broke off and Mayli saw that he was fighting against tears.

She asked herself, "What are we here for?"

But he cried aloud, "What are we fighting for in this damned country? That's what all the fellows said. If we win the war we'll get this country back with all the rest of it. If we lose the war we'll not have this anyway. This isn't the place to fight. Why, we can sink men into this hole by the tens of thousands and never win. It isn't a fit battlefield for white men!"

This she heard, and she did not answer. She looked around the jungle. No, it was not a battlefield. The trees trembled above their heads, and vines swung in the branches. Around them the underbrush spread in a thicket. Great grasses stood high above their heads wherever the trees parted enough for the sun, grasses wet with rain, and leaves as huge as plates. She paused now beside one such big leaf that held water from the last rain like a bowl and kneeling she drank the water from it. There had been three rains in the hours during which they had walked and they had drunk thus again and again. No, it was not a country for a battlefield. But how many had died upon it! She thought of the General and of Chung, and of all those others whom this morning she had left dead and yet she had not the heart to reproach this tired and confused man who walked beside her. He was no more to blame than she was. He had been sent here and he was here.

They took up the march again and for a few moments they did not speak. Then she said gently, "Shall we march all night or dare we rest?"

"Let's keep going," he said, "as long as our legs will move."

From then on they said nothing except what had to be said.

At last it was dark and they could walk no more. "Let's stop here where we are," the Englishman said. "We'll tramp down the grass. I don't think we ought all to sleep. We three men will walk around the rest of you in regular beats and keep off the snakes that way, at least, and hear the beasts if they come near."

"We will all take our turns except Pansiao," Mayli said. "Pansiao must sleep because she is young yet."

"No, nonsense, you women must sleep," he protested, "I assure you—"

But Mayli said, "We are used, we Chinese women, to doing as men do."

Thus passed that night in the jungle, between sleep and walking, and the dawn came early and they went on their way again.

. . . Now what is there to tell of such a journey as theirs? The

233

weariness numbed their brains and dulled the feeling in their flesh and bones. Fatigue passed into deeper fatigue and they grew drowsy while they walked so that the leeches stuck to their ankles and legs and they did not feel them until one saw another's and plucked it off. Blood dripped down from such wounds and the danger was that they would bleed too much and they watched each other the more carefully for that. The skies were cruel today and the rain came down only once so that they were thirsty all day and faint, although they were too weary for hunger, and a great craving for salt fell upon them all more than for food. Today they did not speak to each other except the few words that must be said, for talk took breath and strength. The Englishman held Mayli's compass and they pushed steadily westward and yet who knew whether this jungle stretched north and south or east and west? They could only press on, hoping that somewhere it would end.

Late that evening they came upon a muddy winding river and looking down that river they saw a swinging bridge of bamboo. This cheered them greatly for it meant that men were near, and they went toward it. Yet all knew that the men might be enemies and so they approached the bridge and crossed it half fearfully. A small beaten path led through lower jungle along the other side of the river and this they followed until it came toward a village set beside the river, and on the other side of the river the jungle had been cut back to make small rice fields, now very green with new rice and yellow with harvests, too. For the whole year in this country was so warm and wet that men could sow rice in one field and harvest it in the next, and there were no seasons.

They halted when they were in sight of the village, and talked together of what to do. "We men will go and scout," the Englishman said.

But this Mayli would not allow. "If you are captured or killed then what of us?" she asked.

So it was decided that she and the tall Englishman would go forward and the others would stay behind. If they came back, all would be well, if they did not, then the others must go on as best they could. Yet when Pansiao was told this she would not stay behind and so she went, too.

234

"Your sister?" The Englishman asked, glancing at the slender girl who put her hand in Mayli's.

Mayli was about to answer no, and then she thought of Sheng, of whom she was always thinking now, and she said, "Yes—my sister."

The villagers in that place were only some six or seven families, and they had lived here in great peace and knew nothing of the war except that they had heard of a disturbance beyond the jungle. Not one of them could read or write and they heard nothing from the outside even of the war, nor did any come to them, and so they did not know enough to hate one kind of man and love another. So remote was the village from all the world, that not once a year did a man leave this place to go out nor did a man come here from elsewhere, for what was there to come for since these people only lived to raise food for themselves and there was nothing to buy or sell?

Here Mayli and Pansiao and the Englishman came with steady steps and watchful eyes. It was late afternoon, and the men were in the fields, and the women, too, except a few old ones and children, and when they saw the strangers they let out cries and others came running from the fields, and for a moment they all stood staring at the strangers and making a few sounds of speech to each other, which the three could not understand. But they were kindly looking people, cheerful and childlike, and healthy except for some festering insect bites, and some sores on the men's legs from standing too long in watery rice fields. The more Mayli looked at their faces the easier she was.

"I believe these are only peasants," she said to the Englishman. And she put on a hearty smile and opened her mouth and pointed into it to show she was hungry. Immediately there was a chatter among the women and they climbed the ladders into their little houses set on posts above the river edge and they brought down cold rice and fish in large leaves. This they offered to the three, who when they saw the food felt their hunger grow intense and they took the food and ate it in a moment. At this the villagers laughed out loud.

"We can stay here safely," Mayli said.

235

"Looks like it," the Englishman said.

And Mayli pointed up the river and held up five fingers to show there were five others and they went back again toward where the others were and the villagers followed them at a little distance. When they saw the five then great talk burst out, and they circled them as they went back to the village, laughing and talking and staring very much at the guns the three Englishmen had, but seemingly without knowledge of what these were.

Then the women brought out more food, and all ate and they drank cold fresh water which was very sweet, and in a little while there was great friendliness among them all. The children pressed near to stare and the women laughed and talked together in their own language and the men handled the guns. Now it could be seen that not one of these men had ever seen a gun before and the short Englishman grinning and wanting to amuse them lifted the gun to his shoulder and shot a small bird that sat on a branch and it fell dead. At this the villagers screamed in sorrow and terror and they ran back from the visitors.

"Oh," Mayli cried. "Why did you have to show what you could do with your gun?"

"I was only in fun," the short Englishman stammered. "I thought they'd like to see it."

"Not everybody is as ready to kill as you are," she retorted and she said to the tall Englishman, "Quick—pretend you are angry—pretend to punish him!"

So the tall Englishman strode forward and slapped the other's cheeks. "Take this," he said, "don't utter a word. I've got to do it—she's right." He shouted at the man and jerked his gun away from him and he took the gun and offered it to the oldest man of the village. But this man would not have it and all the villagers backed themselves away from the dreadful thing, and so the Englishman took all three of the guns and set them in a row against a great tree that was there. When the villagers saw this they made much talk among themselves and no one went near the tree, and so at last the danger was past.

Now night came down again, and again food was eaten and a fire was built in the center of the village against the mosquitoes and

236

the men brought out mats and slept near it but the women slept in their houses. No one asked the Chinese women into the houses and Chinese and English slept on the ground to the windward of the fire, on branches they broke from the trees. And they slept as well as though they were on beds for they were fed and the smoke drove the insects from them.

. . . Now they stayed at this village three days in all until they were rested and washed, and all tried to help the villagers as best they could. Mayli used her skill to tend the festering sores the villagers had, and this made them grateful. She had no medicines, but she boiled water and washed out the sores and used a sort of wine they made from soured cooked rice, and she motioned to those who had these sores that they must wash them with boiled water and then with wine and allow the sun to shine into them every day, and they understood her and even in three days she saw these sores begin to heal. Be sure the mothers brought sick children to Mayli, and an old man pointed to his chest and rumbled a deep cough to show her what was wrong with him, but she could not heal them all.

Yet in less than three days she began to be anxious to be gone from the village, for the two white men could not contain themselves but must act as though they were lords of the village. And one began to follow about a pretty girl of the village and Mayli was frightened when she saw this and went to the tall one.

"You must tell this fellow to stay away from the girl," she warned him. "These people will not allow it."

"I'll tell him," he promised.

But of what use is the promise? She saw that these white men without meaning ill, nevertheless angered the villagers in a score of small ways. They did not believe such small brown men were altogether human as they themselves were, and the brown men soon saw this and grew sullen, and on the morning of the third day Mayli said to the tall Englishman, "It is time that we went on before trouble breaks out between them and us."

"They're hot-tempered beggars," he said. "I believe it's their peppery food. They eat too much of it."

At this she lost some of her patience. "You treat these villagers as servants," she said. "You forget we are only guests."

At this he said in a very cold voice, "After all, Burma does belong to us, you know."

She laughed aloud. "Will you never know you are beaten?" she cried.

And suddenly she remembered all that Sheng had said against the white people and at this moment she agreed with him and she went on furiously, "How is it that you cannot understand even now that our lives are dependent on the people? Will nothing ever teach you? Do you wake up only when you are dead, you English?"

Over this honest good young face, so very young, now that he had shaved it with a razor he borrowed from a Burmese that day, she saw a bewildered stubborn surprise. He did not know her meaning and she saw that anger was no use, and scorn was no use, for he did not know why she was angry or why he could be scorned. The words went into his ears but they beat against a wall in him somewhere and came back again without entering or leaving an echo. "Come," she said, "we must be on our way—there is no other salvation."

Nor did she want to stay behind with her women in this village, for what would happen to them if they stayed? No, the white men were their allies after all and they had no others.

So she went that day to the old man who was, she knew by now, the head of the village, and she made signs and asked him for the path, and he understood and made signs that one would guide them out of the jungle to the roads, and so that day they left the village which had treated them so kindly and went on their way again, though what that way was who could tell?

. . . Now Sheng had been traveling too, and those with him. This journey had been made harder by a curious thing. That Indian had begun to show a mighty hatred of the solitary Englishman, so much so that Sheng saw it and he said to Charlie, "This man of India will do harm to the white man if he is left alone with him. Do you see how he has his hand always in his bosom where he keeps his knife?"

238

That Indian did have a knife, but it was a strange short one, not more than four inches long, but the edges of it were ground very fine and sharp.

"I have seen his hatred when he looks secretly at the white man," Charlie said. "It is an evil thing that none of us speak his language to ask him what his hatred is."

"We must keep our eyes on him day and night," Sheng said. "Not for love," he added, "but for justice."

This they did although their task was made harder because the Englishman lived altogether ignorant of the Indian's hatred and came indeed to treat him in small ways like a servant, and the Indian obeyed him when he pointed at something he wanted done, but his eyeballs swelled with fresh hatred when he did so.

Now they pressed steadily north, and though none knew it, the jungle ended much sooner northward than westward, and they struck a clear road which led toward the west. They halted there and took much thought as to whether they would go east or west. Eastward Sheng would have gone if he could, but the first village toward the east was full of the enemy, and luckily they found this out before they went far, because Charlie, who was ahead, saw a handful of enemy men drinking tea at a small roadside inn and he fled back to the others and immediately they all turned westward.

This was the same road to which the villagers had led Mayli and the others, but how could anyone know this? Yet so it was, and so all traveled the same road. But Sheng and the men with him went more quickly than Mayli and the women could go, and each day Sheng came nearer to Mayli, so that the time must come when they would meet. This came about one day near midday at a certain small town, and this was the circumstance.

By now Mayli and her women and the Englishmen had come to a good friendship. That is, each knew the other's faults and could bear with them. Mayli indeed had come to know the English very well and it seemed to her through those men that she knew entirely why the battle of Burma had been lost, and yet why they were not to be wholly despised because they had lost it. She had come to this knowledge by watching and by talk. Thus she saw by watching that these men never lent themselves to any time or place with under-

239

standing, but they were as they had been born, men of England. They were good and they were honest. Never, she told herself, would she have believed that men could be so honorable toward women as these were toward hers, and this in spite of lust enough in them at any time to have done what was evil had they been evil in heart. The short one, indeed, could not keep his eyes from following a woman wherever she walked but he could keep his lust only in his eyes. As for the tall one, and this was the wisest one, he was such that she could not but like him. He was learned, for he had been taught in good schools. "Oxford," he told her when she asked, "and my father and grandfather before me." There was so much delicacy in this man, so much troubled reasoning and so much blindness that sometimes thinking of him in the night she sighed.

"It would be easier for those who live under their yoke," she thought, "if they were all evil."

But no, for every evil white man, she thought, there were a hundred who were only blind, and of the two the blindness was harder to bear. Thus, probing this one with her skillful questions as they walked along the road together, she heard him say, "We have a responsibility to this country."

When he said the word responsibility, he lifted his head and looked over the greenness of Burma through which the road cleft like a silver sword.

"Why," she asked, "why do you feel responsible for this country?"

"Because," he said soberly, "it is part of the Empire."

"But why the Empire?" she persisted. "Why not let these people have their own country to hold and to rule?"

"One cannot simply throw down a responsibility," he said gravely. "One has to fulfill it."

She saw from his honest troubled look that indeed he meant this well and that he felt the weight of duty upon him and upon his own people.

She looked over the green country, too. "It would be a better world for us all," she said at last, "if you and your kind were not so good."

He looked at her and stammered as he always stammered when she was too quick for him. "Wh— what's the meaning of that?"

240

"We could be free if you did not think it your duty to save us," she said, her eyes sad and laughing together. "Your duty keeps you master and makes us slave. We cannot escape your goodness. Your honesty will not let us go. One of these days we shall defy your God and then we shall be free."

"You sound mad," he said astonished. "Do you know what you are talking about?"

"Not quite," she said, "not quite, for I'm not talking out of my head but out of my heart. But I feel you such a weight here." She put her hand on her bosom. "Yes, even just being with you, I feel is a weight on me."

"I'm sorry for that," he said, very grave. "I really like you enormously—"

"Which surprises you for you never thought you could like a Chinese," she said.

He flushed heartily. "I would never have said that," he said. "It's simply that one doesn't expect a Chinese—to—"

"Be wholly human," she finished.

Now as they had talked they came near to a large town and he being absorbed in what they were saying and she in her thoughts that were as large as the world, they entered the town too carelessly, without seeing what the people were, whether friendly or not. So a young yellow-robed priest saw them first, and he ran secretly to his fellows to tell them that Englishmen had come into the town with women who were Chinese and the most evil thoughts came running up from his words like little flames from coals dropped in dried grass, until in less than an hour, while they sat down at a wayside table to eat and drink, the whole town had turned against them and they did not know it. They sat there on wooden benches in the main street, eating rice and curried vegetables which they had bought, and drinking tea. One moment was all peace and the hot sun shining down over the cloth that was spread above them for shade and the next moment they looked into sullen furious faces gathering around them.

"Why—what the devil?" the Englishman muttered. He leaped to his feet with his gun, and so did the other two men, but Mayli put her hand on his arm and turned the bayonet point down. "You and your guns," she murmured, "always a gun for the cure to any trouble! Wait, you fool, and let us see what is the matter."

She searched that crowd for any face that looked Chinese, for often in a town as large as this there was a Chinese merchant, but there was none here. Her heart beat hard once or twice as she thought what she could do in this evil circumstance. Then she said to the Englishman, smiling as she did so into the faces of the mob. "Put down your gun—tell the others to put theirs down. Sit down all of you and go on eating—" This she murmured and unwillingly the men obeyed. Then she held out her hands to the people and showed them empty and bare. She took up a gun, shook her head and put it down. She pointed up the roadway, and signified that they were going on. She took out money and paid the innkeeper for the food. Then she motioned to the others who sat there trying to eat. "Come," she said, "show no fear. Let us go together as though nothing were wrong."

Whether it was her calm, whether it was her voice speaking a language which they did not know, whether it was, after all, the three guns which the men had, the people allowed them to pass but they closed in behind them and pressed close while they walked.

Now while this was happening Sheng and his men and the Englishman with them had entered the town from the other side, and they too were coming up this street and they saw this great crowd and halted.

"Is this the enemy?" Sheng asked Charlie, for the crowd was very great and all along the street others were running to join it.

"Let us turn back and go around a side street," Charlie said, "and come out of the town in a roundabout way and so avoid whatever it is."

This they did, and a few minutes striding along they were nearer the gate than the others were and they went through and were on the other side. At that very moment they heard a voice shouting in English, "Let's run for it!"

"I'll be damned," that Englishman with Sheng now said when he heard this voice, and he stood still and they all stood still and stared behind them. In a moment they saw the three Englishmen holding the hands of women and running toward them and behind them came a shouting yelling mob, now full of desire for attack. Sheng and those with him stood ready across the middle of the road and they fired their guns full over the heads of those fleeing and over the crowd. At the sound of these guns the Englishmen turned and dropping the hands of the women they too fired over the heads of the crowd, and at this 'fire the crowd stopped. Not one had a gun and how could they withstand such weapons?

Had they been a hardier people they might have plunged on. But those people were only mischievous and impetuous as children are and they were not hardy and rather than risk death they let these go on and they turned and went back into their town, laughing and full of good spirits as though they had won a victory.

It was only now that Sheng and Mayli had time to see each other, and for one full instant each stood staring at the other and then Mayli forgetting shame ran forward toward him and Pansiao was just behind her.

"Sheng!" she cried, "it is you! And your arm—is it healed?"

"Brother!" Pansiao screamed. "Brother, how did you come here?"

But Sheng, as soon as he saw Mayli and saw the company she was in, was thrown into a turmoil of jealousy. Who were these white men with whom Mayli traveled? And he remembered with sharp pain how easily she talked with white people and how near she was to such foreigners, and he felt the old wall of difference between him and Mayli. He stood still and looked very cold and he put on a false smile and he said, "Are we met again? I see you are with friends. As for my arm, it is healed enough to fight with."

At this Mayli stopped, too. Here was such folly as she could not imagine. She stamped her foot in the dust of the rough road and she shouted at Sheng, "What do you mean, you Sheng? What are you thinking? How can you speak to me so?"

But Pansiao went up to him and put her hand on his arm and said, "Brother, now that you are here, we can leave these strangers."

"I am not sure you wish to leave them," Sheng said with his great eyes full of anger still on Mayli.

Now Mayli was very hot and weary, how weary she did not know until the anger of the mob was over, and suddenly she felt weary enough to lie down in the road where she stood and die. Her lips began to tremble and it was Charlie who saw it and he said to Sheng,

"Elder Brother, ought you to be angry when we are just escaped so great a danger?" And as he spoke his eyes went sidewise at Pansiao and she looked sidewise at him, although out of politeness neither spoke to the other. When he had overcome his politeness enough he said to her, "Are you well?" And she said, "Yes," and with these few words each felt much was said.

All this time the Englishmen had looked on, much astonished and understanding not one word. That one Englishman who was with Sheng was silent from doubt of himself because he had run away from his army and so he stood behind Sheng and Charlie. But now the tall Englishman saw him clearly and he called out to him and went toward him with his hand outstretched as white men do when they see each other.

"I say, you're English," he said.

That other one put out his hand and smiled eagerly, "Rather," he said and stopped there.

"How did you happen to meet up with these Chinamen?" the first one asked.

"Quite by accident," the other one said.

"So did we with these women," the tall one said. "We were taken prisoner by the Japs but we got away. There were eight of us—the rest weren't so lucky."

"I say," the other one answered, then he went on carefully, "I got lost myself. The retreat was frightful, wasn't it?"

"Frightful," the tall one agreed.

Then those Englishmen all came together, shaking hands and murmuring to each other in low voices, and in a moment the two kinds stood separate again, English and Chinese, and all were full of unease, except for Mayli, and she looked first at these and then at those. It was a strange moment, a moment such as does sometimes fall whole and separate out of flowing time, entire in itself, linked neither to past or future. They endured it in uncertain silence. Around them was the brilliant green of this country which was foreign to them all. There were the low hills and under their feet was the dusty road. The sky above their heads was smooth and blue but in the west thunderheads piled themselves slowly higher and more high on the horizon. There was no one in sight in field or on the road, and the air was silent and hot about them. They were for this round separate moment cut off from the whole world, alone and yet apart. The Englishmen stood together, bearded and filthy and in diffident unease. The Chinese stood together in their faded and torn uniforms, barefoot, bareheaded, their faces brown with the sun, their eyes cool, and behind them was the Indian but none heeded him. Mayli stood between them all. Now she looked at the tall Englishman, now she looked at Sheng. Then she spoke to Sheng.

"Shall we go on?" she asked him.

"Go on with them?" he demanded. He drew down his black brows and thrust out his chin at the Englishmen. "No," he said, "I have had enough."

"What then?" she asked. "Where shall we go?"

"Where do they go?" he asked still scowling.

She turned to the Englishmen and changed her tongue. "Where do you go?" she asked.

The Englishmen murmured together. She heard the fragments of their words. "We'd better clear out—" "Anywhere back to white men—" "Out of this foul country—"

These were the words Mayli could hear. Then the tall one straightened himself. "Westward," he said, "to India."

They turned their eyes westward and there were the thunderheads slowly rising. They were silver-edged against the sun, but on the horizon land they massed black.

"There will be a storm," she said.

"I daresay," the Englishman said, "but it won't be the first we've had."

They hesitated a moment longer. Then the Englishman put his hand into his pocket and took out the compass she had let him carry through the jungle.

"I say, here's your compass—thanks awfully," he said.

She was moved for a moment to tell him to keep it. For indeed those Englishmen looked very helpless, standing there closely together. Could they find their way, unguided? But Chung had given her the compass and she did not wish to give it away forever, and so she took it in silence. Then the Englishman shouldered his gun. His face was pale and tired but his eyes were still resolute. "Well," he said abruptly, "we'd better be moving on."

He turned sharply as he spoke and strode off and behind him the other Englishmen in their dirty sweat-streaked uniforms fell in smartly and so they marched away down the road. Down the road they marched toward India and the Chinese stood watching while the brave and tattered figures grew small against the thunderous sky and then were lost in the rising darkness.

But here was the strangest instant of this strange moment. That man from India who all through these days had followed silently and faithfully behind Sheng now gathered his thin black body together and he leaped into the air as though his legs were springs of steel and he darted out and made after the Englishmen. This he did without a sound, with no cry or word of farewell. No, he only ran into the darkness after the white men, his bare feet silent as a tiger's in the dust.

They saw his wild face for one instant, the whites of his great sad eyes, the flash of his white teeth. Then he, too, was gone.

All were too amazed at first to speak, until Sheng said, looking at Charlie, "That man of India—has he still his knife?"

And Charlie said, "You know he lives with it in his hand and he sleeps with it under his pillow."

"Then the outlook is not good," Sheng said grimly.

Now as the Chinese stood, a deep stealing wind began to come out of the clouds. It rose steadily with a distant roar and hearing it Mayli was troubled and for the first time she was afraid. She turned to Sheng, "Where shall we go?" she asked. "I am afraid of that storm. It does not look as usual as other storms."

"It is a huge storm of some sort," he replied. In anxiety he examined the clouds curling and boiling over the whole western sky. "Certainly we must escape it," he said soberly.

Now they looked toward the east and they saw the sky there was still clear and blue.

"Let us go home," Sheng said suddenly.

And Pansiao hearing this word, "home," cried out, "Oh, I want to go home."

246

"Home—home," the weary women sighed.

But Mayli said sadly, "Between us and home there are hundreds of miles of jungles and mountains and rivers. Can we go so far on foot?"

"I go," Sheng said sturdily.

He set off at once and Pansiao ran after him and Charlie went after her and one by one the women followed until only Mayli still stood, so weary, she told herself, that she could not put out her foot to take up so long a march. Ahead of them the pure bright sky shone still more clear. But was she not too weary to walk toward it? She longed to sleep until she died.

Ahead of her Sheng stopped and looked back. "Do you come with me?" he shouted.

Yet she hesitated. What if they never reached home?

"Sheng!" she cried. "Will you promise me—"

He cut across her pleading voice with harsh and whiplike words. "I make no promises," he shouted. "I am not one of those men who make promises!"

She saw him standing tall and straight in the livid light. If she stayed here, if she ran after those Englishmen, would not the storm overtake her? The sunlight still fell upon the land from the clear sky ahead. What could she do except go with Sheng? And promises were nothing but words, and words were bubbles of air, falling easily from men's lips and broken and gone as though they had never been. She bent her head. No, even though he would not promise—

"I am coming," she said, and so they began the march home.

. . . Far away in Ling Tan's house Jade sat watching her sons play on the threshing floor in front of the door. It was near noon and in a little while the two men, Lao Ta and Lao Er, would come home to their noon meal. They were in the fields, cutting the ripe wheat. It was a heavy harvest and they had twice thinned it secretly, as all the farmers had done in that region under the enemy, so that the enemy inspectors, searching the fields, could not see how good a harvest it was. The secret grain they had threshed by night and it was hidden in the bins in the cave under the kitchen.

Now Jade was sewing on a garment of Lao Er's and despising the stuff of which it was made as she stitched. The cotton stuffs were all worthless now, for this was all the enemy brought them. Some day, she mused, she would weave once more the old fine strong blue cloth that lasted from father to son, some day when they were free again. Yes, they would be free again, she knew it, she felt it. There was no promise for eye to see nor for ear to hear, and yet men and women, in the midst of present evil, had begun to hope out of their own unyielding hearts. Out of such musing she lifted her head from her sewing and saw the two men coming across the fields, their sickles in their hands. They walked side by side, sturdy and strong.

She rose to go into the house and put the meal on the table. Then she stopped for she heard an uproar from her twin sons. They were quarreling, the larger one against the smaller. Now these two were not of one size, the last born was the smaller, and she was about to defend that smaller one against the larger, for he was bawling and weeping and hard pressed. Then she did not. She only stood watching the two while this weeping and roaring went on, waiting to see how they fought this battle.

Suddenly she saw that small fellow stop weeping and she saw his face set itself in fury and he flew at the bigger one with all his strength, his anger bitter in his face and strong in his arm. And she laughed.

"Good, my son!" she called. "Fight for yourself—fight, fight!"

And she went into the house, content.

COLOPHON

This is one of the titles in a series of the Oriental Novels of Pearl S. Buck. Other titles include *Dragon Seed, East Wind: West Wind, The Good Earth, A House Divided, Imperial Woman, Kinfolk, The Living Reed, Mandala, The Mother, Peony, Sons,* and *The Three Daughters of Madame Liang.*

The text was set in Granjon. The typeface was designed by George William Jones (1860-1942) and named after the famous Parisian punch-cutter, Robert Granjon (1513-1589). This face was the model for such popular faces as Times New Roman, Plantin, and Galliard, and was originally designed to compete with Monotype Garamond. The display face is Calligraphy 421 with the folios in Sabon. This book was typeset by Rhode Island Book Composition, Kingston, Rhode Island and printed by McNaughton & Gunn, Saline, Michigan on acid free paper.